NEW YORK REVIEW COMICS

YELLOW NEGROES AND OTHER IMAGINARY CREATURES

YVAN ALAGBÉ was born in Paris and spent three years of his youth in West Africa. Along with Olivier Marboeuf he founded a contemporary visual arts review called *L'oeil carnivore*, a magazine, *Le Cheval sans tête* ("The Headless Horse"), which gained a cult following for its publication of innovative graphic art and comics, and the publishing house Amok, which drew from material serialized in *Le Cheval*, including the first version of *Yellow Negroes*. In 2001, Amok partnered with the publishing group Fréon to establish the Franco-Belgian collaboration Frémok, now one of the most acclaimed European comics publishers. Alagbé's graphic novel *École de la misère* (2013) uses the same characters as *Yellow Negroes*.

DONALD NICHOLSON-SMITH has translated works by Henri Lefebvre, Antonin Artaud, Guillaume Apollinaire, and Guy Debord, among many others. For NYRB Classics he has translated Jean-Patrick Manchette's *Fatale* and *The Mad and the Bad*, Jean-Paul Clébert's *Paris Vagabond*, and the NYR Comics title *The Green Hand and Other Stories,* by Nicole Claveloux.

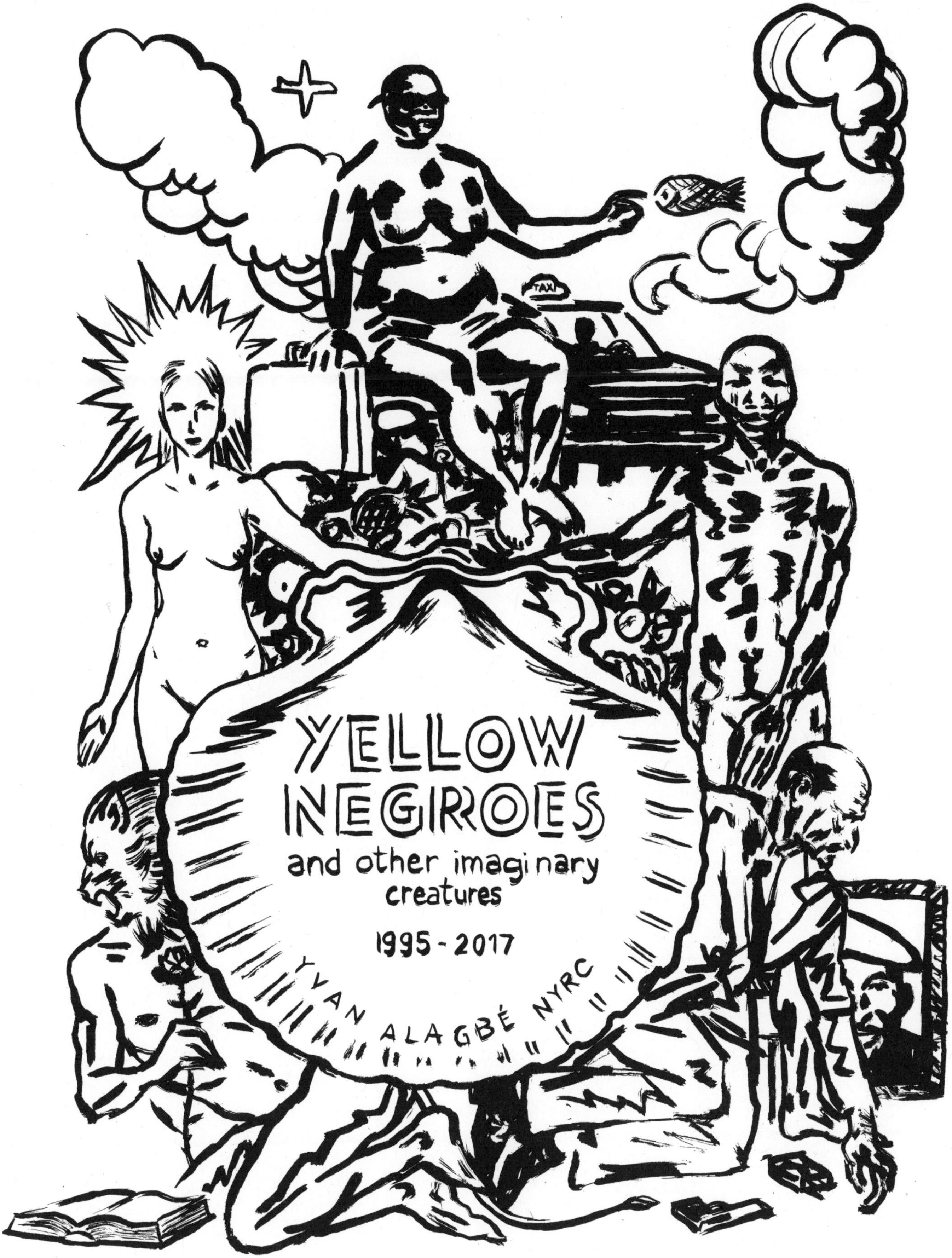
YELLOW
NEGROES
and other imaginary
creatures
1995 - 2017
YVAN ALAGBÉ NYRC
TAXI

THIS IS A NEW YORK REVIEW COMIC
PUBLISHED BY THE NEW YORK REVIEW OF BOOKS
435 Hudson Street, New York, NY 10014
www.nyrb.com

Cover design by Yvan Alagbé

Also by Yvan Alagbé:
Qui a connu le fue/Who has known the fire, with drawings
   by Olivier Bramanti, FRMK, 2007
École de la misère, FRMK, 2013

Library of Congress Cataloging-in-Publication Data

Names: Alagbé, Yvan, author, artist. | Nicholson-Smith, Donald, translator.
Title: Yellow negroes and other imaginary creatures / by Yvan Alagbé ;
  translated by Donald Nicholson-Smith.
Other titles: Nègres jaunes et autres créatures imaginaires. English
Description: New York : New York Review Books, [2017]
Identifiers: LCCN 2017024498 (print) | LCCN 2017029111 (ebook) | ISBN
  9781681371771 (epub) | ISBN 9781681371764 (paperback)
Subjects: LCSH: Comic books, strips, etc. | BISAC: COMICS & GRAPHIC NOVELS /
  Literary. | FICTION / Short Stories (single author).
Classification: LCC PN6747.A53 (ebook) | LCC PN6747.A53 N4413 2017 (print) |
  DDC 741.5/944—dc23
LC record available at https://lccn.loc.gov/2017024498

ISBN 978-1-68137-176-4
Available as an electronic book; 978-1-68137-177-1

Printed in Italy
10 9 8 7 6 5 4 3 2 1

LOVE

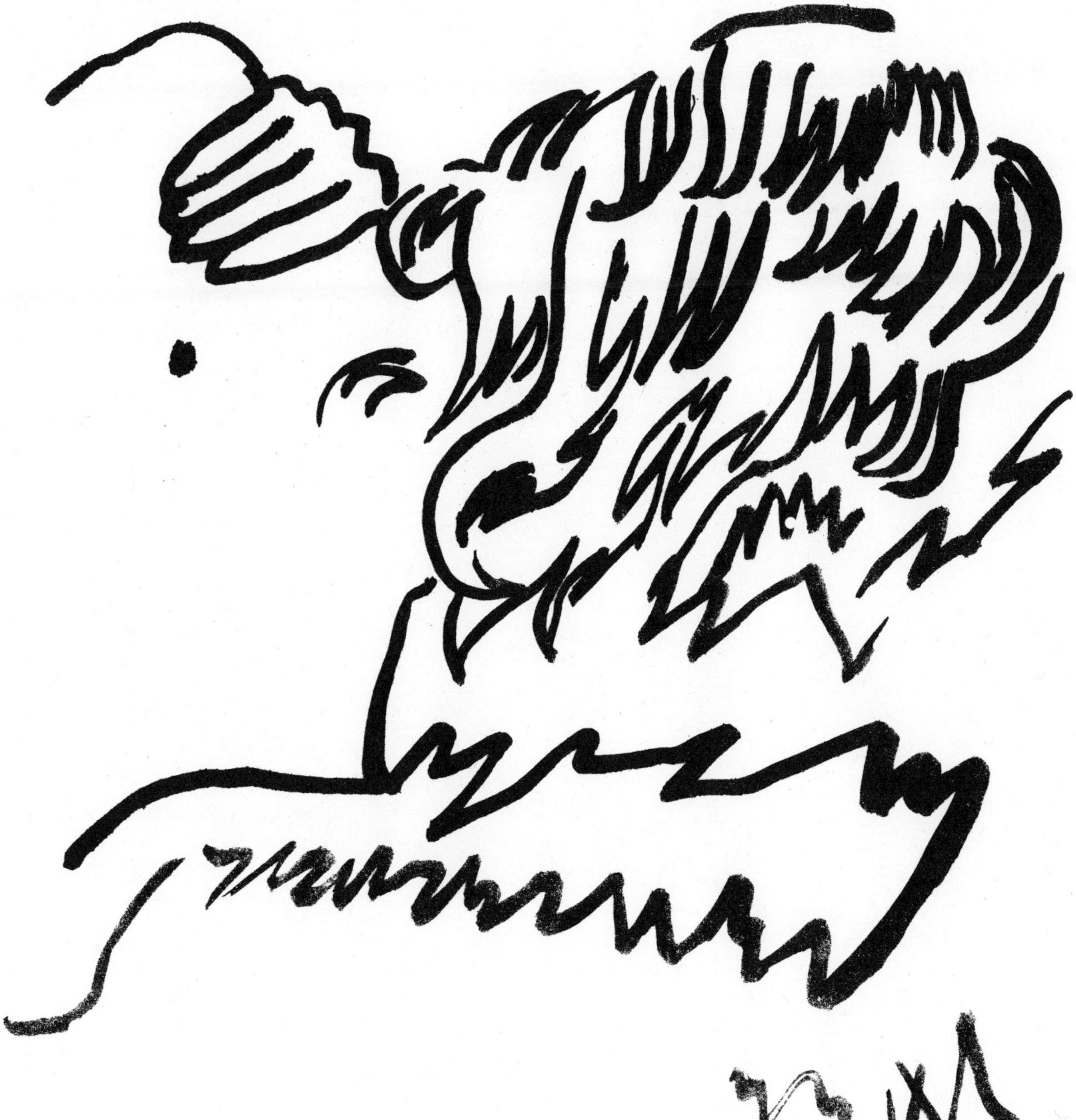

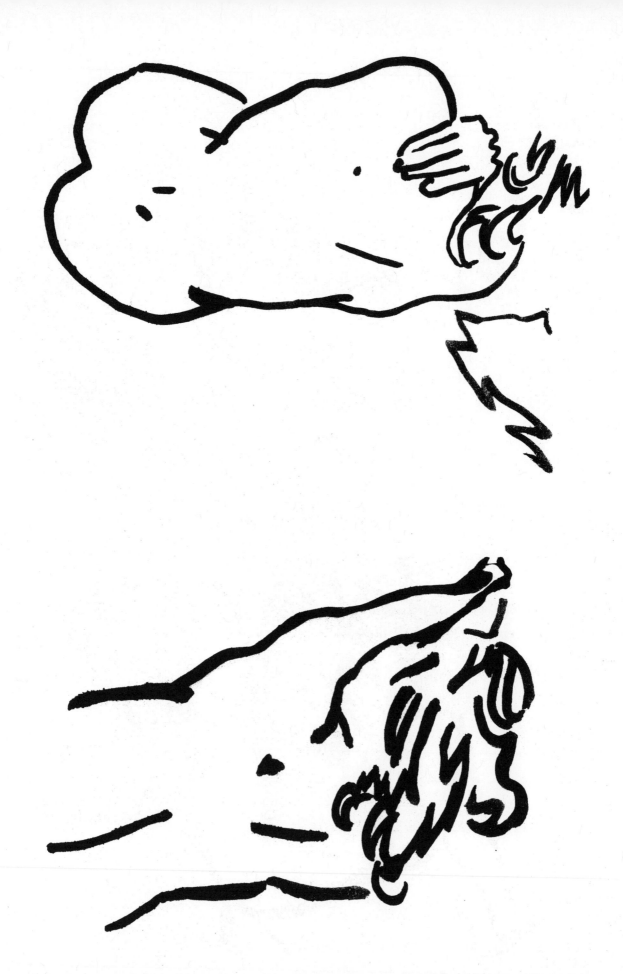

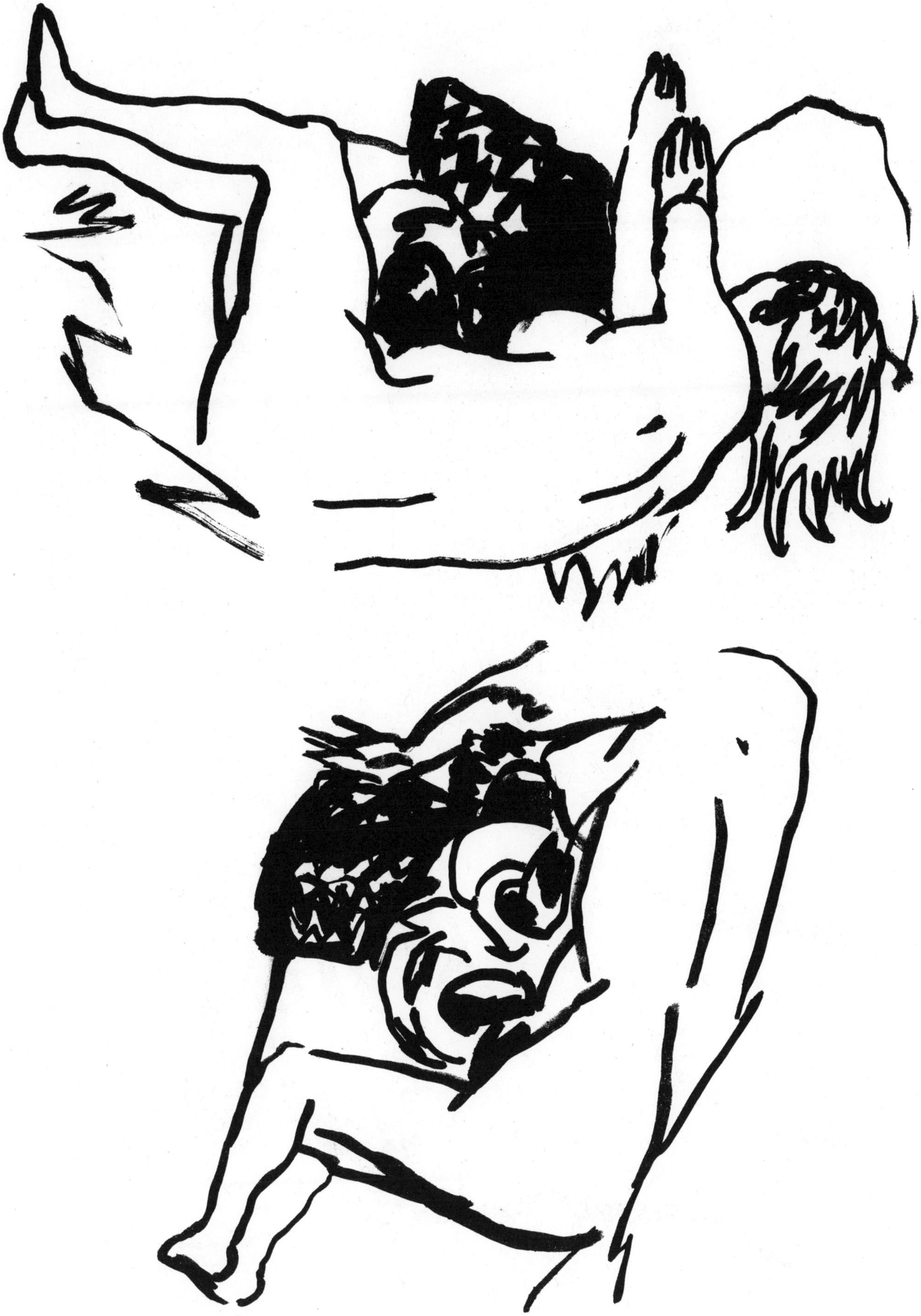

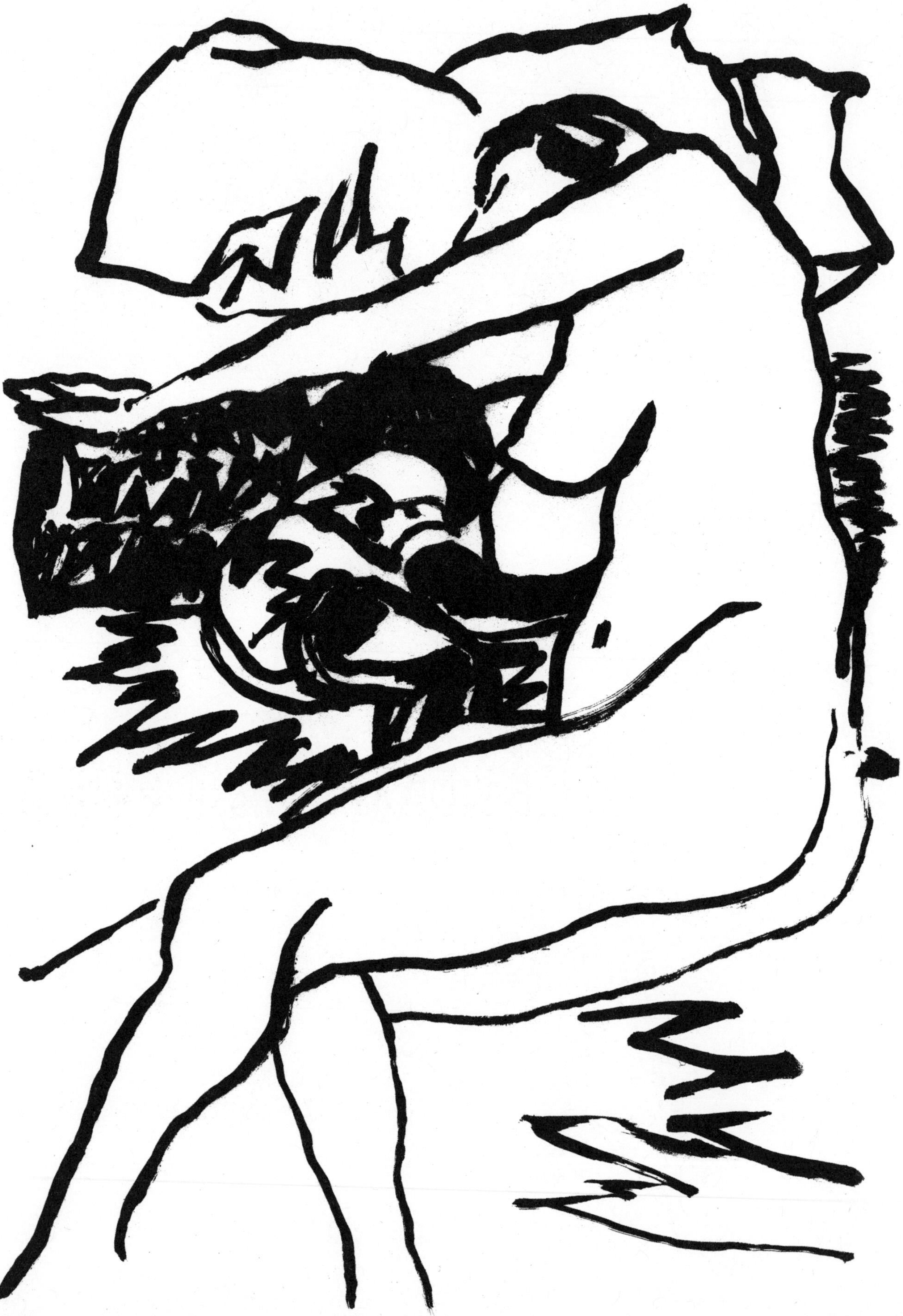

YELLOW NEGROES

THE LEPER WAS GROANING. THE CORNERS OF HIS MOUTH WERE DRAWN
BACK FROM HIS TEETH, A RAPID DEATH RATTLE SHOOK HIS CHEST, AND
WITH EACH INTAKE OF BREATH HIS BELLY HOLLOWED TOWARDS HIS
SPINE. THEN HE CLOSED HIS EYES.
-"I FEEL AS IF ICE WERE IN MY BONES! COME HERE NEXT TO ME!"
AND JULIAN, PULLING ASIDE THE COVERS, LAY DOWN ON THE DEAD
LEAVES NEXT TO HIM, AND THEY WERE SIDE BY SIDE.
THE LEPER TURNED HIS HEAD.
-"UNDRESS, SO THAT I MAY HAVE THE WARMTH OF YOUR BODY!"
JULIAN TOOK OFF HIS CLOTHES AND THEN, AS NAKED AS THE DAY HE WAS BORN,
GOT BACK INTO THE BED; AND AGAINST HIS THIGH HE FELT THE LEPER'S SKIN,
COLDER THAN A SNAKE AND ROUGHER THAN A RASP.
HE TRIED TO ENCOURAGE THE MAN, WHO REPLIED, PANTING,
"OH, I AM DYING! COME CLOSER TO ME, WARM ME UP! NOT WITH YOUR
HANDS! NO! WITH YOUR WHOLE BODY!"

GUSTAVE FLAUBERT, "THE LEGEND OF SAINT JULIAN THE HOSPITALER"

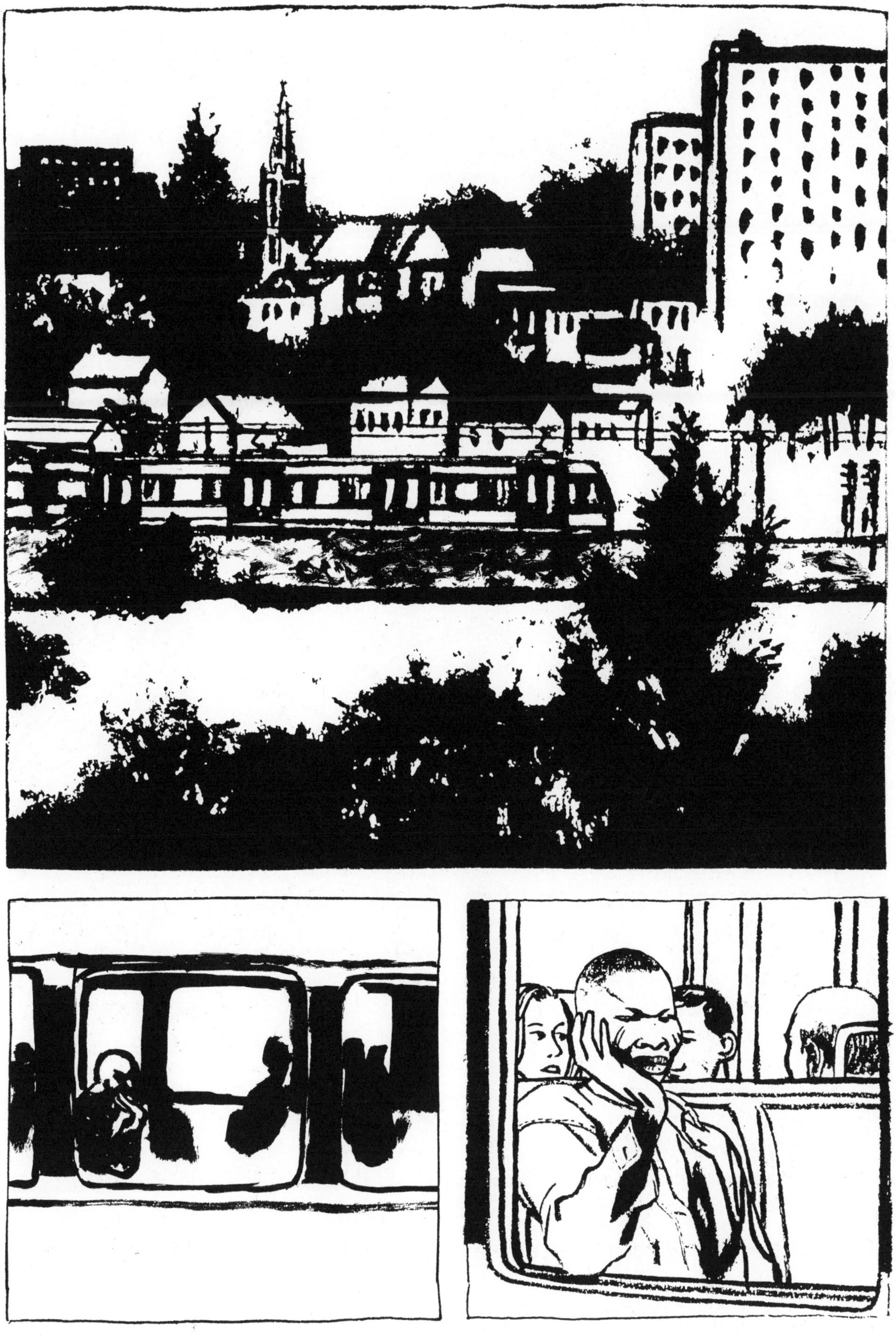

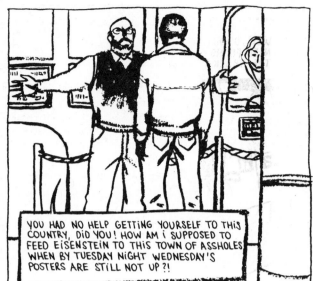

FUCK ME, YOU JUST WON'T DO SHIT! YOU HAVE TO GET EVERYTHING HANDED TO YOU ON A PLATTER!! STUCK RIGHT UNDER YOUR STUPID NOSE!! I GIVE YOU WORK WHEN YOU DON'T EVEN HAVE PAPERS, I PAY YOU, AND I STILL HAVE TO DO THE JOB MYSELF!!

YOU HAD NO HELP GETTING YOURSELF TO THIS COUNTRY, DID YOU! HOW AM I SUPPOSED TO FEED EISENSTEIN TO THIS TOWN OF ASSHOLES WHEN BY TUESDAY NIGHT WEDNESDAY'S POSTERS ARE STILL NOT UP?!

ALL MY PROGRAMMING DOWN THE TOILET! SHIT! YOU GET IT?!

WHAT THE FUCK'S BETWEEN YOUR EARS, HUH? YOU'D BETTER WATCH OUT THOUGH. WATCH YOURSELF. NO PAPERS - I'M A NICE GUY, I HIRE YOU. WE DO EVERY-THING TO HELP YOU, SO MAKE AN EFFORT, GODDAMMIT! OR ELSE STAY HOME, FOR SHIT'S SAKE!

GO AHEAD, TAKE OFF! YOU'RE REALLY TOO DUMB, YOU POOR FOOL! IF YOU LEAVE NOW DON'T BOTHER COMING BACK NEXT WEEK. THERE ARE PLENTY OF GUYS WHO WANT TO WORK!

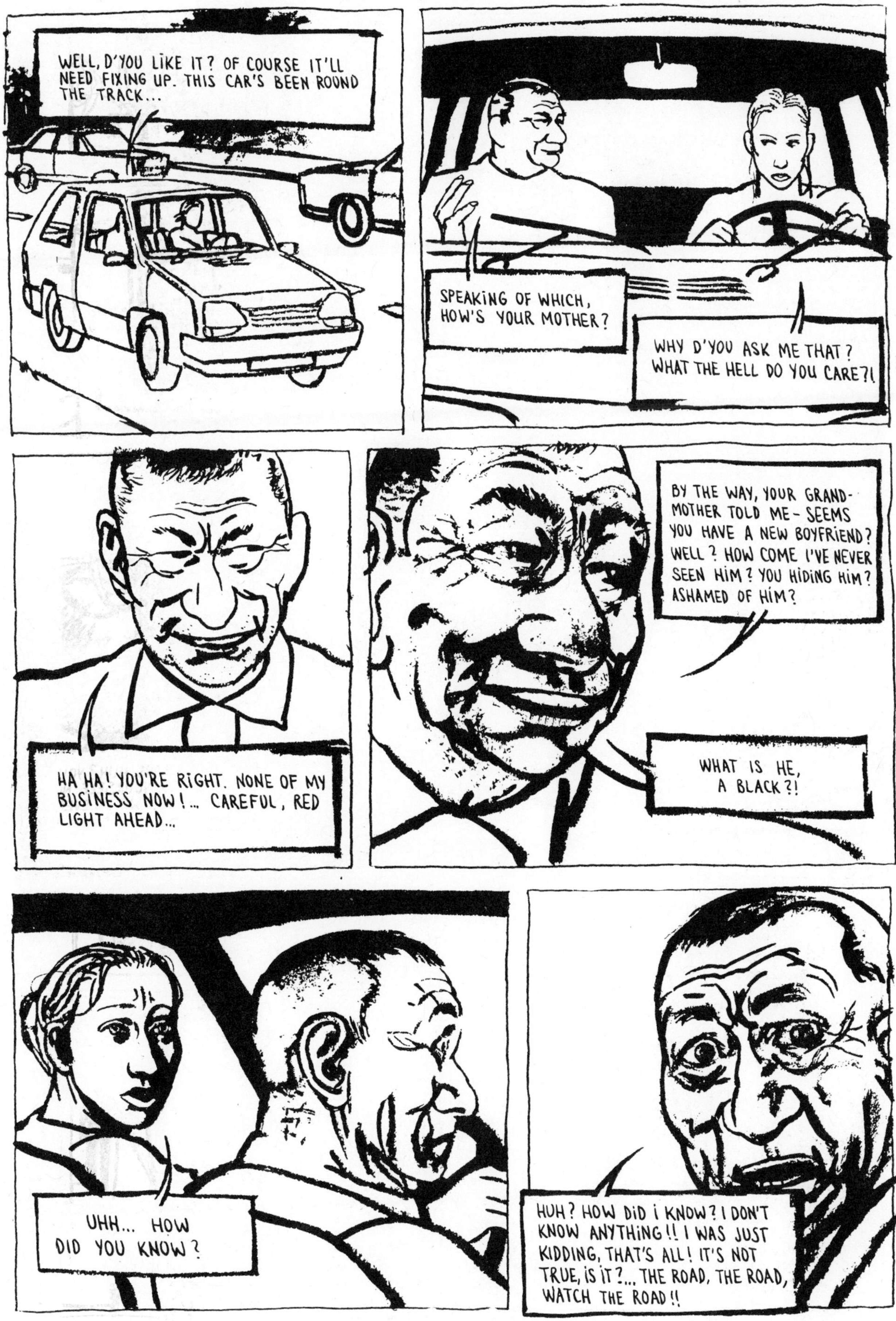

WELL, D'YOU LIKE IT? OF COURSE IT'LL NEED FIXING UP. THIS CAR'S BEEN ROUND THE TRACK...
SPEAKING OF WHICH, HOW'S YOUR MOTHER?
WHY D'YOU ASK ME THAT? WHAT THE HELL DO YOU CARE?!
HA HA! YOU'RE RIGHT. NONE OF MY BUSINESS NOW!... CAREFUL, RED LIGHT AHEAD...
BY THE WAY, YOUR GRAND-MOTHER TOLD ME - SEEMS YOU HAVE A NEW BOYFRIEND? WELL? HOW COME I'VE NEVER SEEN HIM? YOU HIDING HIM? ASHAMED OF HIM?
WHAT IS HE, A BLACK?!
UHH... HOW DID YOU KNOW?
HUH? HOW DID I KNOW? I DON'T KNOW ANYTHING!! I WAS JUST KIDDING, THAT'S ALL! IT'S NOT TRUE, IS IT?... THE ROAD, THE ROAD, WATCH THE ROAD!!

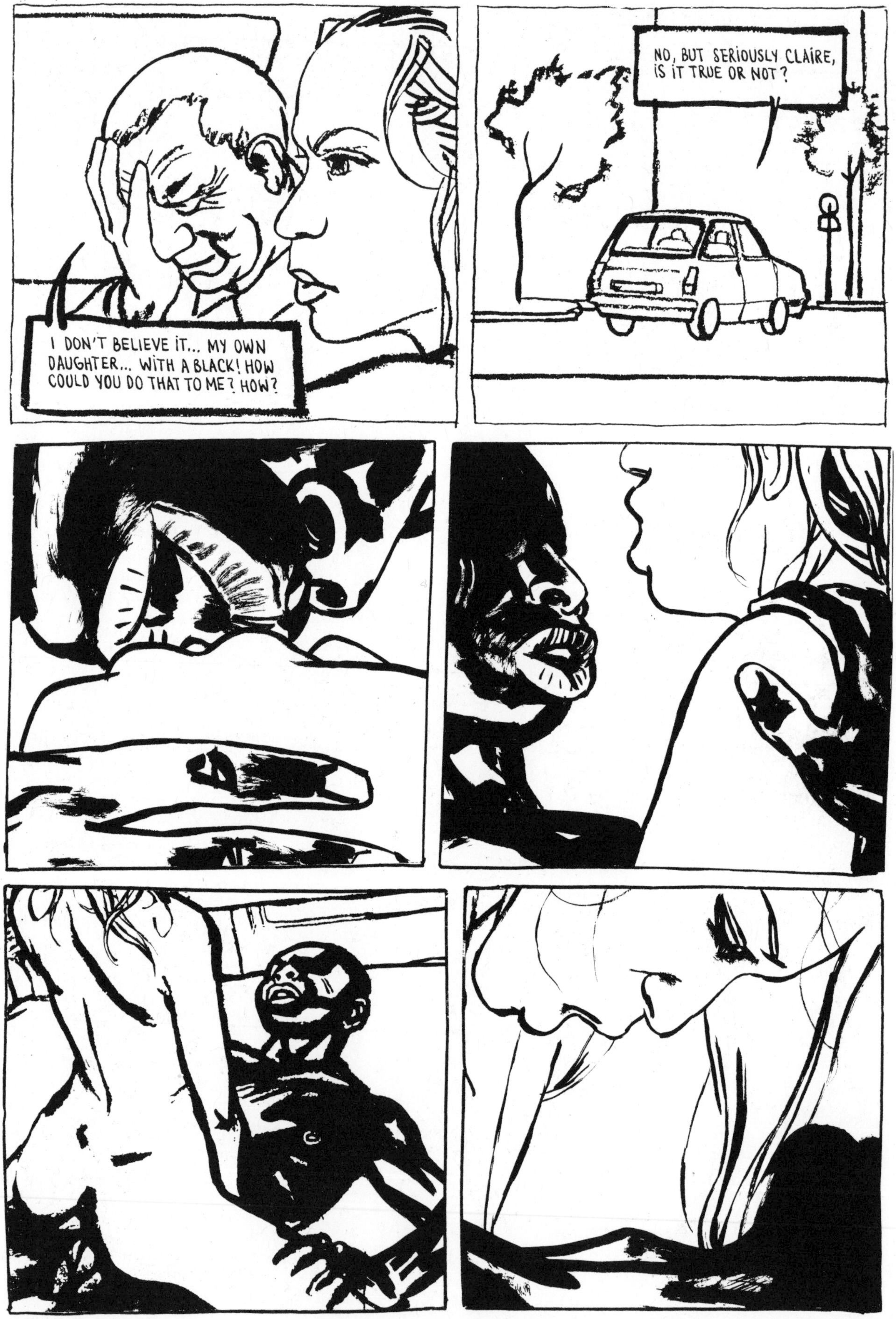
I DON'T BELIEVE IT... MY OWN DAUGHTER... WITH A BLACK! HOW COULD YOU DO THAT TO ME? HOW?
NO, BUT SERIOUSLY CLAIRE, IS IT TRUE OR NOT?

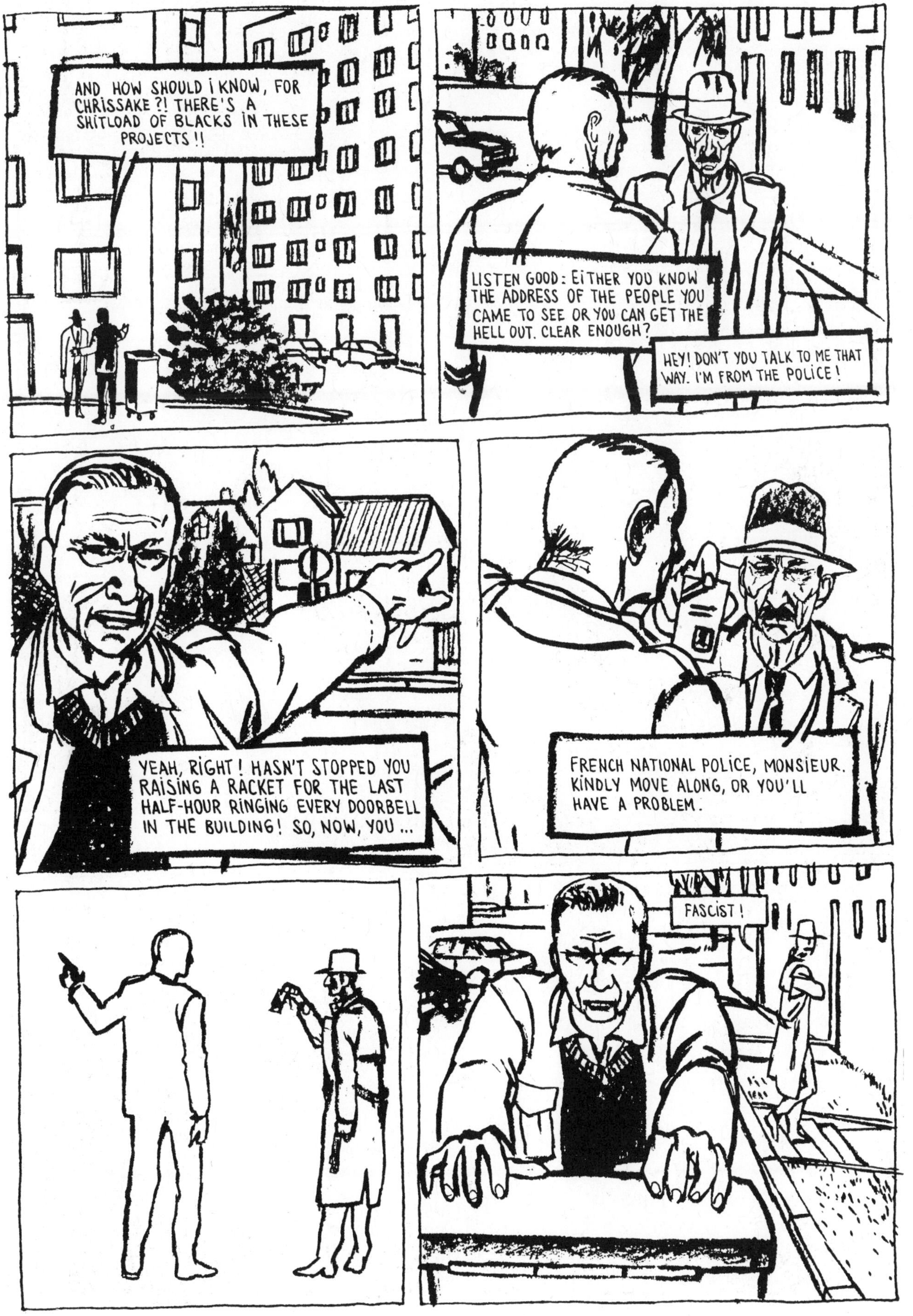
AND HOW SHOULD I KNOW, FOR CHRISSAKE?! THERE'S A SHITLOAD OF BLACKS IN THESE PROJECTS!!
LISTEN GOOD: EITHER YOU KNOW THE ADDRESS OF THE PEOPLE YOU CAME TO SEE OR YOU CAN GET THE HELL OUT. CLEAR ENOUGH?
HEY! DON'T YOU TALK TO ME THAT WAY. I'M FROM THE POLICE!
YEAH, RIGHT! HASN'T STOPPED YOU RAISING A RACKET FOR THE LAST HALF-HOUR RINGING EVERY DOORBELL IN THE BUILDING! SO, NOW, YOU ...
FRENCH NATIONAL POLICE, MONSIEUR. KINDLY MOVE ALONG, OR YOU'LL HAVE A PROBLEM.
FASCIST!

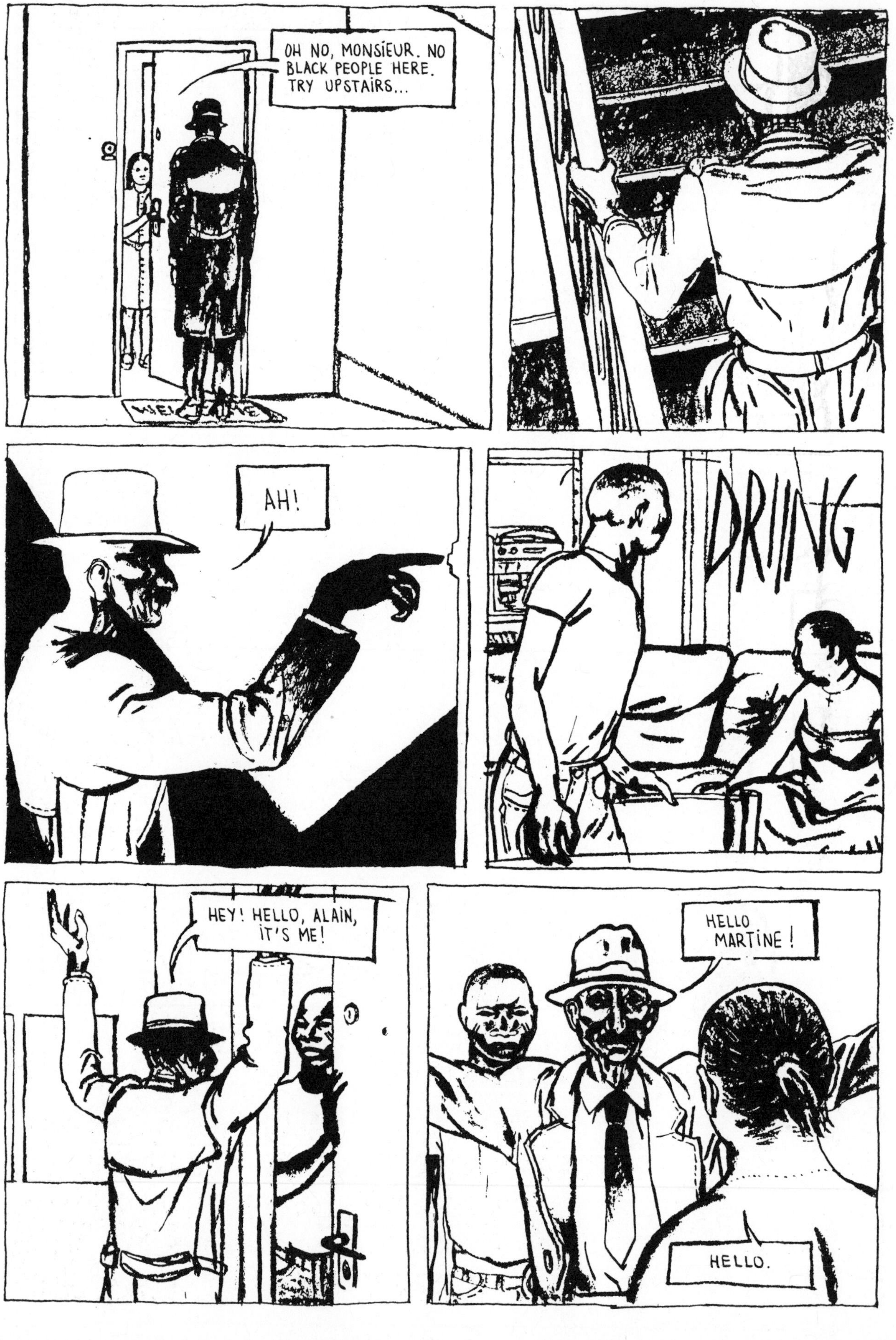
OH NO, MONSIEUR. NO BLACK PEOPLE HERE. TRY UPSTAIRS...
AH!
DRING
HEY! HELLO, ALAIN, IT'S ME!
HELLO MARTINE!
HELLO.

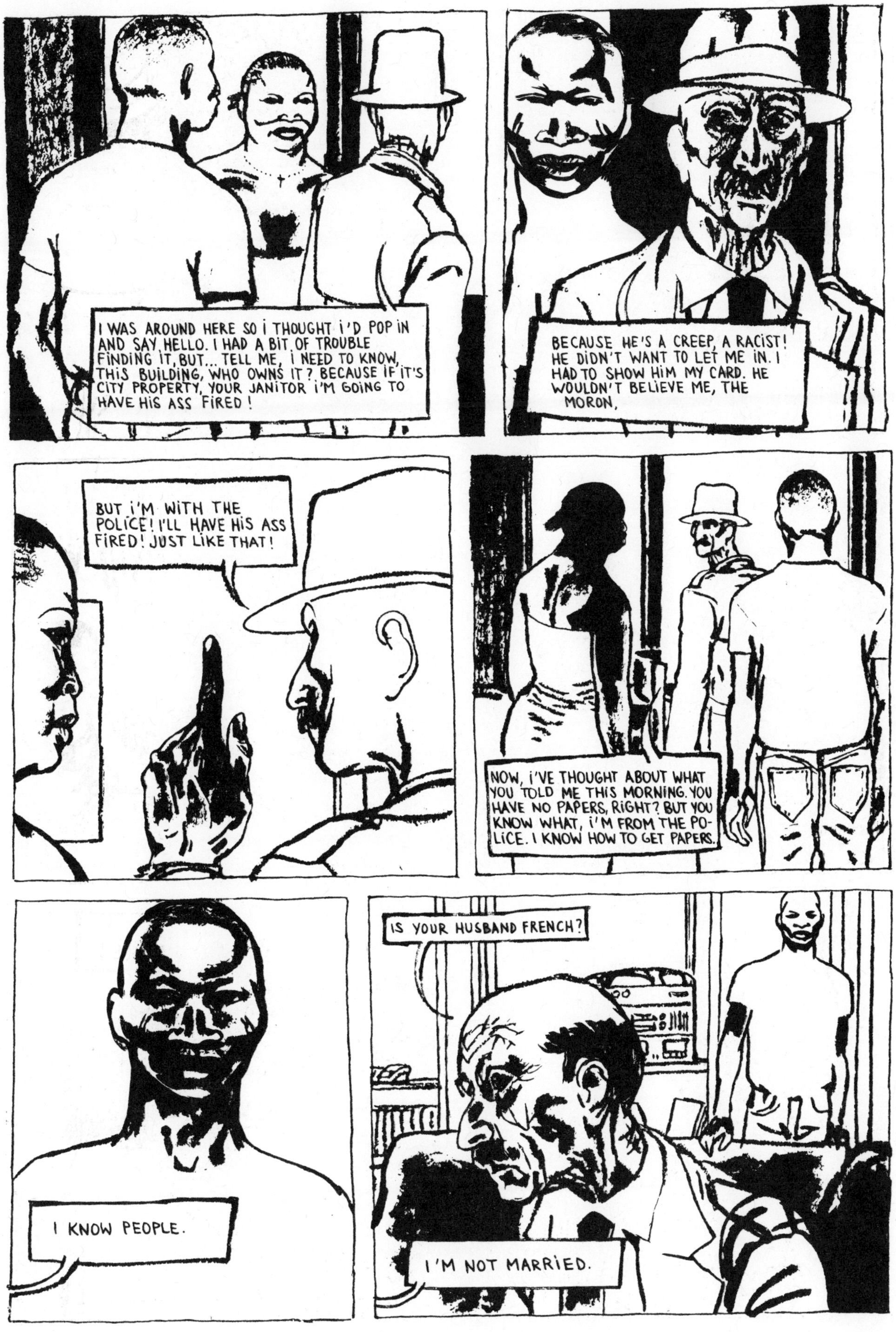
I WAS AROUND HERE SO I THOUGHT I'D POP IN AND SAY HELLO. I HAD A BIT OF TROUBLE FINDING IT, BUT... TELL ME, I NEED TO KNOW, THIS BUILDING, WHO OWNS IT? BECAUSE IF IT'S CITY PROPERTY, YOUR JANITOR I'M GOING TO HAVE HIS ASS FIRED!
BECAUSE HE'S A CREEP, A RACIST! HE DIDN'T WANT TO LET ME IN. I HAD TO SHOW HIM MY CARD. HE WOULDN'T BELIEVE ME, THE MORON.
BUT I'M WITH THE POLICE! I'LL HAVE HIS ASS FIRED! JUST LIKE THAT!
NOW, I'VE THOUGHT ABOUT WHAT YOU TOLD ME THIS MORNING. YOU HAVE NO PAPERS, RIGHT? BUT YOU KNOW WHAT, I'M FROM THE POLICE. I KNOW HOW TO GET PAPERS.
I KNOW PEOPLE.
IS YOUR HUSBAND FRENCH?
I'M NOT MARRIED.

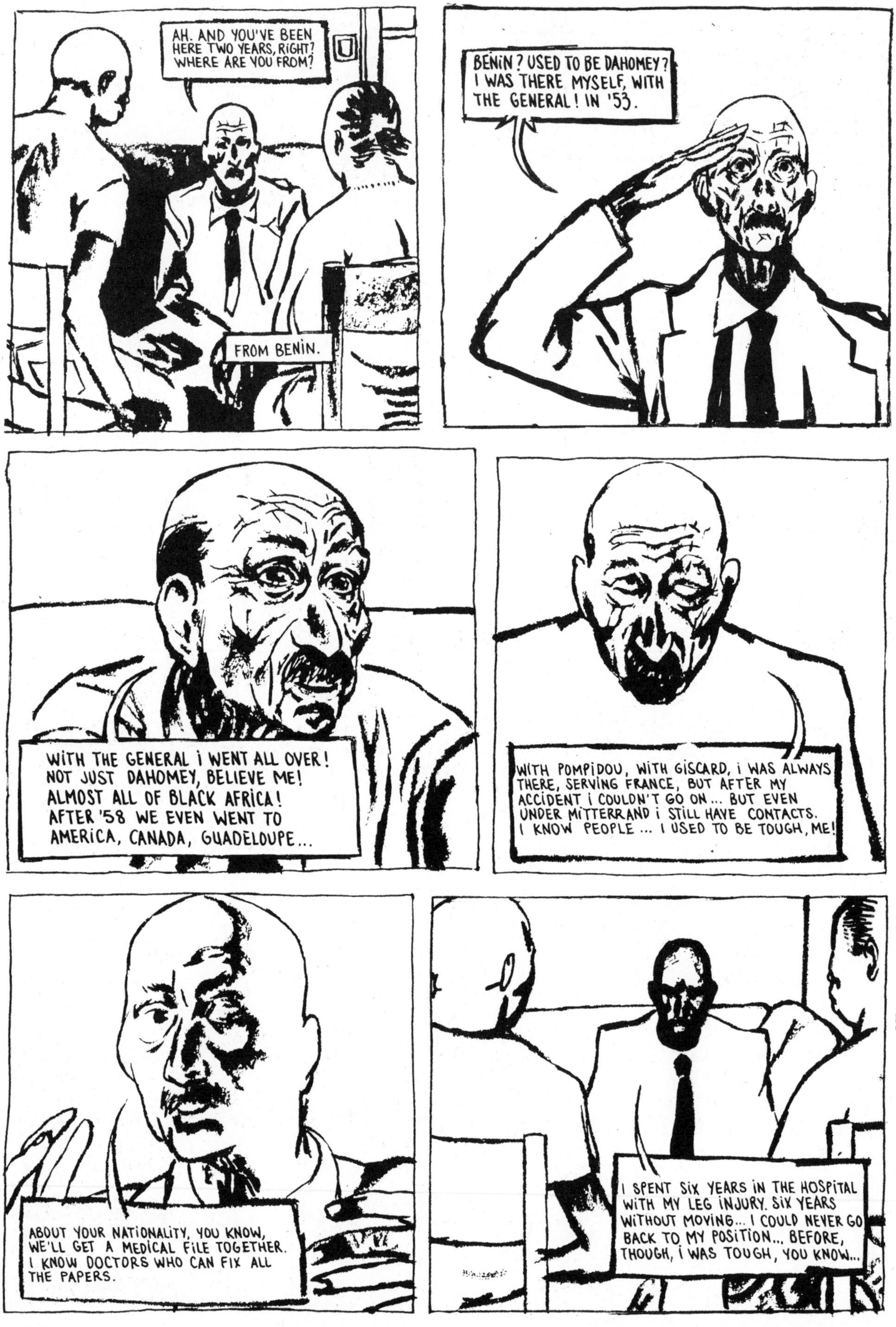
AH. AND YOU'VE BEEN HERE TWO YEARS, RIGHT? WHERE ARE YOU FROM?
FROM BENIN.
BENIN? USED TO BE DAHOMEY? I WAS THERE MYSELF, WITH THE GENERAL! IN '53.
WITH THE GENERAL I WENT ALL OVER! NOT JUST DAHOMEY, BELIEVE ME! ALMOST ALL OF BLACK AFRICA! AFTER '58 WE EVEN WENT TO AMERICA, CANADA, GUADELOUPE...
WITH POMPIDOU, WITH GISCARD, I WAS ALWAYS THERE, SERVING FRANCE, BUT AFTER MY ACCIDENT I COULDN'T GO ON... BUT EVEN UNDER MITTERRAND I STILL HAVE CONTACTS. I KNOW PEOPLE... I USED TO BE TOUGH, ME!
ABOUT YOUR NATIONALITY, YOU KNOW, WE'LL GET A MEDICAL FILE TOGETHER. I KNOW DOCTORS WHO CAN FIX ALL THE PAPERS.
I SPENT SIX YEARS IN THE HOSPITAL WITH MY LEG INJURY. SIX YEARS WITHOUT MOVING... I COULD NEVER GO BACK TO MY POSITION... BEFORE, THOUGH, I WAS TOUGH, YOU KNOW...

WE'LL SAY YOU SPENT TWO YEARS IN THE HOSPITAL AND SINCE YOU KNEW NO ONE YOU COULDN'T RENEW YOUR VISA. SIX YEARS I WAS IN THE HOSPITAL MYSELF...

AND WHILE I WAS THERE MY WIFE LEFT ME...

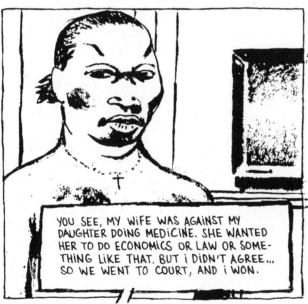

YOU SEE, MY WIFE WAS AGAINST MY DAUGHTER DOING MEDICINE. SHE WANTED HER TO DO ECONOMICS OR LAW OR SOMETHING LIKE THAT. BUT I DIDN'T AGREE... SO WE WENT TO COURT, AND I WON.

THE JUDGES FOUND FOR ME. THEY SAW THERE WERE GROUNDS FOR DIVORCE... SO WE GOT DIVORCED. LEGALLY I WAS IN THE RIGHT... AND THANKS TO ME MY DAUGHTER COULD GO ON WITH HER STUDIES.

NOW SHE'S A GYNECOLOGIST IN METZ. SHE HAS HER OWN PRACTICE AND MAKES A GOOD LIVING, RIGHT! THIRTY THOUSAND FRANCS A CONSULTATION AND SHE'S BOOKED UP FOR THREE MONTHS!

HELLO, I'M MARIO. ARE YOU AN ARTIST? IS THAT YOUR JOB?

SORT OF.

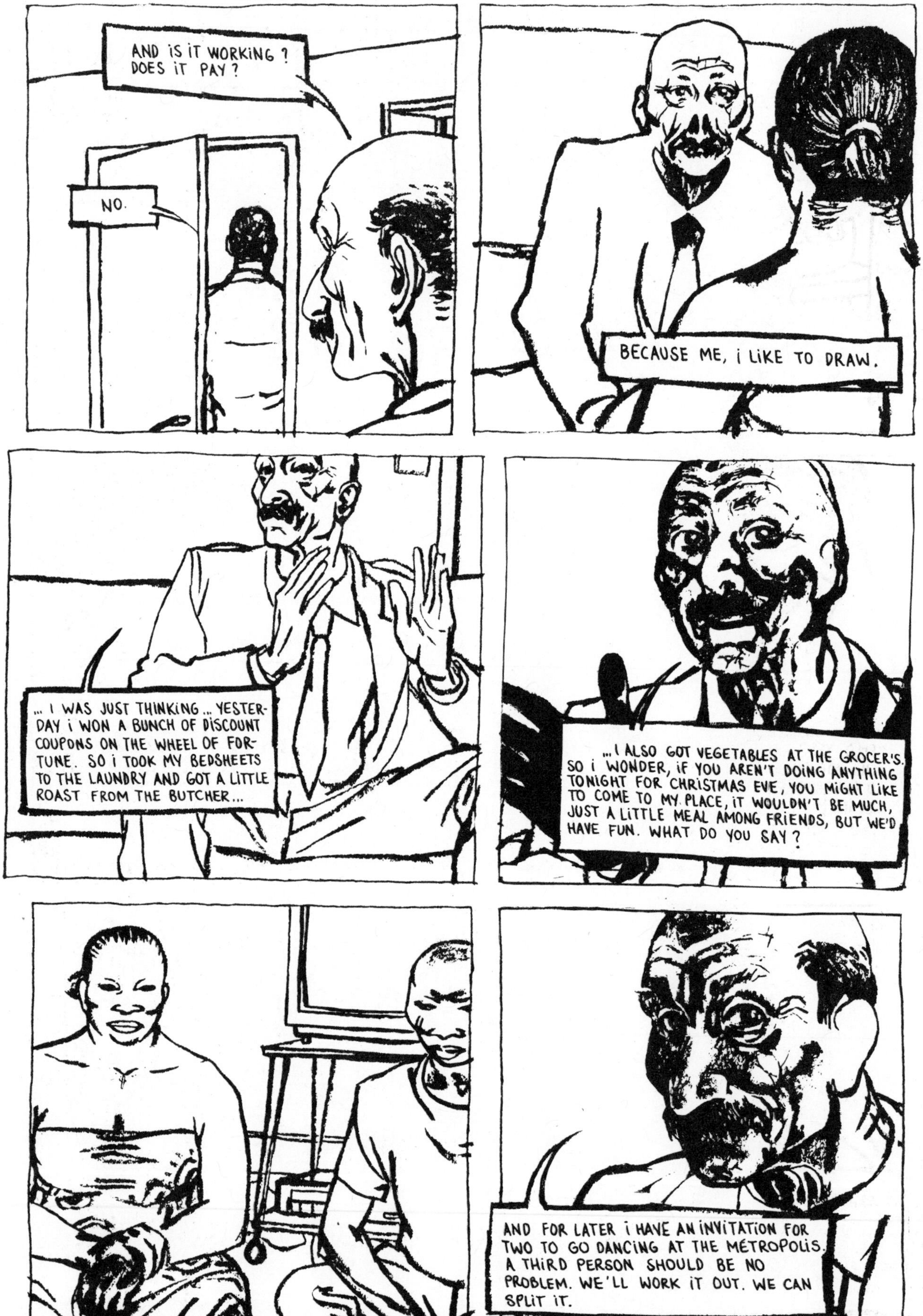
AND IS IT WORKING ? DOES IT PAY ?
NO.
BECAUSE ME, I LIKE TO DRAW.
... I WAS JUST THINKING ... YESTERDAY I WON A BUNCH OF DISCOUNT COUPONS ON THE WHEEL OF FORTUNE. SO I TOOK MY BEDSHEETS TO THE LAUNDRY AND GOT A LITTLE ROAST FROM THE BUTCHER...
... I ALSO GOT VEGETABLES AT THE GROCER'S. SO I WONDER, IF YOU AREN'T DOING ANYTHING TONIGHT FOR CHRISTMAS EVE, YOU MIGHT LIKE TO COME TO MY PLACE, IT WOULDN'T BE MUCH, JUST A LITTLE MEAL AMONG FRIENDS, BUT WE'D HAVE FUN. WHAT DO YOU SAY ?
AND FOR LATER I HAVE AN INVITATION FOR TWO TO GO DANCING AT THE MÉTROPOLIS. A THIRD PERSON SHOULD BE NO PROBLEM. WE'LL WORK IT OUT. WE CAN SPLIT IT.

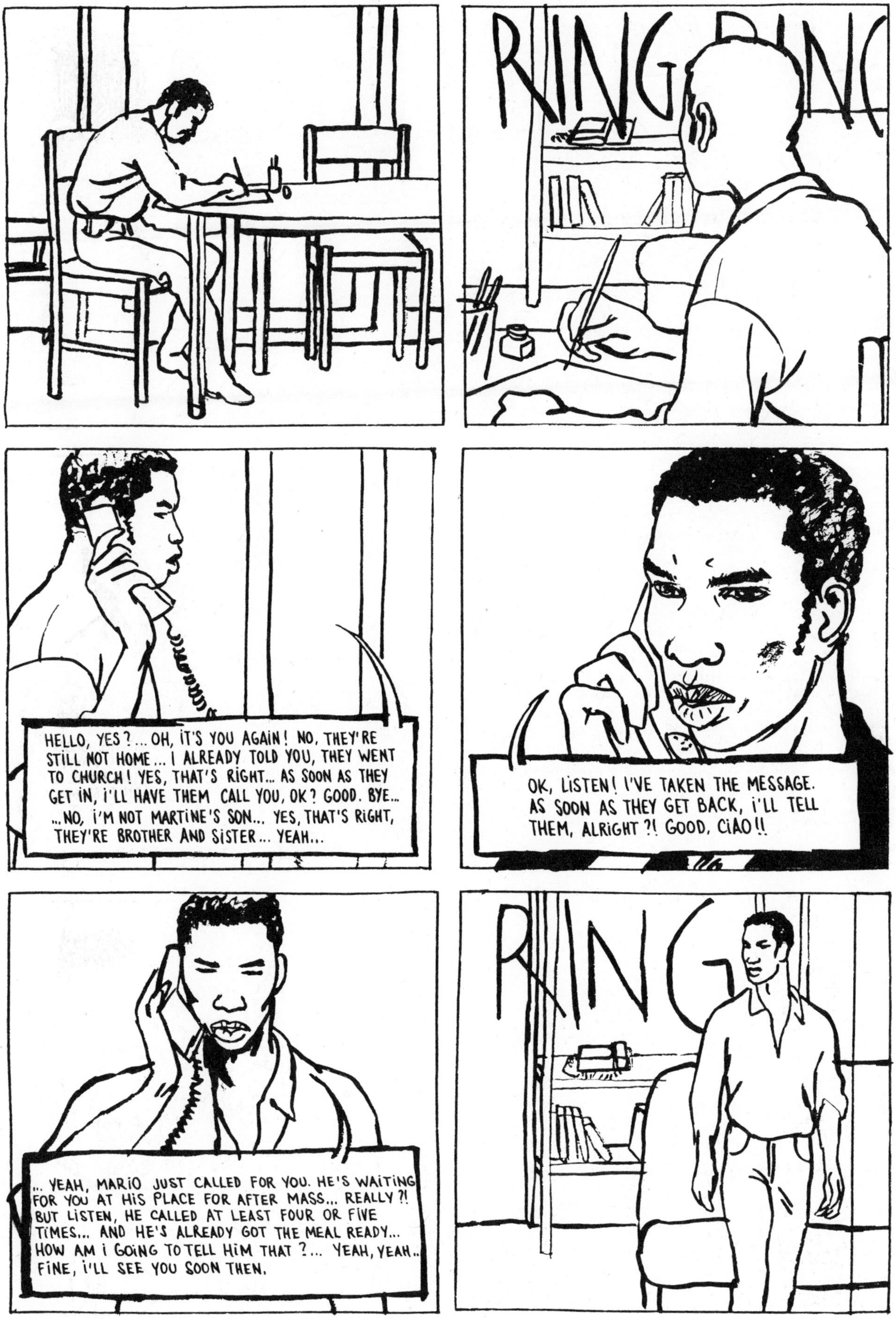
RING RING
HELLO, YES?... OH, IT'S YOU AGAIN! NO, THEY'RE STILL NOT HOME... I ALREADY TOLD YOU, THEY WENT TO CHURCH! YES, THAT'S RIGHT... AS SOON AS THEY GET IN, I'LL HAVE THEM CALL YOU, OK? GOOD. BYE... ...NO, I'M NOT MARTINE'S SON... YES, THAT'S RIGHT, THEY'RE BROTHER AND SISTER... YEAH...
OK, LISTEN! I'VE TAKEN THE MESSAGE. AS SOON AS THEY GET BACK, I'LL TELL THEM, ALRIGHT?! GOOD, CIAO!!
... YEAH, MARIO JUST CALLED FOR YOU. HE'S WAITING FOR YOU AT HIS PLACE FOR AFTER MASS... REALLY?! BUT LISTEN, HE CALLED AT LEAST FOUR OR FIVE TIMES... AND HE'S ALREADY GOT THE MEAL READY... HOW AM I GOING TO TELL HIM THAT?... YEAH, YEAH.. FINE, I'LL SEE YOU SOON THEN.
RING

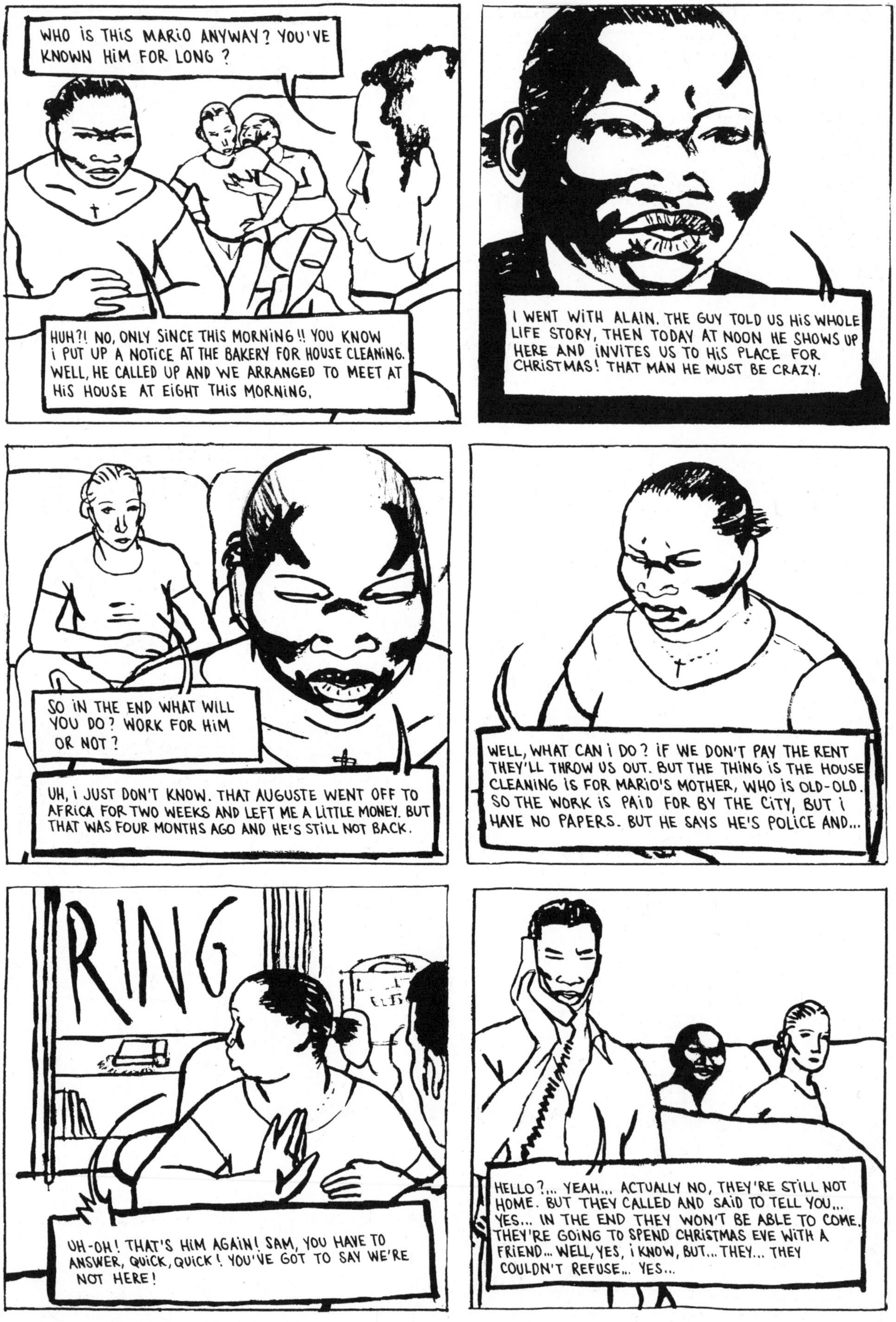
WHO IS THIS MARIO ANYWAY? YOU'VE KNOWN HIM FOR LONG?
HUH?! NO, ONLY SINCE THIS MORNING!! YOU KNOW I PUT UP A NOTICE AT THE BAKERY FOR HOUSE CLEANING. WELL, HE CALLED UP AND WE ARRANGED TO MEET AT HIS HOUSE AT EIGHT THIS MORNING.
I WENT WITH ALAIN. THE GUY TOLD US HIS WHOLE LIFE STORY, THEN TODAY AT NOON HE SHOWS UP HERE AND INVITES US TO HIS PLACE FOR CHRISTMAS! THAT MAN HE MUST BE CRAZY.
SO IN THE END WHAT WILL YOU DO? WORK FOR HIM OR NOT?
UH, I JUST DON'T KNOW. THAT AUGUSTE WENT OFF TO AFRICA FOR TWO WEEKS AND LEFT ME A LITTLE MONEY. BUT THAT WAS FOUR MONTHS AGO AND HE'S STILL NOT BACK.
WELL, WHAT CAN I DO? IF WE DON'T PAY THE RENT THEY'LL THROW US OUT. BUT THE THING IS THE HOUSE CLEANING IS FOR MARIO'S MOTHER, WHO IS OLD-OLD. SO THE WORK IS PAID FOR BY THE CITY, BUT I HAVE NO PAPERS. BUT HE SAYS HE'S POLICE AND...
RING
UH-OH! THAT'S HIM AGAIN! SAM, YOU HAVE TO ANSWER, QUICK, QUICK! YOU'VE GOT TO SAY WE'RE NOT HERE!
HELLO?... YEAH... ACTUALLY NO, THEY'RE STILL NOT HOME. BUT THEY CALLED AND SAID TO TELL YOU... YES... IN THE END THEY WON'T BE ABLE TO COME. THEY'RE GOING TO SPEND CHRISTMAS EVE WITH A FRIEND... WELL, YES, I KNOW, BUT... THEY... THEY COULDN'T REFUSE... YES...

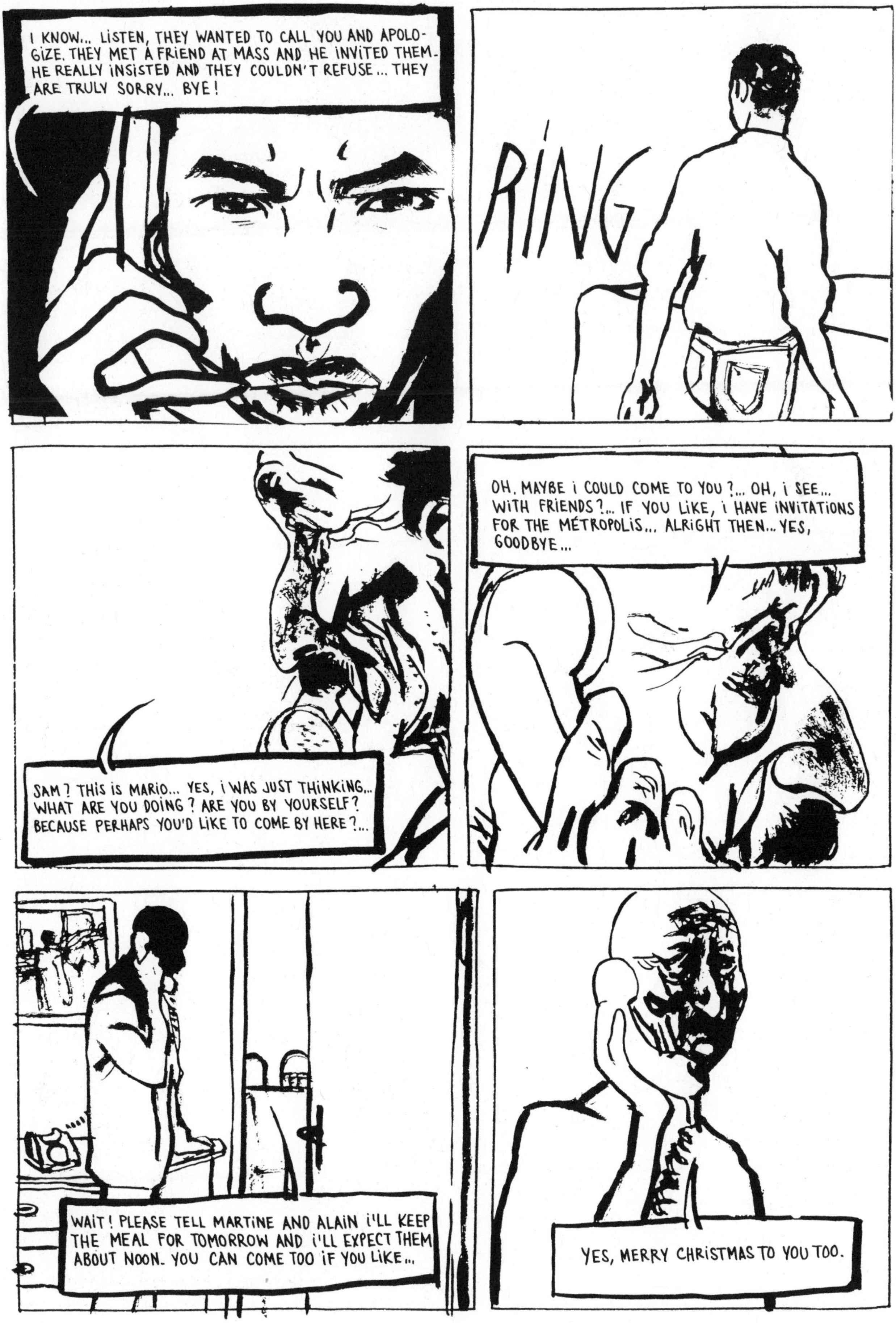
I KNOW... LISTEN, THEY WANTED TO CALL YOU AND APOLOGIZE. THEY MET A FRIEND AT MASS AND HE INVITED THEM. HE REALLY INSISTED AND THEY COULDN'T REFUSE... THEY ARE TRULY SORRY... BYE!
RING
SAM? THIS IS MARIO... YES, I WAS JUST THINKING... WHAT ARE YOU DOING? ARE YOU BY YOURSELF? BECAUSE PERHAPS YOU'D LIKE TO COME BY HERE?...
OH, MAYBE I COULD COME TO YOU?... OH, I SEE... WITH FRIENDS?... IF YOU LIKE, I HAVE INVITATIONS FOR THE MÉTROPOLIS... ALRIGHT THEN... YES, GOODBYE...
WAIT! PLEASE TELL MARTINE AND ALAIN I'LL KEEP THE MEAL FOR TOMORROW AND I'LL EXPECT THEM ABOUT NOON. YOU CAN COME TOO IF YOU LIKE...
YES, MERRY CHRISTMAS TO YOU TOO.

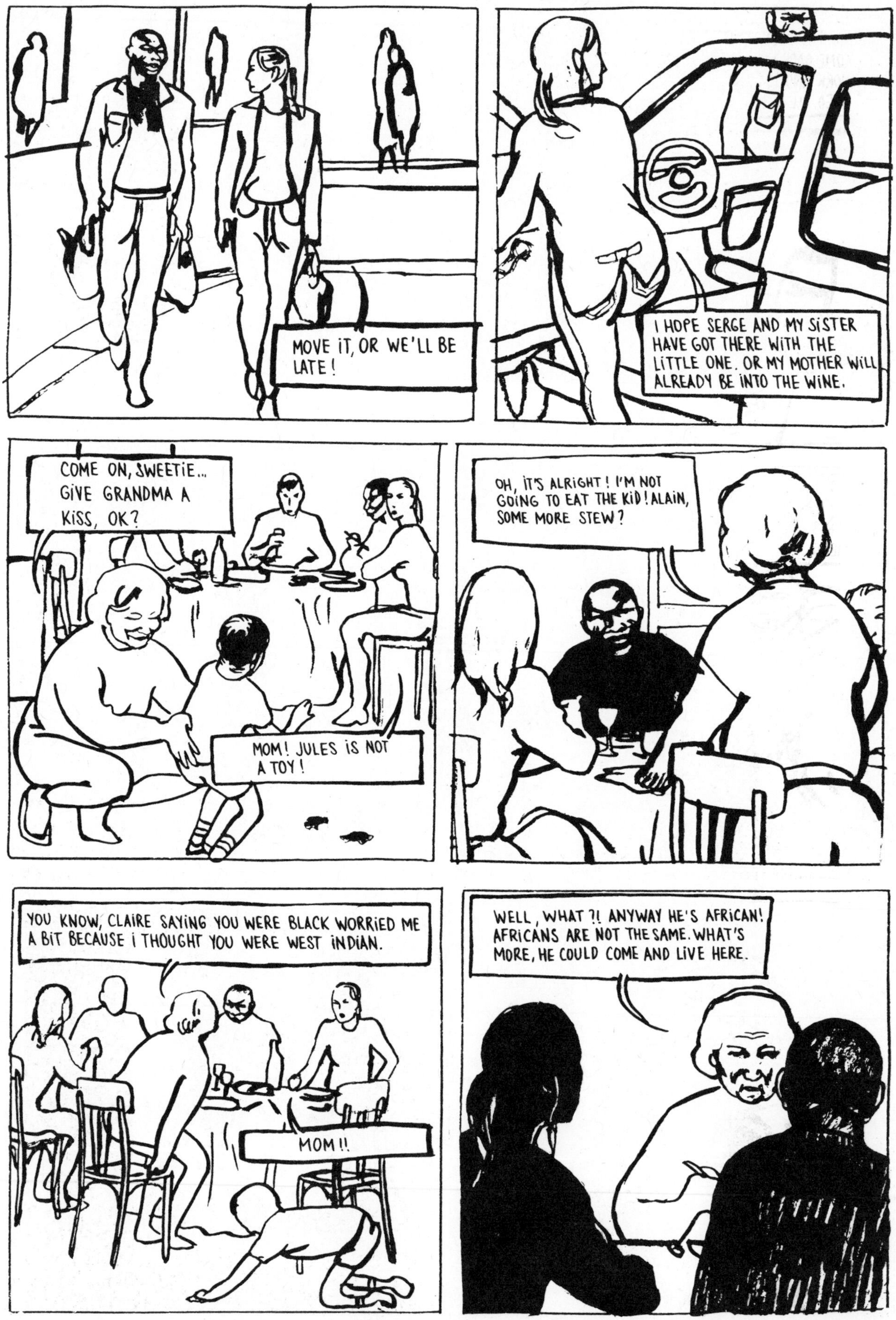
MOVE IT, OR WE'LL BE LATE!
I HOPE SERGE AND MY SISTER HAVE GOT THERE WITH THE LITTLE ONE. OR MY MOTHER WILL ALREADY BE INTO THE WINE.
COME ON, SWEETIE... GIVE GRANDMA A KISS, OK?
MOM! JULES IS NOT A TOY!
OH, IT'S ALRIGHT! I'M NOT GOING TO EAT THE KID! ALAIN, SOME MORE STEW?
YOU KNOW, CLAIRE SAYING YOU WERE BLACK WORRIED ME A BIT BECAUSE I THOUGHT YOU WERE WEST INDIAN.
MOM!!
WELL, WHAT ?! ANYWAY HE'S AFRICAN! AFRICANS ARE NOT THE SAME. WHAT'S MORE, HE COULD COME AND LIVE HERE.

AND I'VE BEEN THINKING, SERGE AND CECILE COULD COME BACK TOO... BECAUSE MYSELF I'M FED UP WITH WORK AND I'M STOPPING. GETTING MYSELF REASSIGNED. I'LL BE MAKING 40% OF WHAT I MAKE NOW.

WHAT'S ALL THIS NONSENSE?! WHAT ABOUT ALL YOUR BILLS?

WELL, THAT'S JUST IT... I THOUGHT YOU COULD TAKE OVER THE MORTGAGE AND WE'D ALL LIVE HERE. THERE'S ENOUGH ROOM... QUITE POSSIBLE IF EVERYONE CHIPS IN...

SHE SAYS A LOT OF STUPID THINGS, MY MOTHER, BUT... WE COULD GET MARRIED... FOR YOUR PAPERS, I MEAN...

NO.

NO, THAT'S NOT WHY YOU GET MARRIED... NOT FOR THAT...

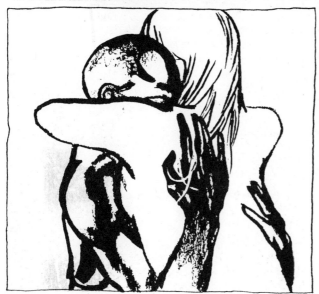

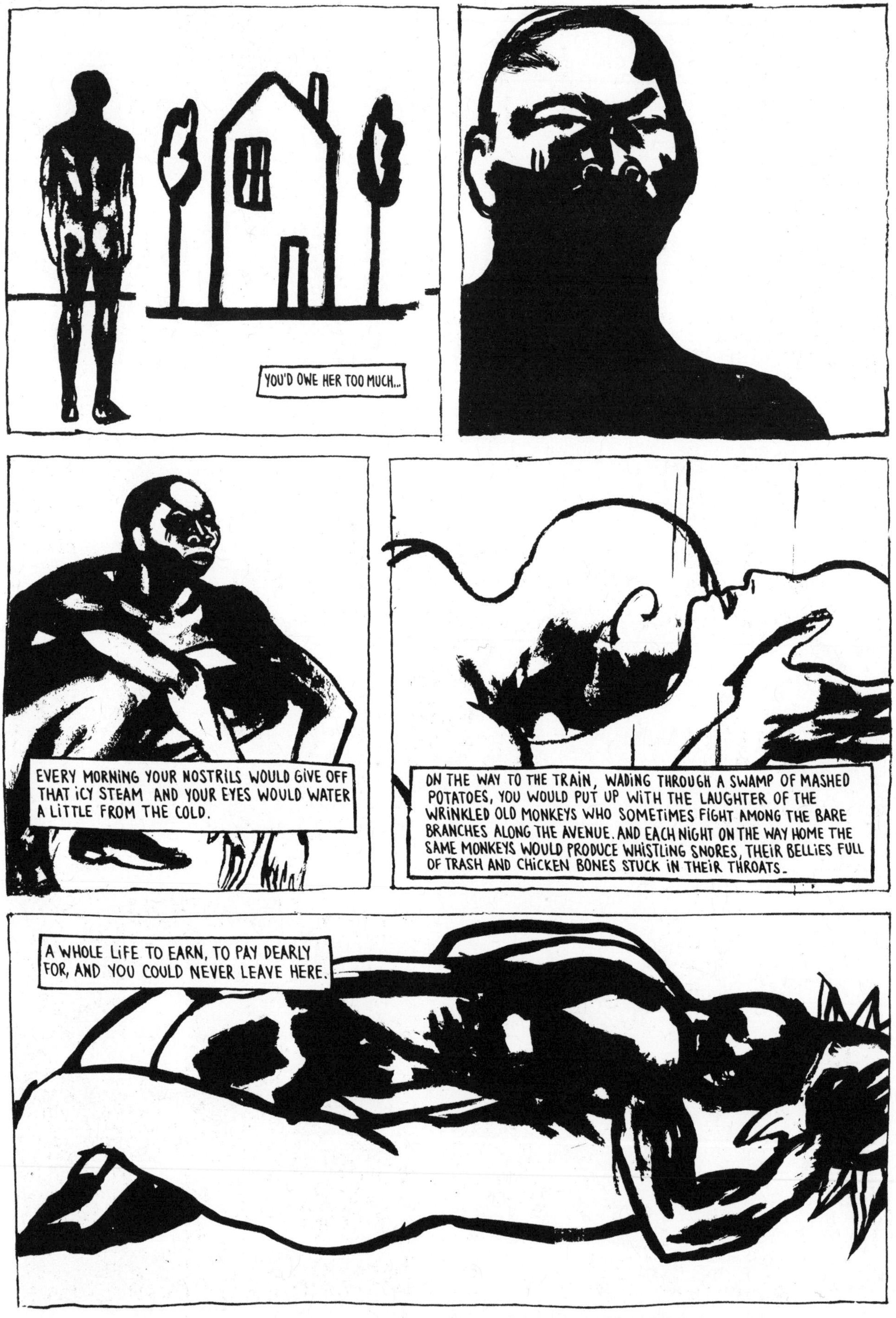
YOU'D OWE HER TOO MUCH...
EVERY MORNING YOUR NOSTRILS WOULD GIVE OFF THAT iCY STEAM AND YOUR EYES WOULD WATER A LiTTLE FROM THE COLD.
ON THE WAY TO THE TRAiN, WADiNG THROUGH A SWAMP OF MASHED POTATOES, YOU WOULD PUT UP WiTH THE LAUGHTER OF THE WRiNKLED OLD MONKEYS WHO SOMETiMES FiGHT AMONG THE BARE BRANCHES ALONG THE AVENUE. AND EACH NiGHT ON THE WAY HOME THE SAME MONKEYS WOULD PRODUCE WHiSTLiNG SNORES, THEiR BELLiES FULL OF TRASH AND CHiCKEN BONES STUCK iN THEiR THROATS.
A WHOLE LiFE TO EARN, TO PAY DEARLY FOR, AND YOU COULD NEVER LEAVE HERE.

AND SO, ALMOST EVERY DAY, ALAIN WALKED UP THE HILL TO A GRAY DETACHED HOUSE WHERE THE MAN SAT HIM DOWN IN AN ANCIENT ARMCHAIR AND TOLD OF COUNTLESS MIRACLES.

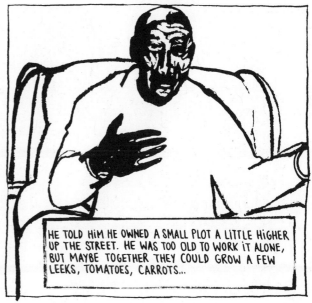

HE TOLD HIM HE OWNED A SMALL PLOT A LITTLE HIGHER UP THE STREET. HE WAS TOO OLD TO WORK IT ALONE, BUT MAYBE TOGETHER THEY COULD GROW A FEW LEEKS, TOMATOES, CARROTS...

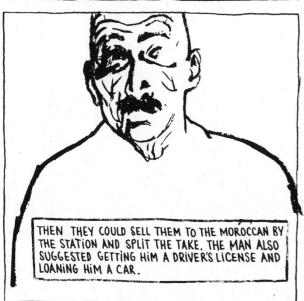

THEN THEY COULD SELL THEM TO THE MOROCCAN BY THE STATION AND SPLIT THE TAKE. THE MAN ALSO SUGGESTED GETTING HIM A DRIVER'S LICENSE AND LOANING HIM A CAR.

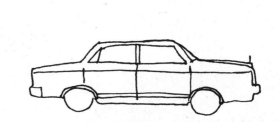

A CAR, WHY NOT ? ALAIN ALREADY SAW HIMSELF, RINGS ON EVERY FINGER, BEHIND THE WHEEL OF A MERCEDES. ALL THE VILLAGE KIDS RUNNING AFTER HIM IN THE RED DUST OF THE ROAD. MONSIEUR TOOTS HIS HORN AND EVERYONE BEGINS TO DANCE. BUT ALAIN KNOWS THAT EVEN WITH PAPERS HE'LL FIND IT HARD TO GET A GOOD JOB. "WHITES ARE TRICKY, AREN'T THEY, AND IT'S TOO HARD FOR US HERE."

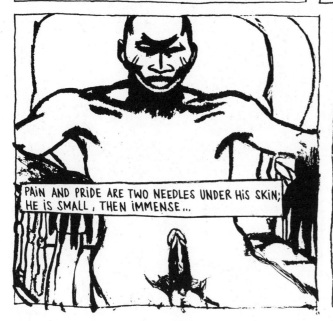

PAIN AND PRIDE ARE TWO NEEDLES UNDER HIS SKIN; HE IS SMALL, THEN IMMENSE...

... HE DREAMS OF BROAD-HIPPED WOMEN.

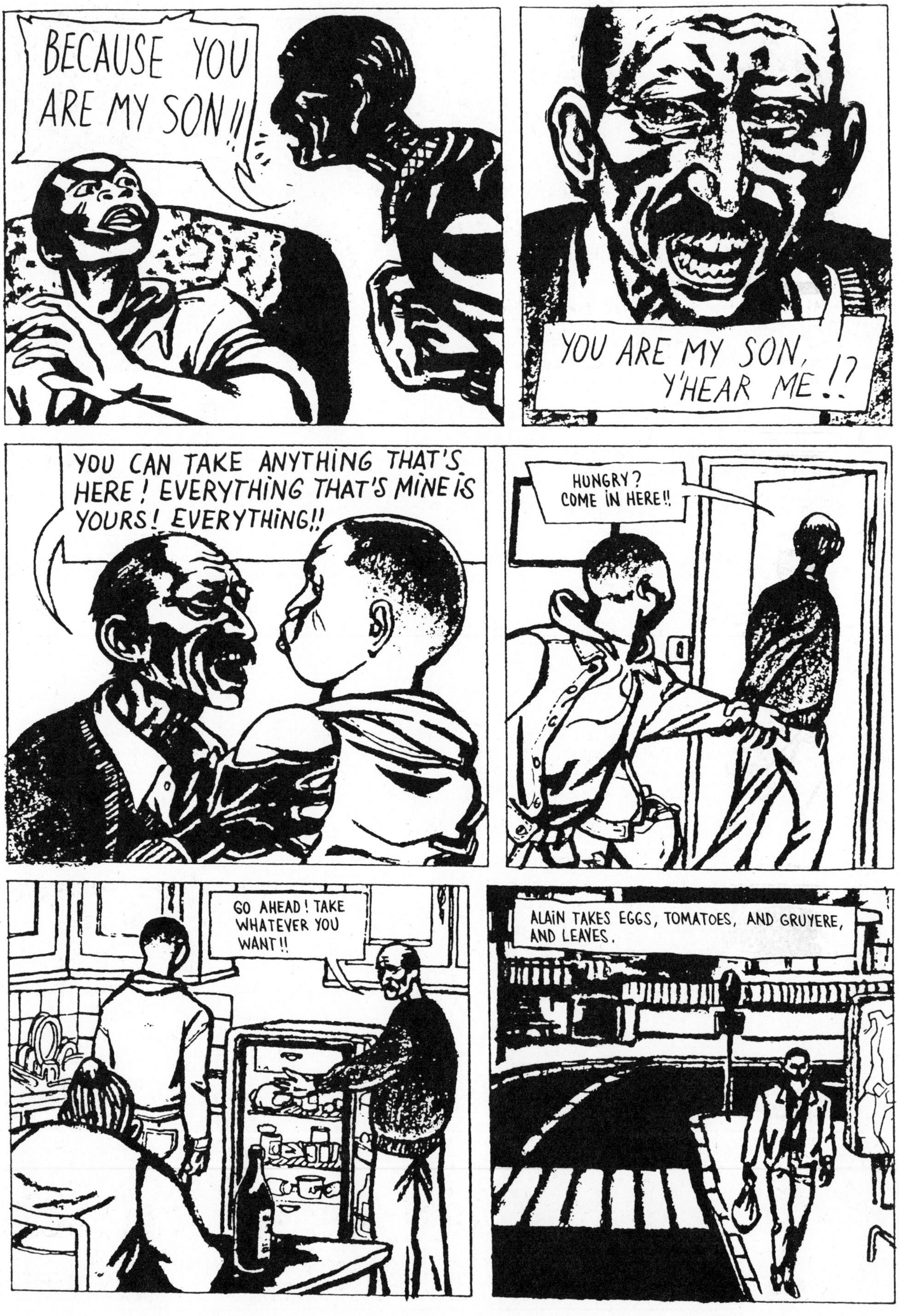
BECAUSE YOU ARE MY SON!!
YOU ARE MY SON, Y'HEAR ME!?
YOU CAN TAKE ANYTHING THAT'S HERE! EVERYTHING THAT'S MINE IS YOURS! EVERYTHING!!
HUNGRY? COME IN HERE!!
GO AHEAD! TAKE WHATEVER YOU WANT!!
ALAIN TAKES EGGS, TOMATOES, AND GRUYERE, AND LEAVES.

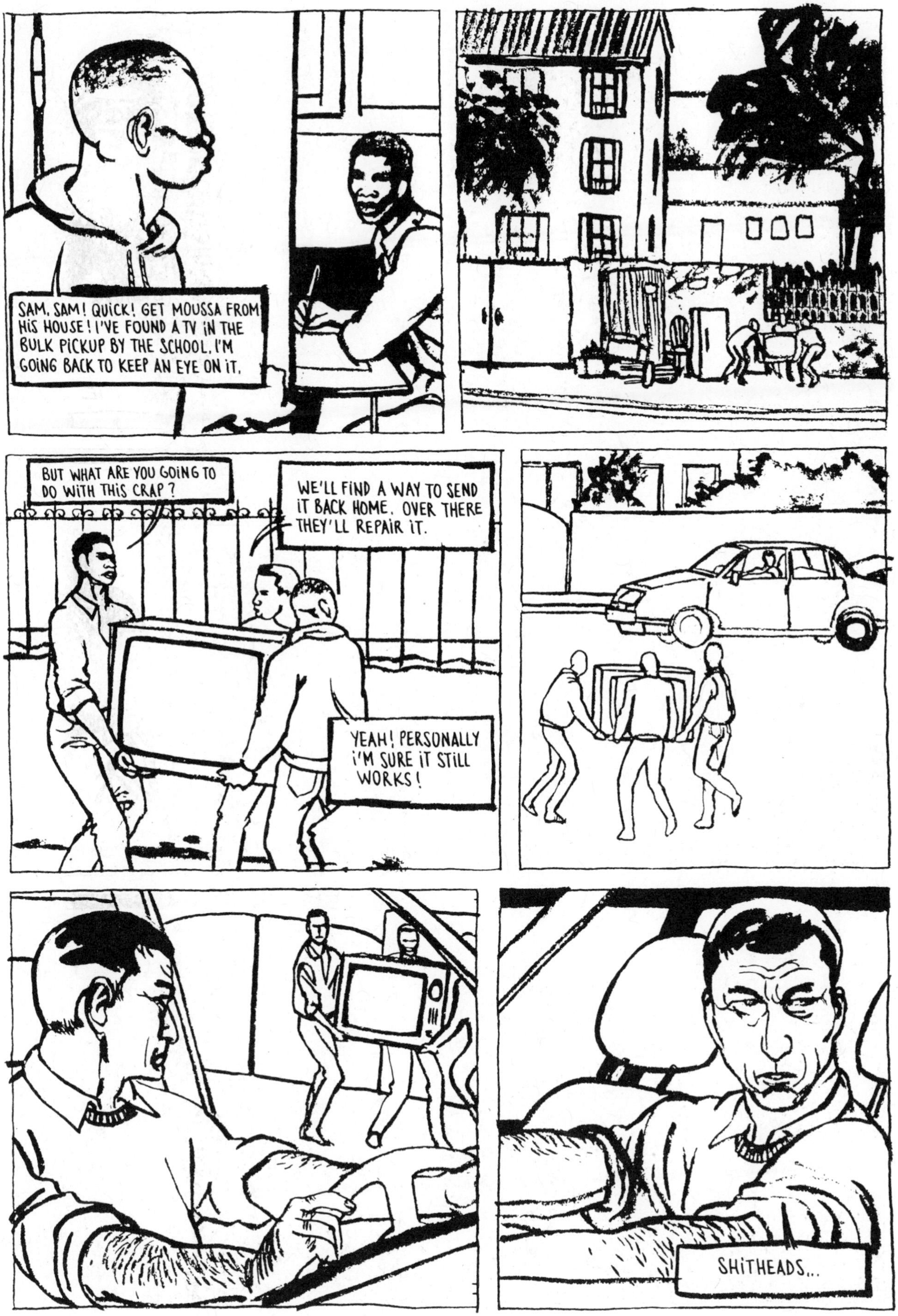
SAM, SAM! QUICK! GET MOUSSA FROM HIS HOUSE! I'VE FOUND A TV IN THE BULK PICKUP BY THE SCHOOL. I'M GOING BACK TO KEEP AN EYE ON IT.
BUT WHAT ARE YOU GOING TO DO WITH THIS CRAP?
WE'LL FIND A WAY TO SEND IT BACK HOME. OVER THERE THEY'LL REPAIR IT.
YEAH! PERSONALLY I'M SURE IT STILL WORKS!
SHITHEADS...

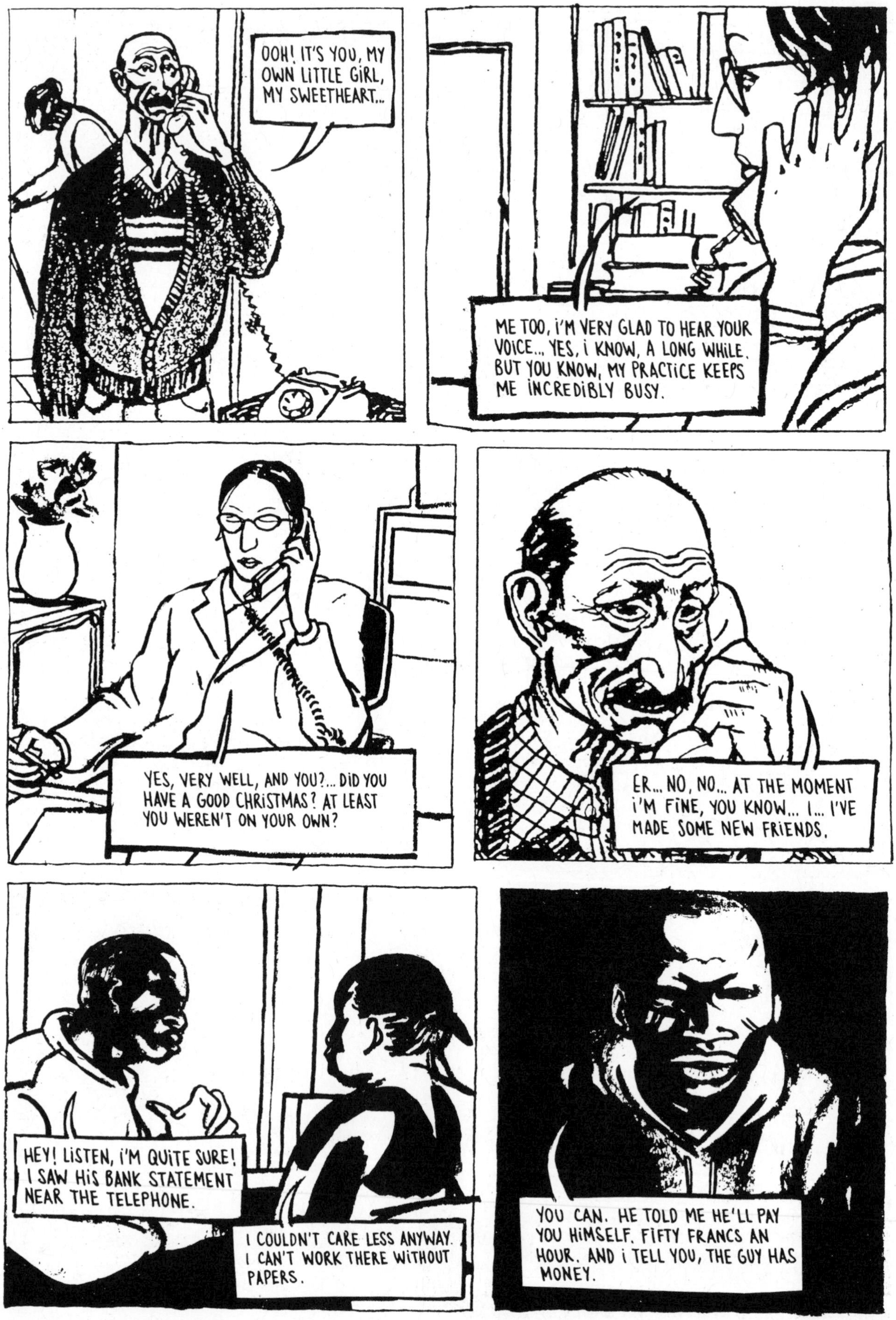

OOH! IT'S YOU, MY OWN LITTLE GIRL, MY SWEETHEART...
ME TOO, I'M VERY GLAD TO HEAR YOUR VOICE... YES, I KNOW, A LONG WHILE. BUT YOU KNOW, MY PRACTICE KEEPS ME INCREDIBLY BUSY.
YES, VERY WELL, AND YOU?... DID YOU HAVE A GOOD CHRISTMAS? AT LEAST YOU WEREN'T ON YOUR OWN?
ER... NO, NO... AT THE MOMENT I'M FINE, YOU KNOW... I... I'VE MADE SOME NEW FRIENDS.
HEY! LISTEN, I'M QUITE SURE! I SAW HIS BANK STATEMENT NEAR THE TELEPHONE.
I COULDN'T CARE LESS ANYWAY. I CAN'T WORK THERE WITHOUT PAPERS.
YOU CAN. HE TOLD ME HE'LL PAY YOU HIMSELF. FIFTY FRANCS AN HOUR. AND I TELL YOU, THE GUY HAS MONEY.

LAST NIGHT I SAW A DOCUMENTARY ON ATOMS, CELLS AND ALL THAT...

YOU SEE, ALL THIS ORGANIZATION, ALL THESE CELLS ARE LIKE PLANETS IN THE UNIVERSE. AND WE ALWAYS THINK THAT ALL THIS IS JUST SO WE CAN EXIST, AS HUMANS.

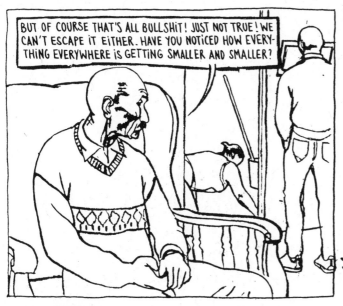

BUT OF COURSE THAT'S ALL BULLSHIT! JUST NOT TRUE! WE CAN'T ESCAPE IT EITHER. HAVE YOU NOTICED HOW EVERYTHING EVERYWHERE IS GETTING SMALLER AND SMALLER?

NOW YOU CAN GO ANYWHERE IN THE WORLD. THE WORLD IS UNIFIED, NOT JUST THE PLANET BUT ALL THE PARTICLES, INFINITELY SMALL OR INFINITELY LARGE, THE UNIVERSE...

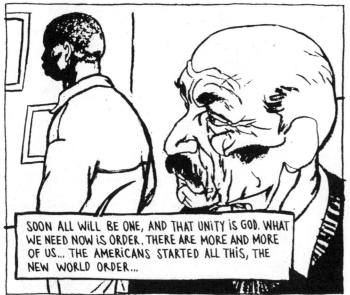

SOON ALL WILL BE ONE, AND THAT UNITY IS GOD. WHAT WE NEED NOW IS ORDER. THERE ARE MORE AND MORE OF US... THE AMERICANS STARTED ALL THIS, THE NEW WORLD ORDER...

THE JAPANESE GET IT TOO. BUT ME I THINK FRANCE HAS A PART TO PLAY. IN FACT, AS DE GAULLE ALWAYS USED TO SAY... YOU ALWAYS NEED LEADERS...

YOU SEE, EVERYTHING HAS TO BE STANDARDIZED. EVERYONE IN THEIR PLACE. THAT'S THE WAY THINGS WORK BEST...

LOOK AT THE PASSAGEWAYS IN THE METRO AT RUSH HOUR, OR AT A HIGHWAY CROWDED WITH CARS. IT'S LIKE CELLS - RED BLOOD CELLS... NOBEL PRIZEWINNERS ARE GRAY CELLS, YOU SEE...

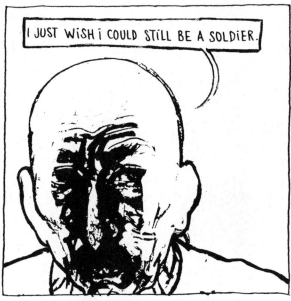

I JUST WISH I COULD STILL BE A SOLDIER.

IT'S ALL POSSIBLE WITH ORDER AND DISCI-PLINE. LIKE THE ARMY, A SINGLE BODY, A SINGLE MAN. WE'LL ALL BE PARTS OF A WHOLE AND ALL EQUAL. ALL BROTHERS...

AND OF COURSE EVERYWHERE IN THE WORLD WE'LL HAVE THE SAME RIGHTS. WE'LL LIVE IN THE SAME HOUSES, WE'LL DRESS THE SAME WAY, OR RATHER WEAR A UNIFORM SUITED TO OUR FUNCTION.

AND ONCE EVERYTHING IS PERFECTLY ORGANIZED, THE ACTIVITY OF ALL OF US WILL GIVE BIRTH TO DIVINE STATES OF AWARENESS...

BECAUSE WE'LL BE CELLS OF THOSE SUPERIOR BEINGS... THOSE DEMIGODS, THOSE TITANS...

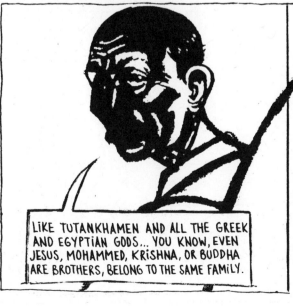

LIKE TUTANKHAMEN AND ALL THE GREEK AND EGYPTIAN GODS... YOU KNOW, EVEN JESUS, MOHAMMED, KRISHNA, OR BUDDHA ARE BROTHERS, BELONG TO THE SAME FAMILY.

US, WE'RE JUST LINKS IN ALL THAT. WHEN OUR WORK IS DONE, AND WE ARE ALL IN OUR PLACES, THEY TOO CAN START TO DO WHAT THEY HAVE TO DO.

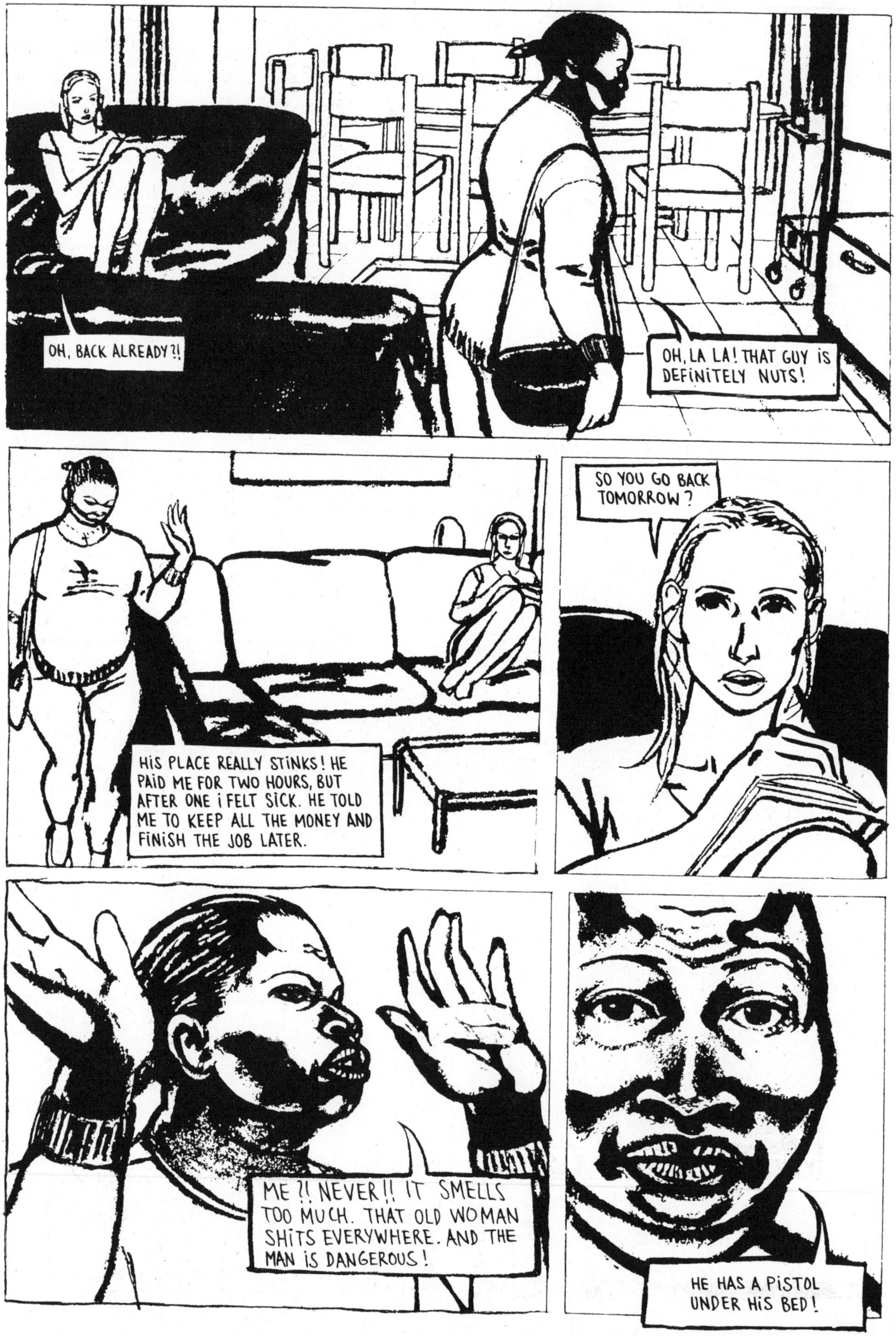
OH, BACK ALREADY?!
OH, LA LA! THAT GUY IS DEFINITELY NUTS!
HIS PLACE REALLY STINKS! HE PAID ME FOR TWO HOURS, BUT AFTER ONE I FELT SICK. HE TOLD ME TO KEEP ALL THE MONEY AND FINISH THE JOB LATER.
SO YOU GO BACK TOMORROW?
ME?! NEVER!! IT SMELLS TOO MUCH. THAT OLD WOMAN SHITS EVERYWHERE. AND THE MAN IS DANGEROUS!
HE HAS A PISTOL UNDER HIS BED!

I KNOW WHO YOU ARE, MARIO. I'VE DONE SOME RESEARCH...

IN NOVEMBER 1959, MAURICE PAPON, PARIS PREFECT OF POLICE, CREATED AN AUXILIARY FORCE MADE UP OF ALGERIANS.

n lins en place par Maurice Papon présente de
vice de coordination des affaires algériennes (SCA
d'assistance technique aux Français-Musulma
TFMA). Le SCAA est composé de spécialistes de
pale, de la police judiciaire et des renseignemer
mission est répressive. Cette direction opérationne
section de renseignement, une section d'opératio
(brigade des agressions et violences) et une briga
'est en liaison avec le SCAA que furent organisé
les policières qui précédèrent le référendum de se
Les Algériens interpellés étaient dirigés, pour inte
s le Vélodrome d'hiver, qui retrouvait ainsi
vait été la sienne durant l'Occupation. Ils étaie

THE UNIT HAD CARTE BLANCHE TO BREAK UP THE NATIONAL LIBERATION FRONT'S NETWORKS IN PARIS AND "FREE THE NORTH AFRICANS FROM RACKETEERS, TORTURERS AND FELLAGHA MURDERERS."

c ou de Saint-Maurice-l'Ardoise. Parfois, ils disp

chaque trottoir, mitraillette en bandoulière. Ils font
sites nocturnes dans les bidonvilles. Les Algériens qu'i
ent sont fouillés, parfois délestés de leur portefeuille,
hmenés dans les caves de leurs hôtels, où ils sont soum
ice de l'eau de Javel, de la bouteille dans l'an
mechoui'' : pieds et poings liés, l'homme est attaché à
ue l'on tourne à toute vitesse, en le bourrant de coups
iciés peuvent passer des semaines entières dans les ''
antent'', ainsi baptisées par les habitants du quartier
musique que les harkis prennent soin de faire hurler
rturent leurs prisonniers[48]. »
Début 1961, on comptait des FPA dans tous les qu

THE SQUAD WOULD HELP REPRESS THE ALGERIAN DEMONSTRATIONS OF OCTOBER 17 AND 18, 1961. MARIO (OR MORE PRECISELY LIEUTENANT "JEAN-RENÉ" NÉOUCHE) WAS ONE OF THE ONLY ALGERIAN OFFICERS LEADING THIS HARKI GROUP.

Paris sont transformées en de véritables champs de t

TONIGHT THE LIEUTENANT HAS SLIPPED SILENTLY OUT OF HIS HOUSE WITH MONEY FILCHED FROM HIS MOTHER. THIS TIME HE WILL NOT BE SUCKING ON THE HEAVY BREASTS OF A GHANAIAN : HE HAS ENOUGH FOR A WHITE WOMAN.

250 FRANCS. HE AGREES AND FOLLOWS HER. THEY RETURN TO THE MAIN STREET WHERE DIMLY ILLUMI-NATED FACES FILE BY THE CARS LIKE MALICIOUS RUMORS. (HOW MANY SODDEN CORPSES CARRIED ALONG BY THE CALM WATERS OF THE SEINE?)

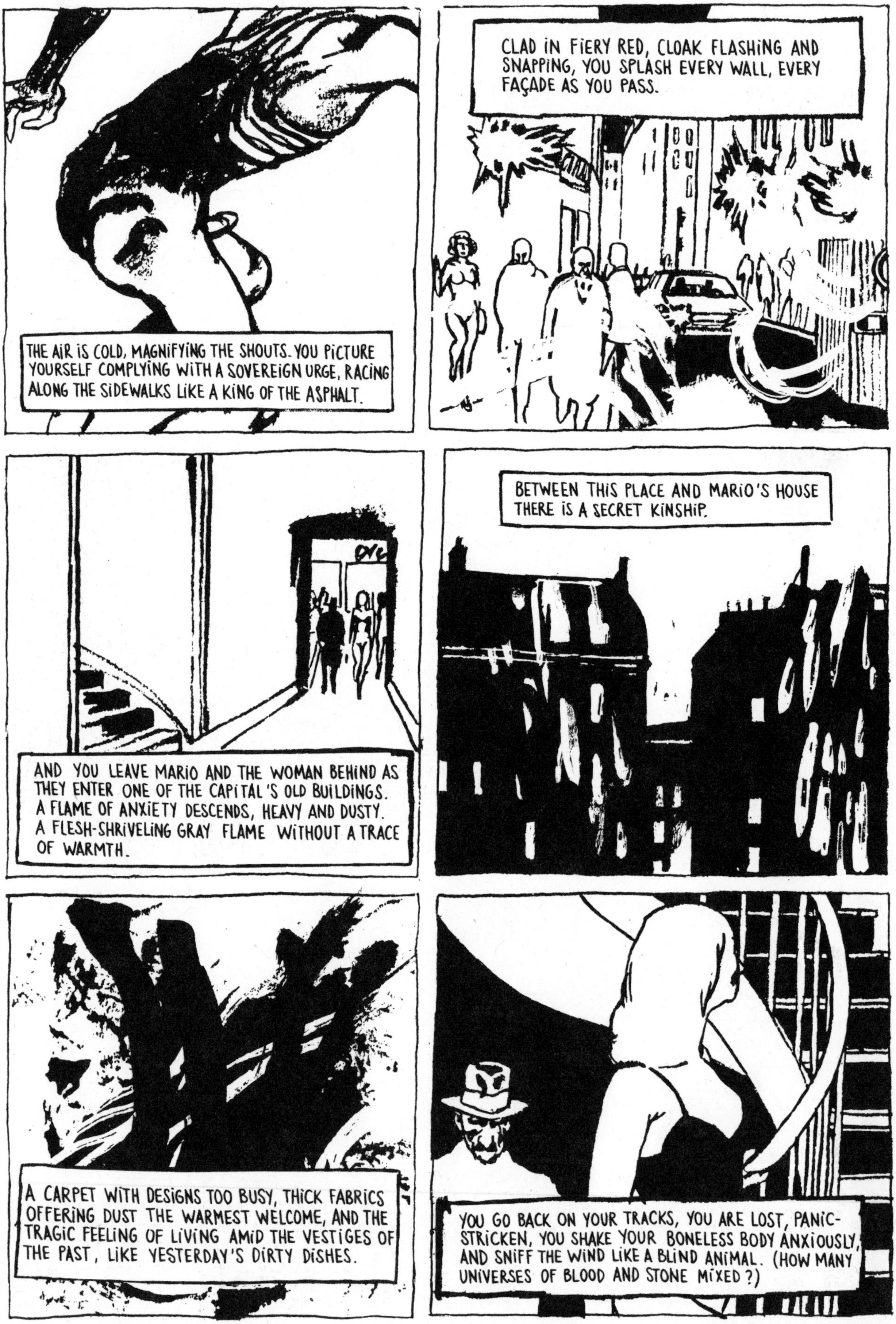
THE AIR IS COLD, MAGNIFYING THE SHOUTS. YOU PICTURE YOURSELF COMPLYING WITH A SOVEREIGN URGE, RACING ALONG THE SIDEWALKS LIKE A KING OF THE ASPHALT.
CLAD IN FIERY RED, CLOAK FLASHING AND SNAPPING, YOU SPLASH EVERY WALL, EVERY FAÇADE AS YOU PASS.
AND YOU LEAVE MARIO AND THE WOMAN BEHIND AS THEY ENTER ONE OF THE CAPITAL'S OLD BUILDINGS. A FLAME OF ANXIETY DESCENDS, HEAVY AND DUSTY. A FLESH-SHRIVELING GRAY FLAME WITHOUT A TRACE OF WARMTH.
BETWEEN THIS PLACE AND MARIO'S HOUSE THERE IS A SECRET KINSHIP.
A CARPET WITH DESIGNS TOO BUSY, THICK FABRICS OFFERING DUST THE WARMEST WELCOME, AND THE TRAGIC FEELING OF LIVING AMID THE VESTIGES OF THE PAST, LIKE YESTERDAY'S DIRTY DISHES.
YOU GO BACK ON YOUR TRACKS, YOU ARE LOST, PANIC-STRICKEN, YOU SHAKE YOUR BONELESS BODY ANXIOUSLY, AND SNIFF THE WIND LIKE A BLIND ANIMAL. (HOW MANY UNIVERSES OF BLOOD AND STONE MIXED?)

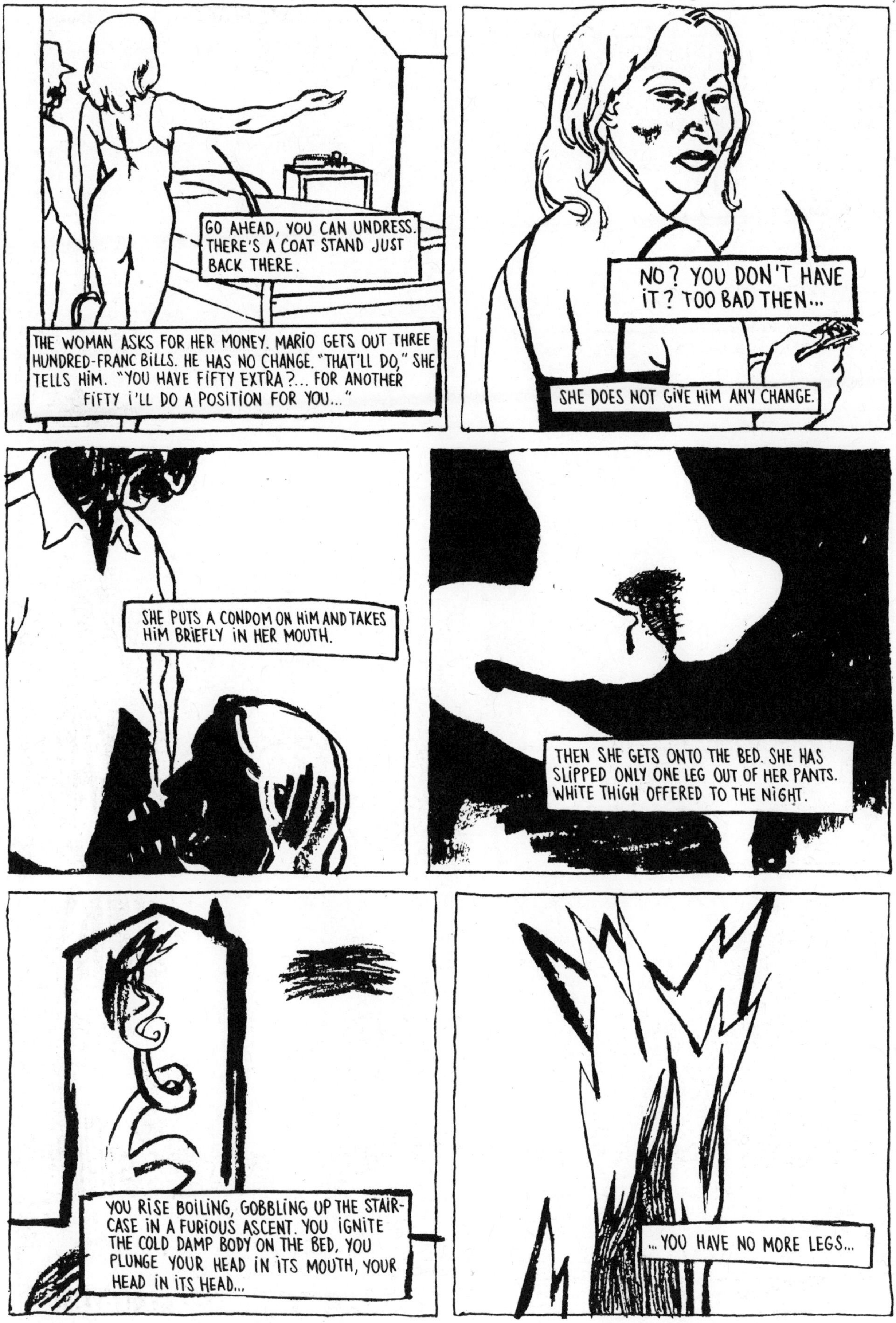
GO AHEAD, YOU CAN UNDRESS. THERE'S A COAT STAND JUST BACK THERE.
THE WOMAN ASKS FOR HER MONEY. MARIO GETS OUT THREE HUNDRED-FRANC BILLS. HE HAS NO CHANGE. "THAT'LL DO," SHE TELLS HIM. "YOU HAVE FIFTY EXTRA?... FOR ANOTHER FIFTY I'LL DO A POSITION FOR YOU..."
NO? YOU DON'T HAVE IT? TOO BAD THEN...
SHE DOES NOT GIVE HIM ANY CHANGE.
SHE PUTS A CONDOM ON HIM AND TAKES HIM BRIEFLY IN HER MOUTH.
THEN SHE GETS ONTO THE BED. SHE HAS SLIPPED ONLY ONE LEG OUT OF HER PANTS. WHITE THIGH OFFERED TO THE NIGHT.
YOU RISE BOILING, GOBBLING UP THE STAIRCASE IN A FURIOUS ASCENT. YOU IGNITE THE COLD DAMP BODY ON THE BED, YOU PLUNGE YOUR HEAD IN ITS MOUTH, YOUR HEAD IN ITS HEAD...
...YOU HAVE NO MORE LEGS...

MARIO SENSES THAT HE ISN'T GOING TO COME. HE STRAINS ALL HIS MUSCLES, BUT HIS STOMACH IS COILED UP LIKE A SNAKE. (HOW MANY LIMBS CUT OFF? HOW MANY CORPSES ENHANCED BY UNKNOWN FORMS, SUBSTANCES, COLORS?)

HE LEANS DOWN TO KISS HER. BUT SHE TURNS HER HEAD AWAY "NO."

WELL, LISTEN IT'S NOT MY FAULT. NORMALLY IT'S A QUARTER OF AN HOUR AND WE'RE ALREADY OVER TWENTY MINUTES.

MAYBE IF WE TRIED WITHOUT A CONDOM...

AND WHAT ELSE?! I DON'T WANT TO PICK UP YOUR DISGUSTING DISEASES!

GIVE ME BACK MY MONEY THEN.

YOU MUST BE JOKING!!

PLEASE... JUST... JUST MY FIFTY FRANCS...

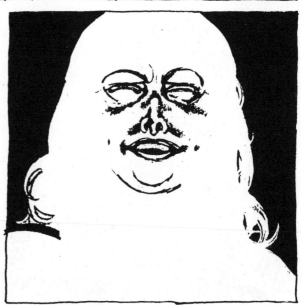

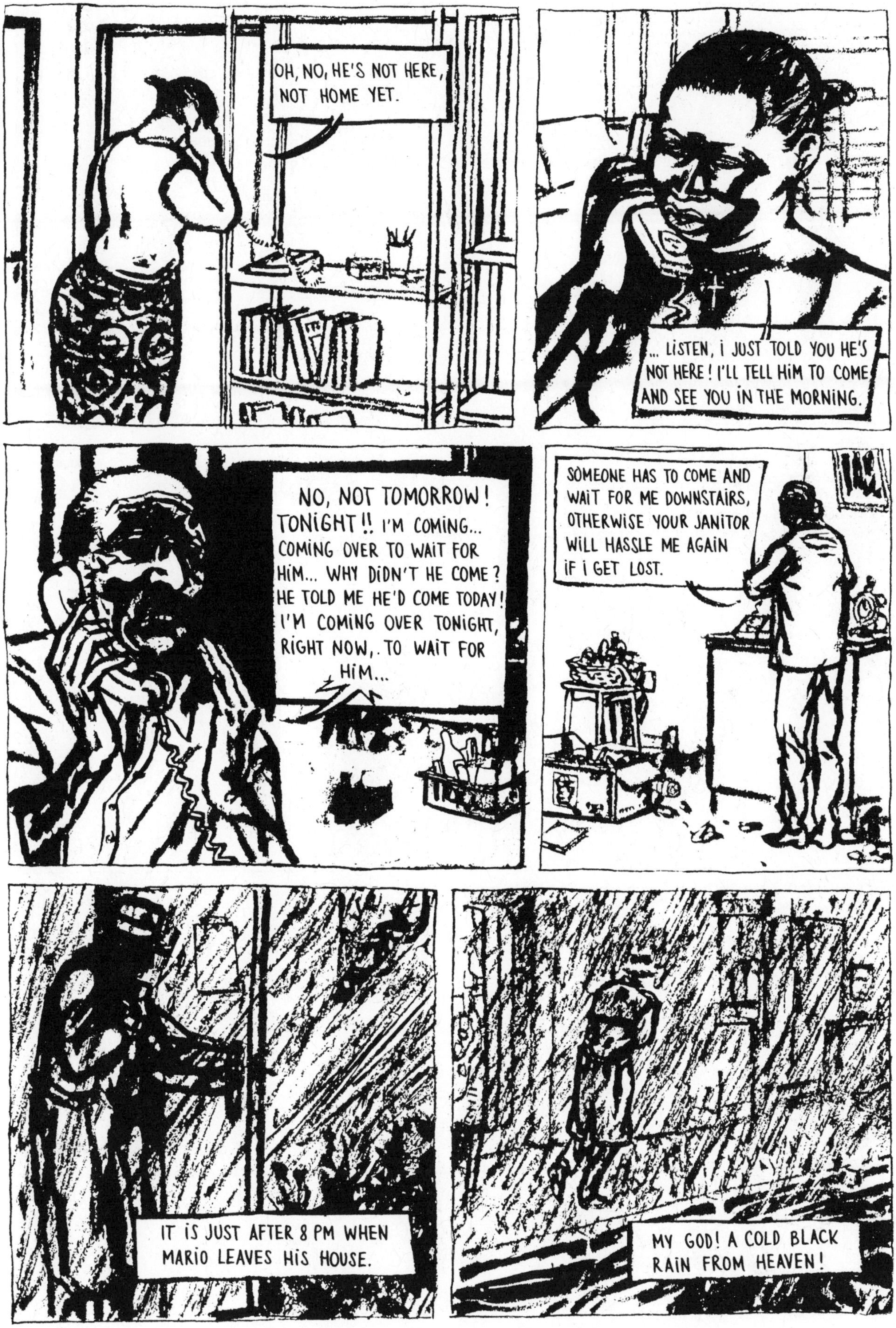
OH, NO, HE'S NOT HERE, NOT HOME YET.
... LISTEN, I JUST TOLD YOU HE'S NOT HERE! I'LL TELL HIM TO COME AND SEE YOU IN THE MORNING.
NO, NOT TOMORROW! TONIGHT!! I'M COMING... COMING OVER TO WAIT FOR HIM... WHY DIDN'T HE COME? HE TOLD ME HE'D COME TODAY! I'M COMING OVER TONIGHT, RIGHT NOW,. TO WAIT FOR HIM...
SOMEONE HAS TO COME AND WAIT FOR ME DOWNSTAIRS, OTHERWISE YOUR JANITOR WILL HASSLE ME AGAIN IF I GET LOST.
IT IS JUST AFTER 8 PM WHEN MARIO LEAVES HIS HOUSE.
MY GOD! A COLD BLACK RAIN FROM HEAVEN!

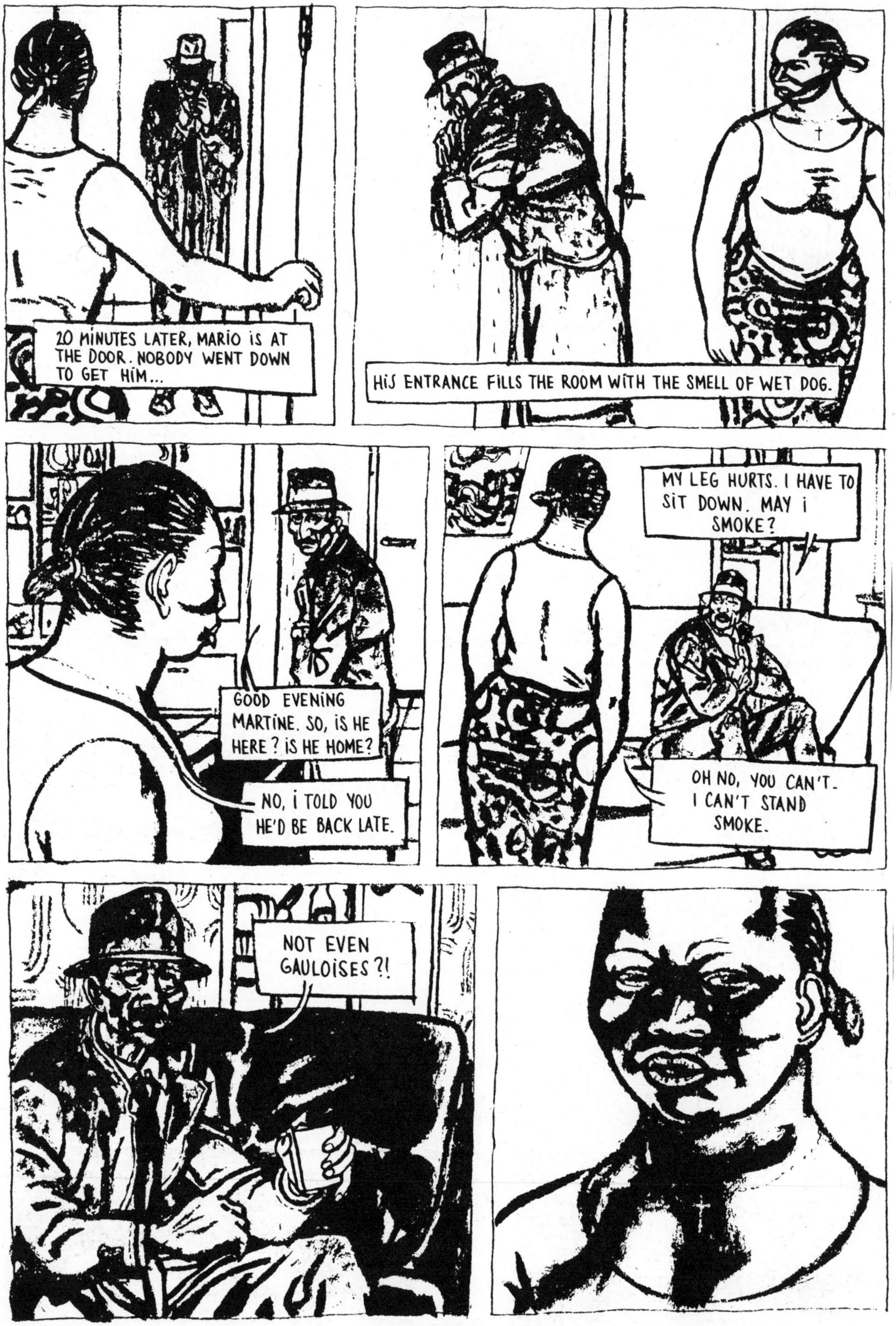
20 MINUTES LATER, MARIO IS AT THE DOOR. NOBODY WENT DOWN TO GET HIM...
HIS ENTRANCE FILLS THE ROOM WITH THE SMELL OF WET DOG.
GOOD EVENING MARTINE. SO, IS HE HERE? IS HE HOME?
NO, I TOLD YOU HE'D BE BACK LATE.
MY LEG HURTS. I HAVE TO SIT DOWN. MAY I SMOKE?
OH NO, YOU CAN'T. I CAN'T STAND SMOKE.
NOT EVEN GAULOISES?!

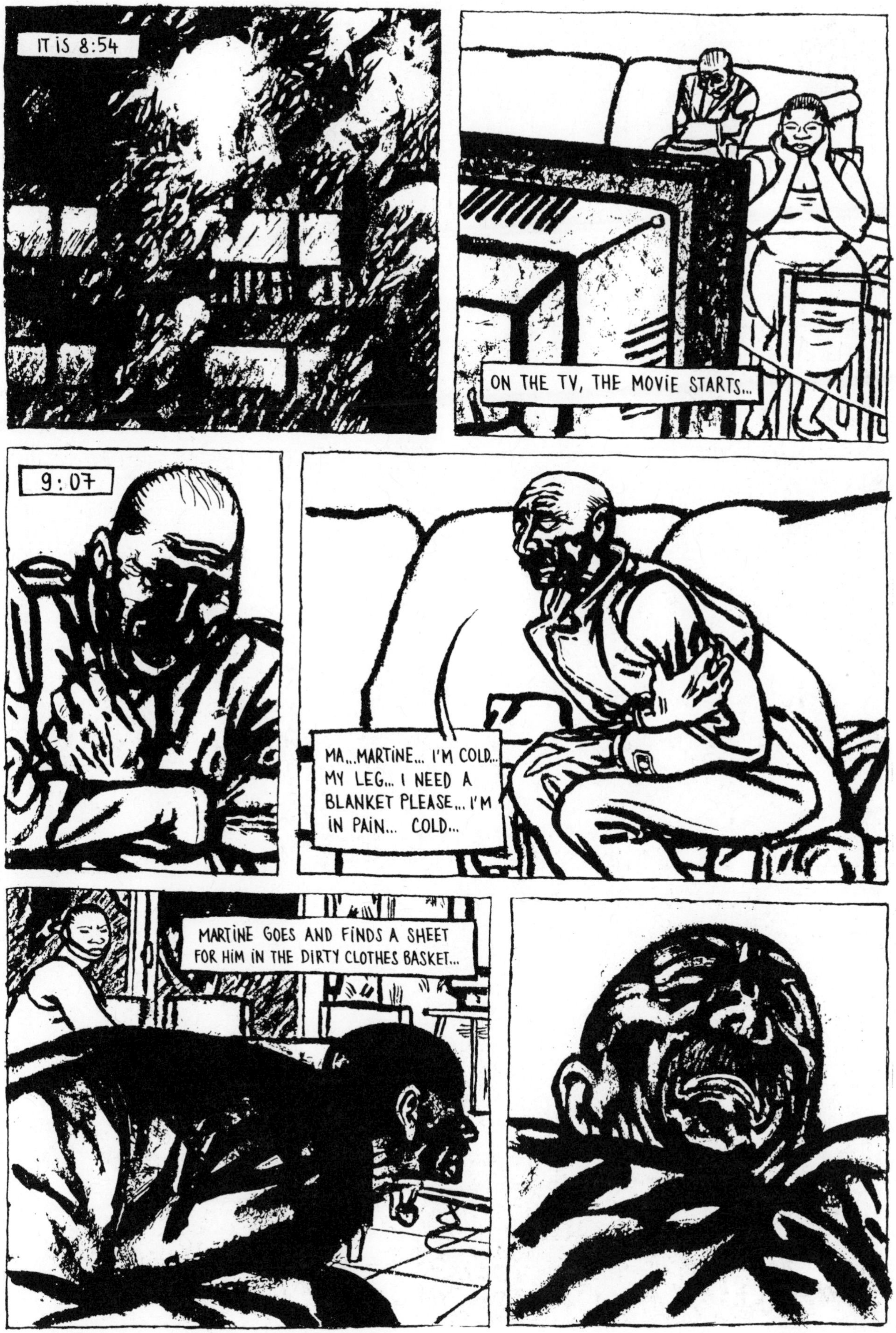
IT IS 8:54
ON THE TV, THE MOVIE STARTS...
9:07
MA... MARTINE... I'M COLD... MY LEG... I NEED A BLANKET PLEASE... I'M IN PAIN... COLD...
MARTINE GOES AND FINDS A SHEET FOR HIM IN THE DIRTY CLOTHES BASKET...

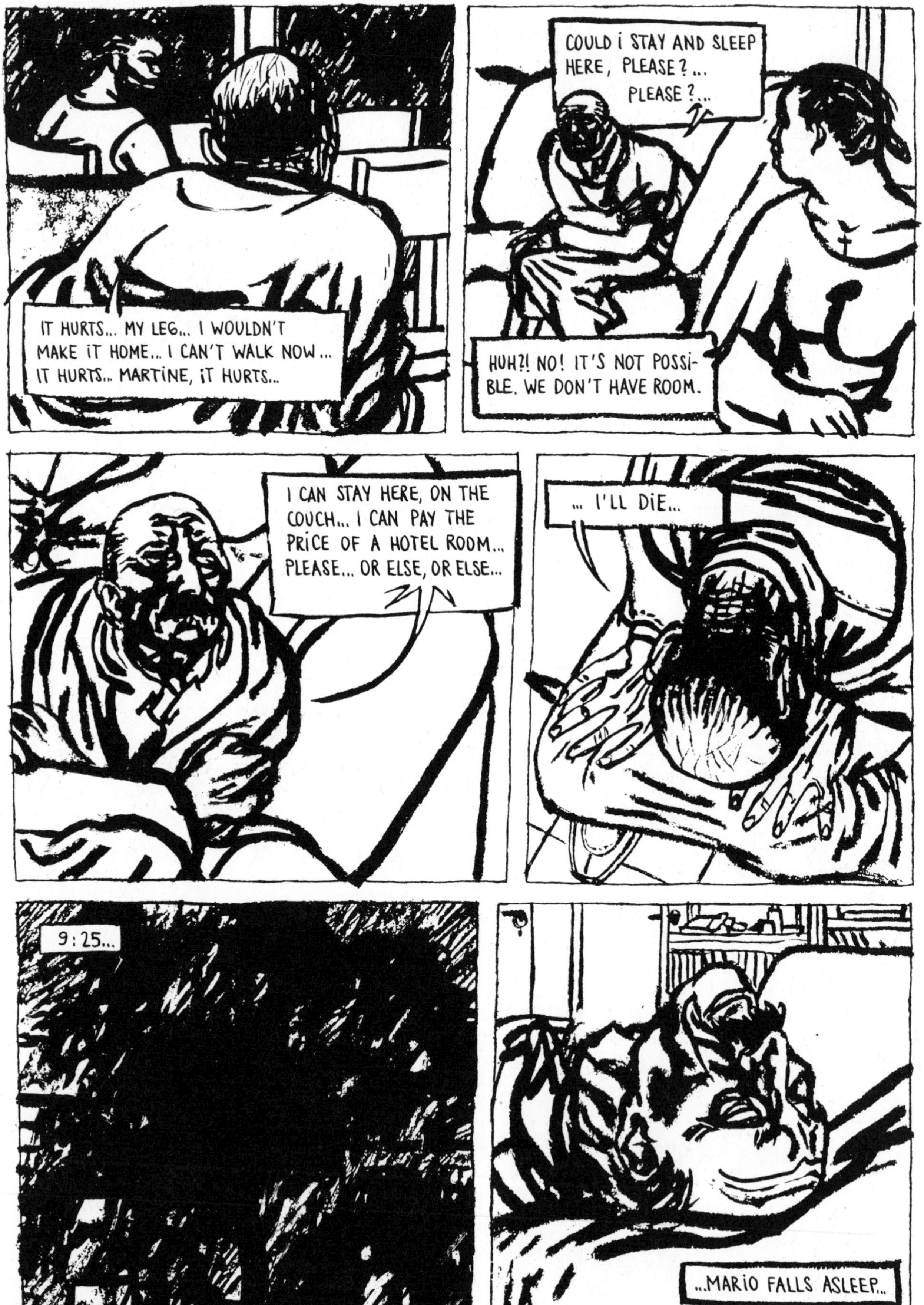
IT HURTS... MY LEG... I WOULDN'T MAKE IT HOME... I CAN'T WALK NOW... IT HURTS... MARTINE, IT HURTS...
COULD I STAY AND SLEEP HERE, PLEASE?...
PLEASE?...
HUH?! NO! IT'S NOT POSSIBLE. WE DON'T HAVE ROOM.
I CAN STAY HERE, ON THE COUCH... I CAN PAY THE PRICE OF A HOTEL ROOM... PLEASE... OR ELSE, OR ELSE...
... I'LL DIE...
9:25...
...MARIO FALLS ASLEEP...

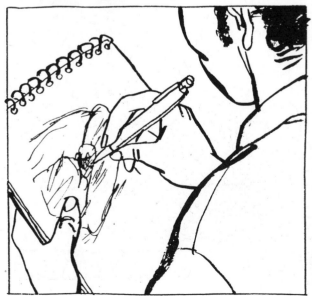

AT 10:11, MARTINE CALLS MOUSSA, WHO DRIVES MARIO HOME.

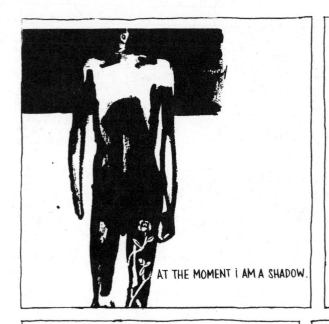

AT THE MOMENT I AM A SHADOW.

I COME IN THE NAME OF PAIN, TO SHARPEN MY SONG, THE TONGUE THAT BLEEDS. I CANNOT IMAGINE HIM QUIET, SLEEPING PEACEFULLY. HE GROANS, GRIMACES, AND OPENS HIS EYES WITHOUT AWAKENING.

I SLEEP ALONGSIDE HIM. MY BREATH THE BREATH OF THE VICTIMS. LOVING OR HATING HIM, WHAT DOES IT MATTER? PITY TORTURES HORROR. GOODWILL IS ATTACHED TO DISGUST LIKE A ROSE CLIMBING UP MY LEG.

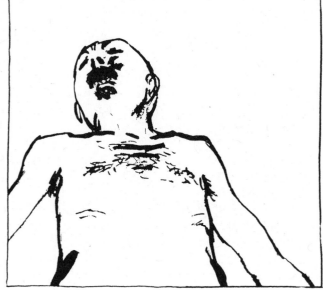

MY LOVE IS SO BRIEF...

,, I'VE SWORN THAT YOU'LL DIE, MARIO.

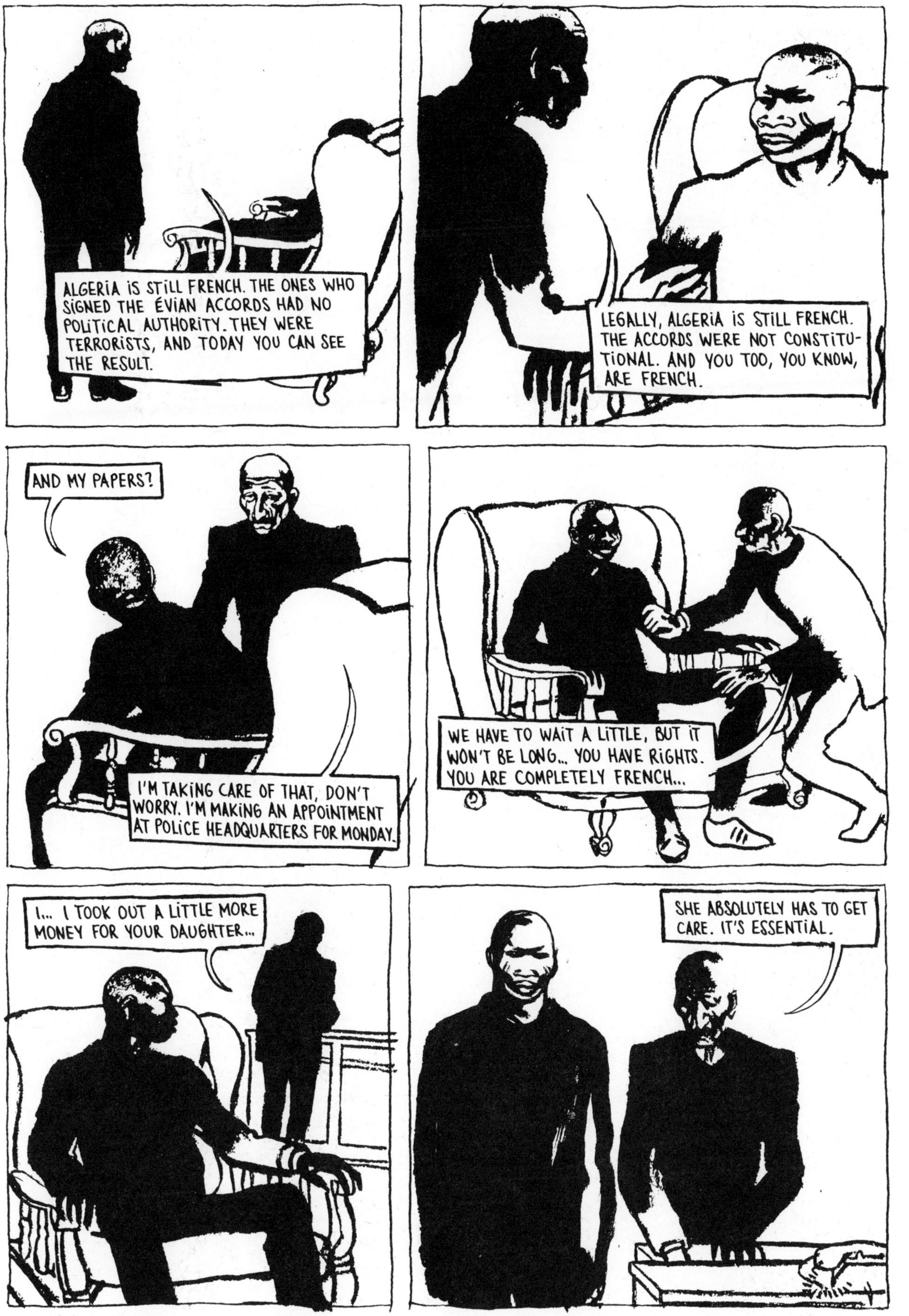
ALGERIA IS STILL FRENCH. THE ONES WHO SIGNED THE ÉVIAN ACCORDS HAD NO POLITICAL AUTHORITY. THEY WERE TERRORISTS, AND TODAY YOU CAN SEE THE RESULT.
LEGALLY, ALGERIA IS STILL FRENCH. THE ACCORDS WERE NOT CONSTITUTIONAL. AND YOU TOO, YOU KNOW, ARE FRENCH.
AND MY PAPERS?
I'M TAKING CARE OF THAT, DON'T WORRY. I'M MAKING AN APPOINTMENT AT POLICE HEADQUARTERS FOR MONDAY.
WE HAVE TO WAIT A LITTLE, BUT IT WON'T BE LONG... YOU HAVE RIGHTS. YOU ARE COMPLETELY FRENCH...
I... I TOOK OUT A LITTLE MORE MONEY FOR YOUR DAUGHTER...
SHE ABSOLUTELY HAS TO GET CARE. IT'S ESSENTIAL.

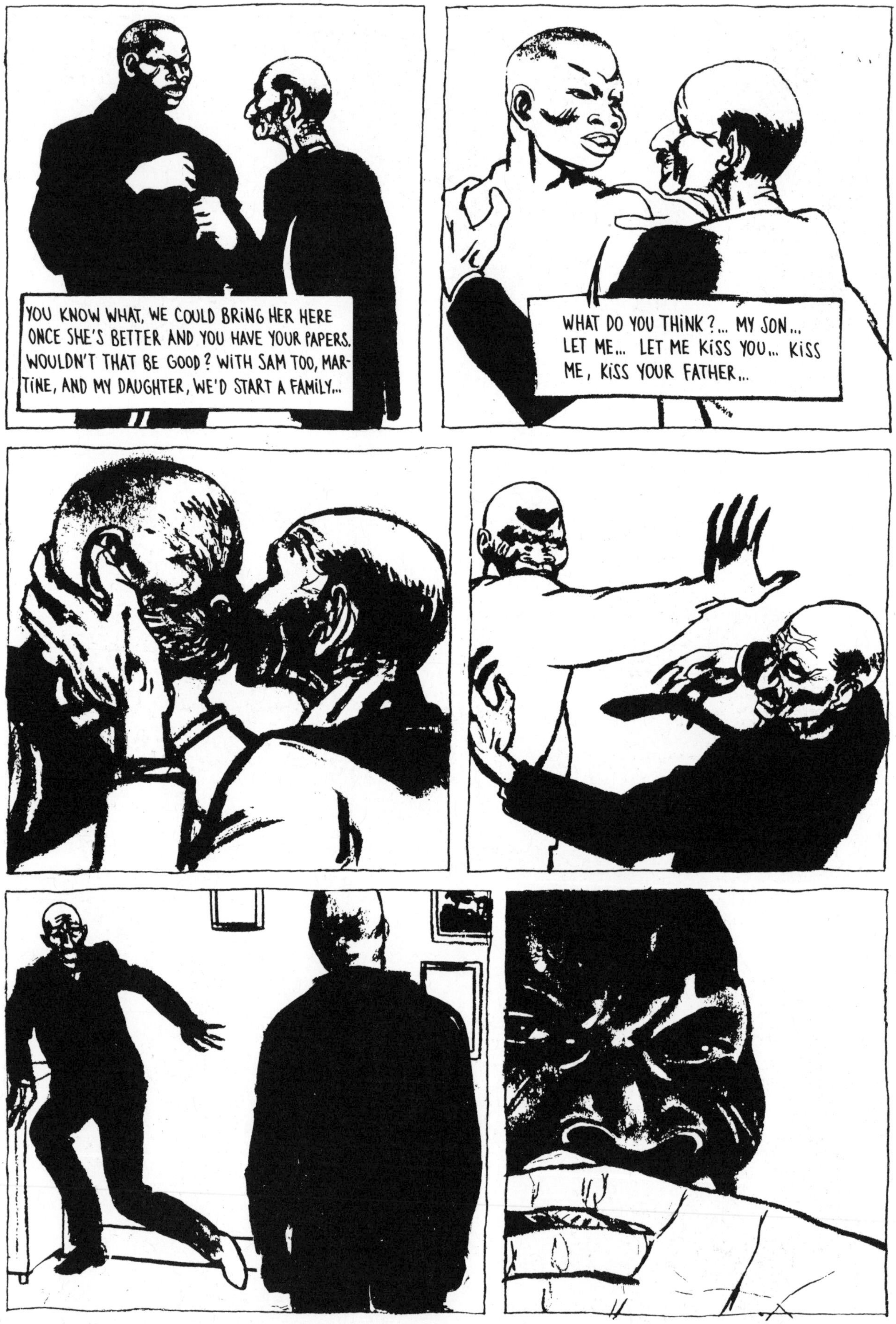
YOU KNOW WHAT, WE COULD BRING HER HERE ONCE SHE'S BETTER AND YOU HAVE YOUR PAPERS. WOULDN'T THAT BE GOOD? WITH SAM TOO, MARTINE, AND MY DAUGHTER, WE'D START A FAMILY...
WHAT DO YOU THINK?... MY SON... LET ME... LET ME KISS YOU... KISS ME, KISS YOUR FATHER...

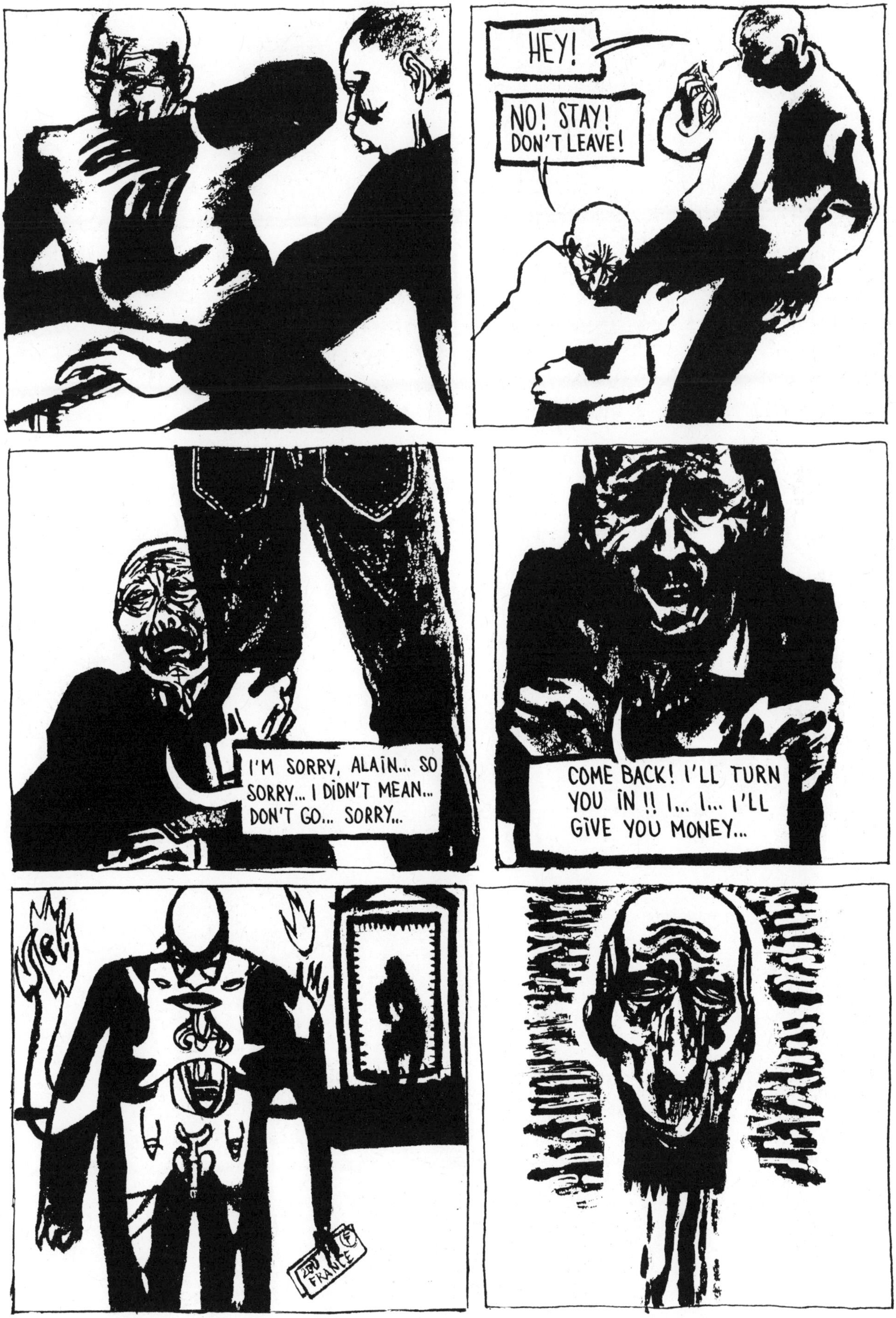
HEY!
NO! STAY! DON'T LEAVE!
I'M SORRY, ALAIN... SO SORRY... I DIDN'T MEAN... DON'T GO... SORRY...
COME BACK! I'LL TURN YOU IN!! I... I... I'LL GIVE YOU MONEY...

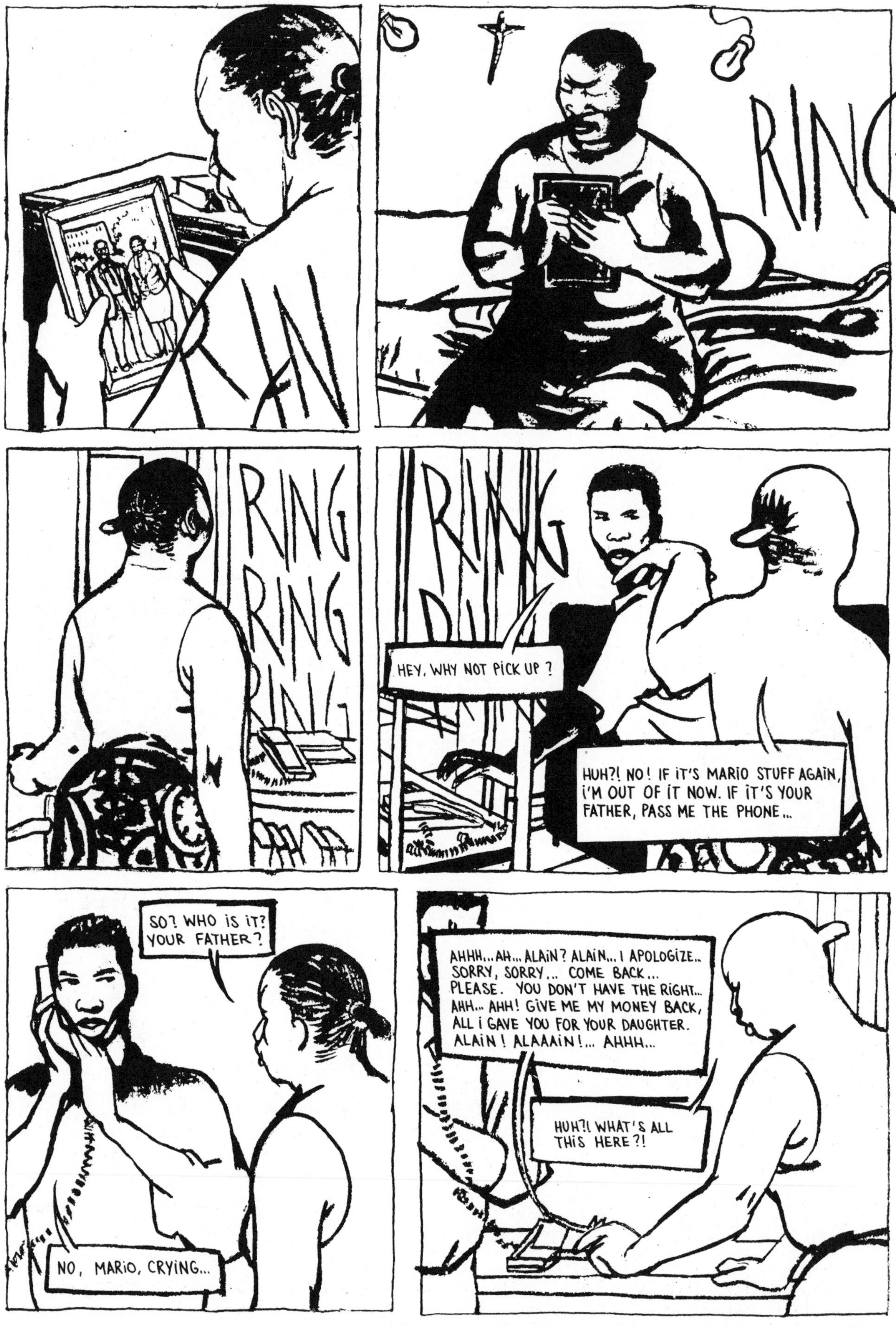

RING
RING
RING
RING
HEY, WHY NOT PICK UP ?
HUH?! NO! IF IT'S MARIO STUFF AGAIN, I'M OUT OF IT NOW. IF IT'S YOUR FATHER, PASS ME THE PHONE...
SO? WHO IS IT? YOUR FATHER?
NO, MARIO, CRYING...
AHHH... AH... ALAIN? ALAIN... I APOLOGIZE.. SORRY, SORRY,... COME BACK... PLEASE. YOU DON'T HAVE THE RIGHT... AHH... AHH! GIVE ME MY MONEY BACK, ALL I GAVE YOU FOR YOUR DAUGHTER. ALAIN! ALAAAIN!... AHHH...
HUH?! WHAT'S ALL THIS HERE?!

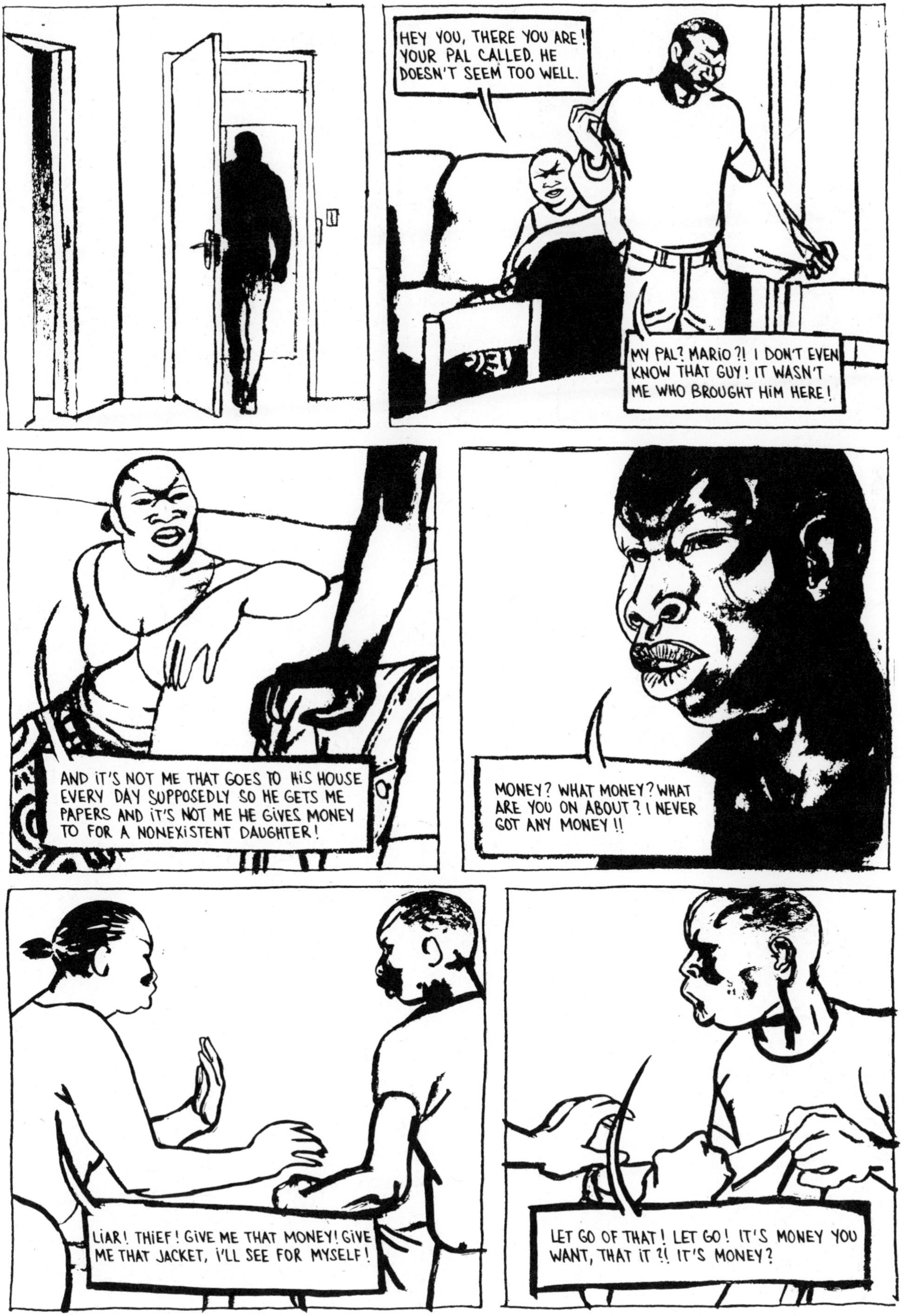
HEY YOU, THERE YOU ARE! YOUR PAL CALLED. HE DOESN'T SEEM TOO WELL.
MY PAL? MARIO?! I DON'T EVEN KNOW THAT GUY! IT WASN'T ME WHO BROUGHT HIM HERE!
AND IT'S NOT ME THAT GOES TO HIS HOUSE EVERY DAY SUPPOSEDLY SO HE GETS ME PAPERS AND IT'S NOT ME HE GIVES MONEY TO FOR A NONEXISTENT DAUGHTER!
MONEY? WHAT MONEY? WHAT ARE YOU ON ABOUT? I NEVER GOT ANY MONEY!!
LIAR! THIEF! GIVE ME THAT MONEY! GIVE ME THAT JACKET, I'LL SEE FOR MYSELF!
LET GO OF THAT! LET GO! IT'S MONEY YOU WANT, THAT IT?! IT'S MONEY?

HERE! HERE!! TAKE IT ALL! I DON'T WANT TO OWE YOU ANYTHING ANYMORE, OR EVEN SEE YOU, I'M LEAVING!!

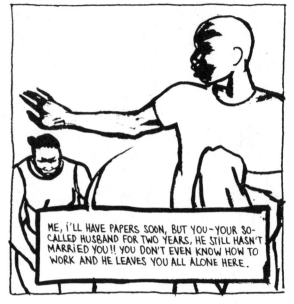

ME, I'LL HAVE PAPERS SOON, BUT YOU-YOUR SO-CALLED HUSBAND FOR TWO YEARS, HE STILL HASN'T MARRIED YOU!! YOU DON'T EVEN KNOW HOW TO WORK AND HE LEAVES YOU ALL ALONE HERE.

THE TRUTH IS THAT YOU'RE HERE DYING OF HUNGER AND COLD AND HE'S IN AFRICA EATING GRILLED FISH AND STUFFING MONEY UP WOMEN'S ASSES!!

RING

RING
RING

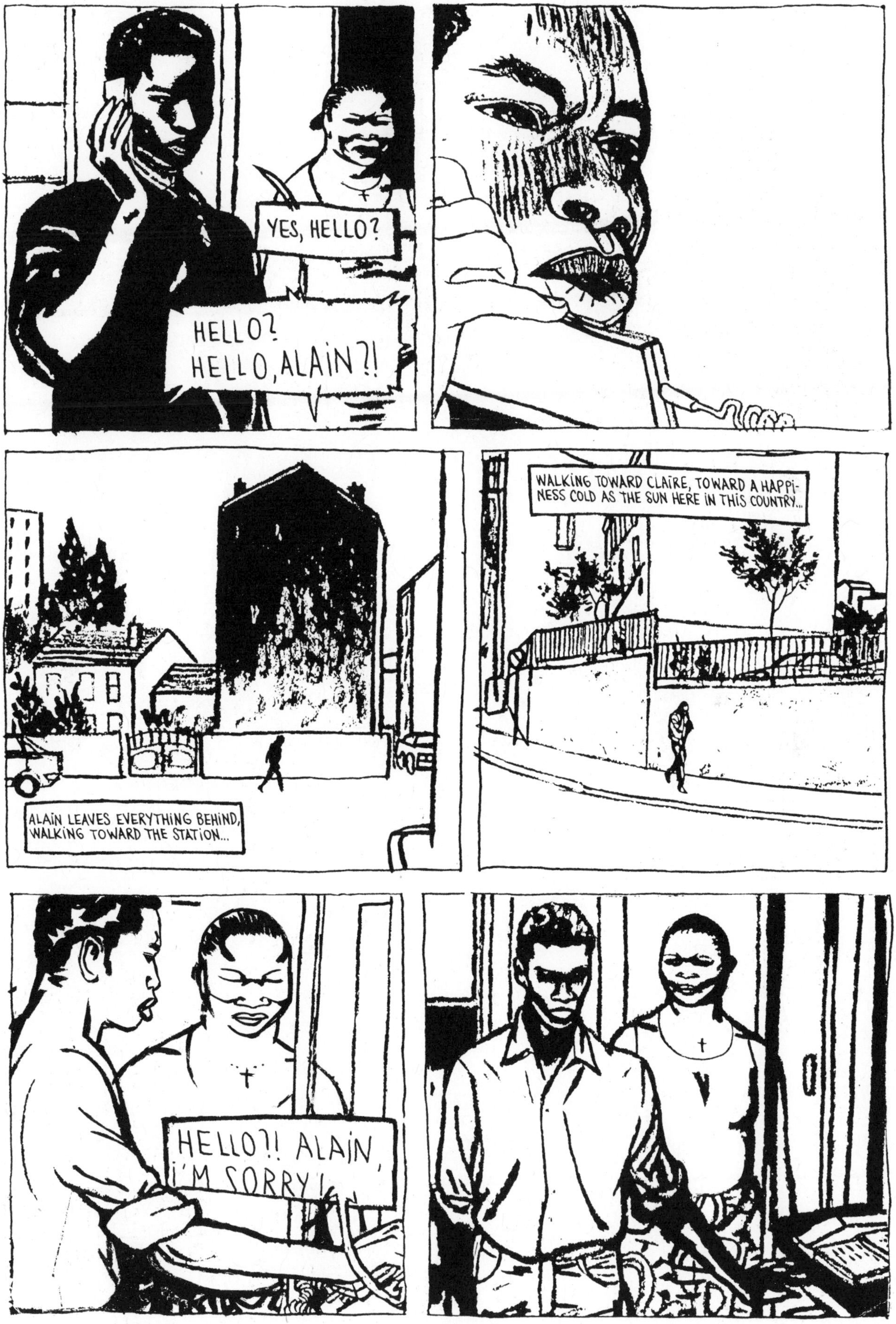
YES, HELLO?
HELLO? HELLO, ALAIN?!
ALAIN LEAVES EVERYTHING BEHIND, WALKING TOWARD THE STATION...
WALKING TOWARD CLAIRE, TOWARD A HAPPINESS COLD AS THE SUN HERE IN THIS COUNTRY...
HELLO?! ALAIN, I'M SORRY!

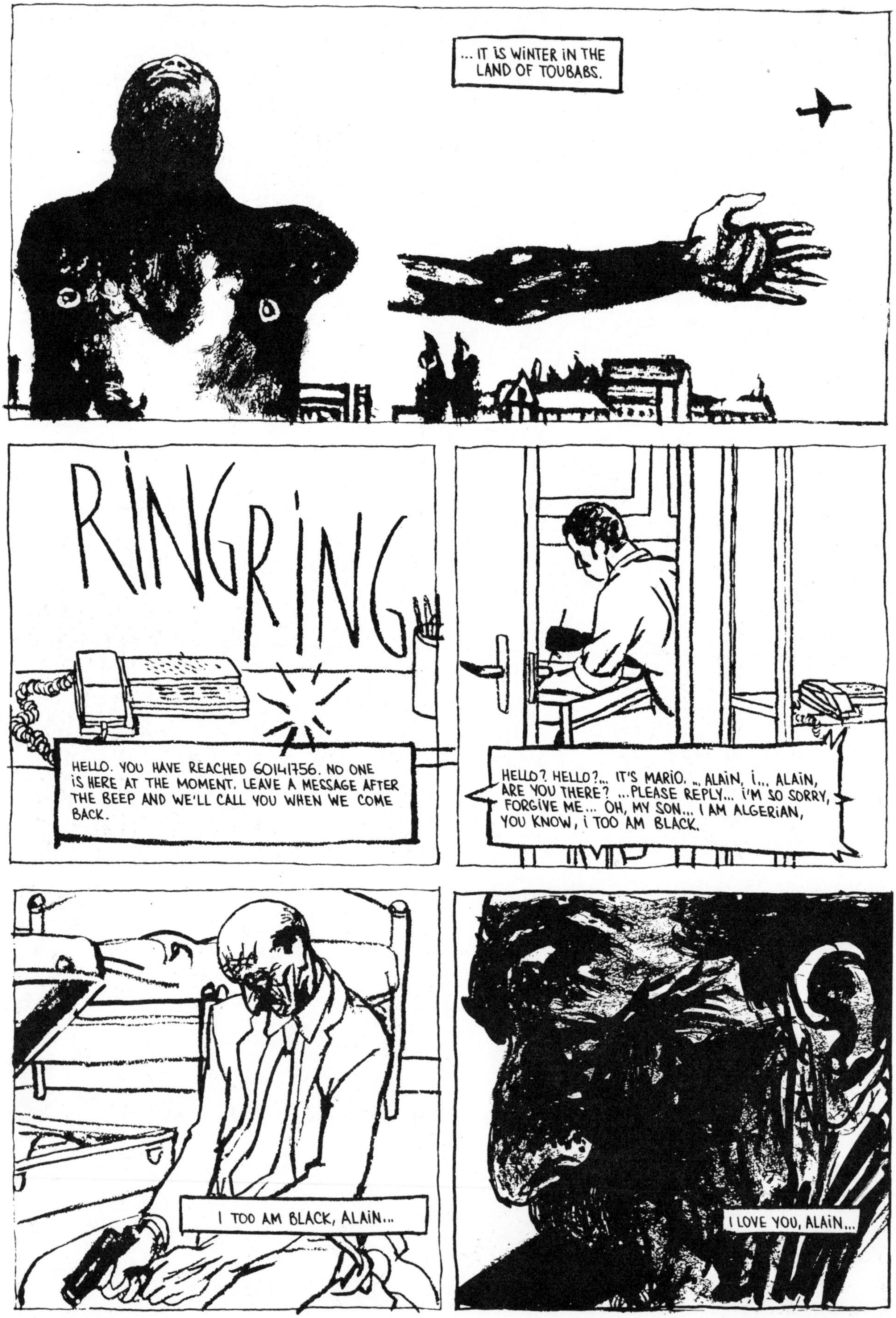
... IT IS WINTER IN THE LAND OF TOUBABS.
RING RING
HELLO. YOU HAVE REACHED 60141756. NO ONE IS HERE AT THE MOMENT. LEAVE A MESSAGE AFTER THE BEEP AND WE'LL CALL YOU WHEN WE COME BACK.
HELLO? HELLO?... IT'S MARIO. ... ALAIN, I... ALAIN, ARE YOU THERE? ...PLEASE REPLY... I'M SO SORRY, FORGIVE ME... OH, MY SON... I AM ALGERIAN, YOU KNOW, I TOO AM BLACK.
I TOO AM BLACK, ALAIN...
I LOVE YOU, ALAIN...

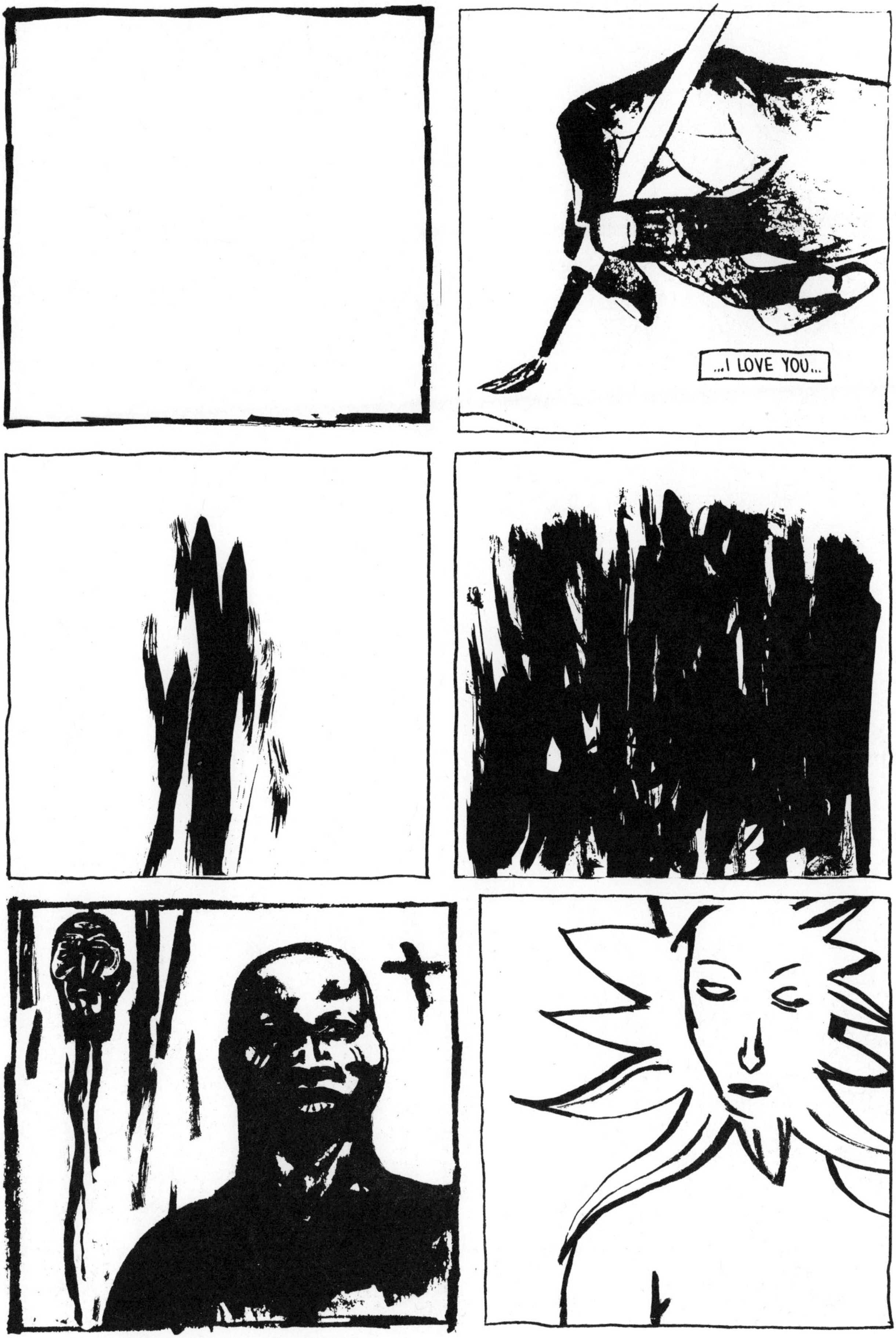
...I LOVE YOU...

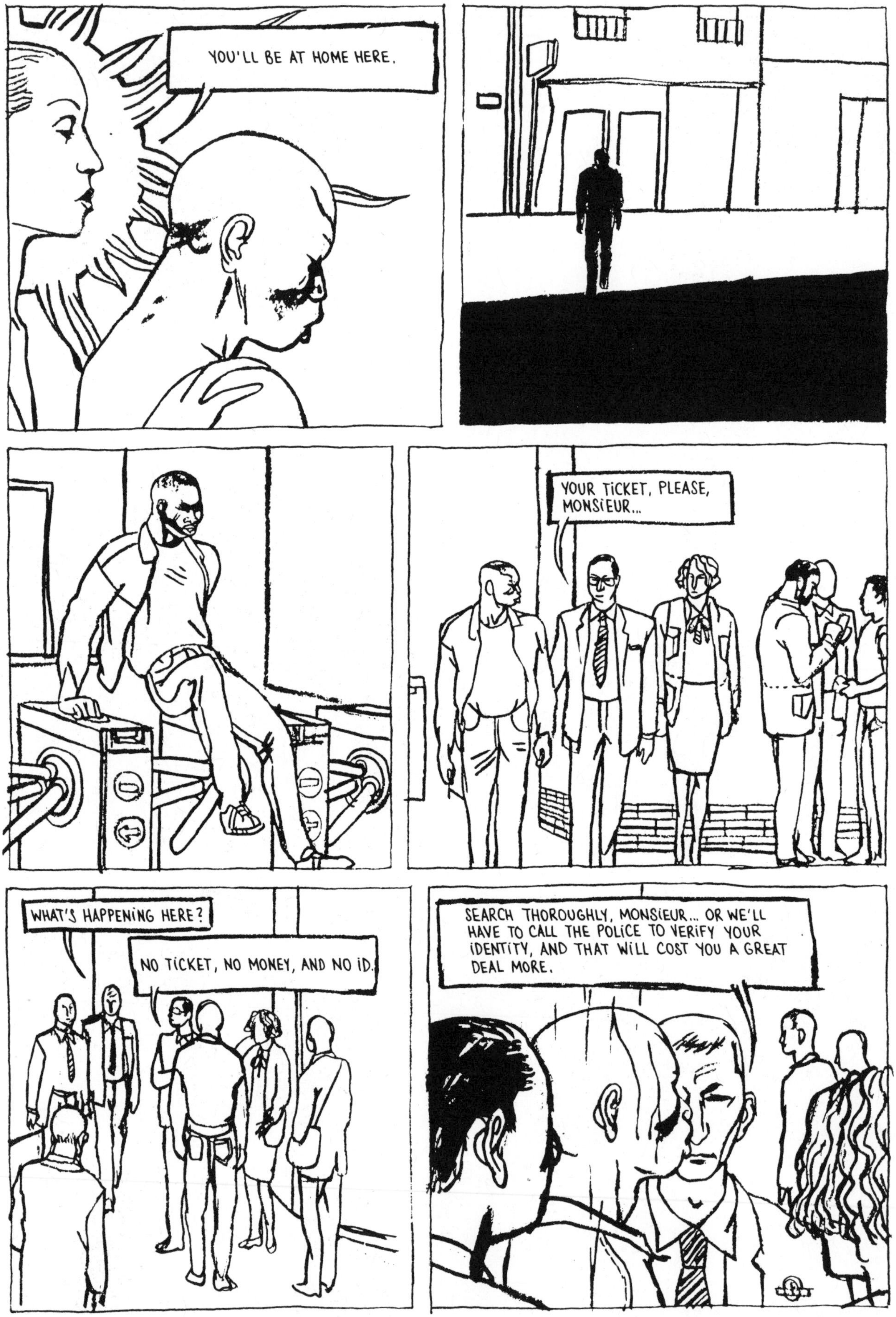
YOU'LL BE AT HOME HERE.
YOUR TICKET, PLEASE, MONSIEUR...
WHAT'S HAPPENING HERE?
NO TICKET, NO MONEY, AND NO ID.
SEARCH THOROUGHLY, MONSIEUR... OR WE'LL HAVE TO CALL THE POLICE TO VERIFY YOUR IDENTITY, AND THAT WILL COST YOU A GREAT DEAL MORE.

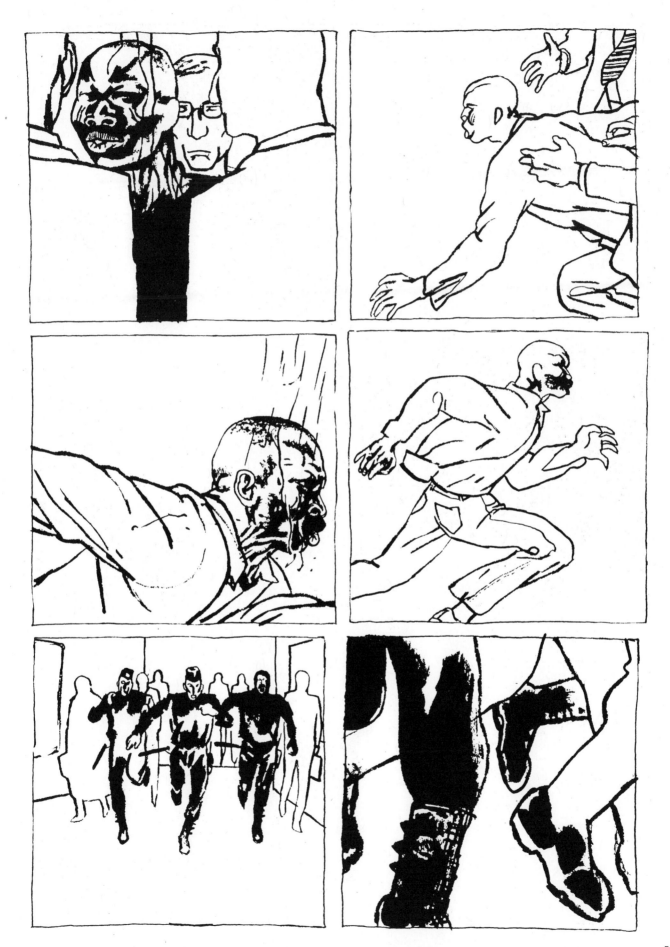

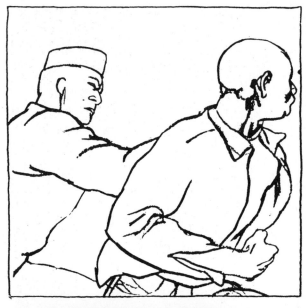

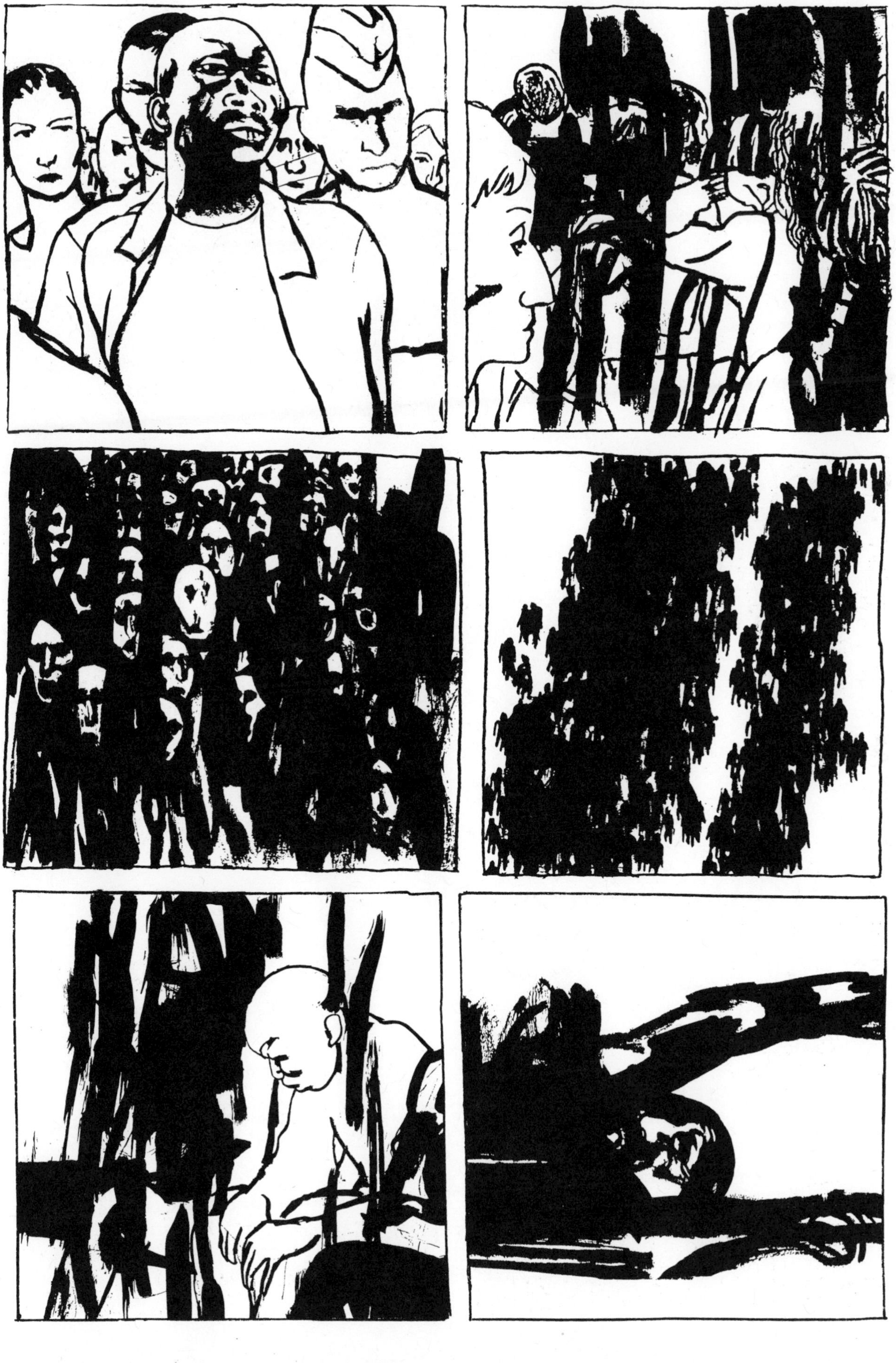

DYAA

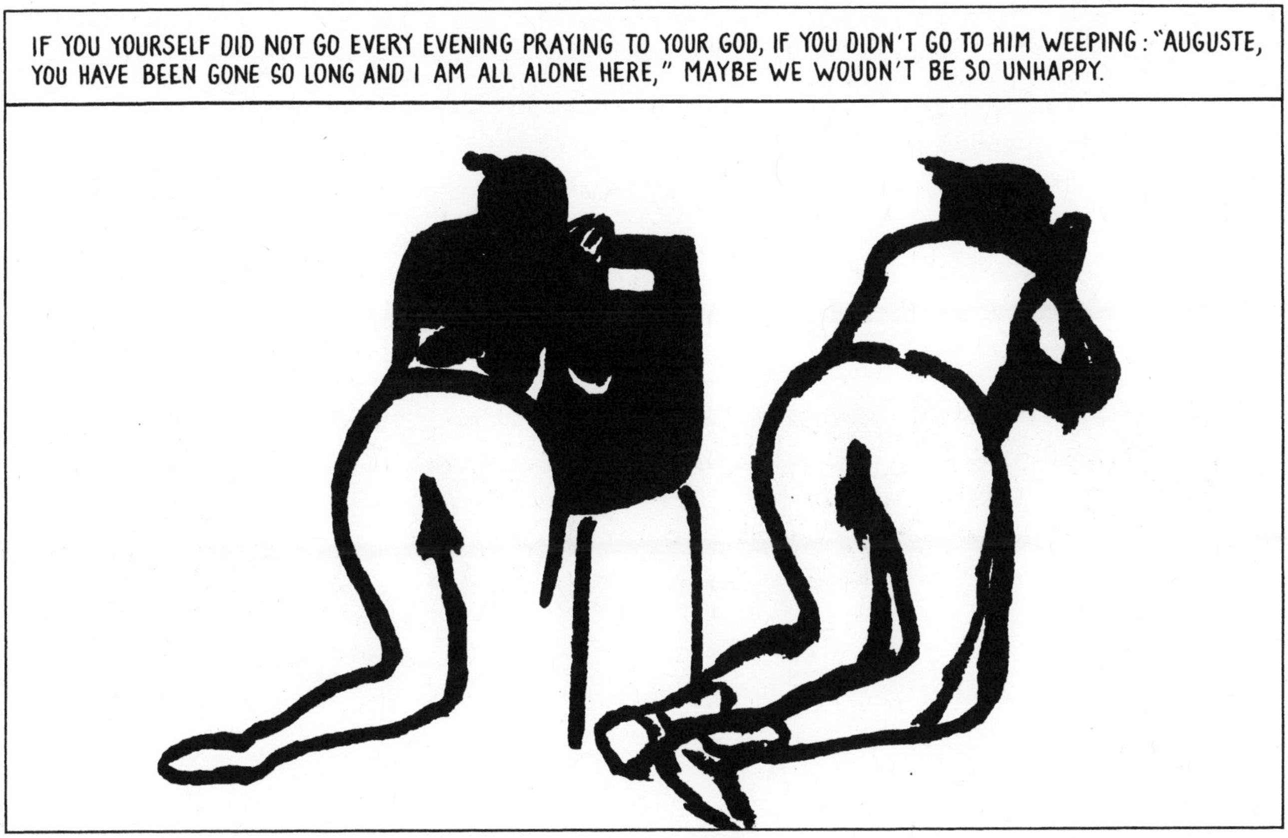
IF YOU YOURSELF DID NOT GO EVERY EVENING PRAYING TO YOUR GOD, IF YOU DIDN'T GO TO HIM WEEPING: "AUGUSTE, YOU HAVE BEEN GONE SO LONG AND I AM ALL ALONE HERE," MAYBE WE WOUDN'T BE SO UNHAPPY.

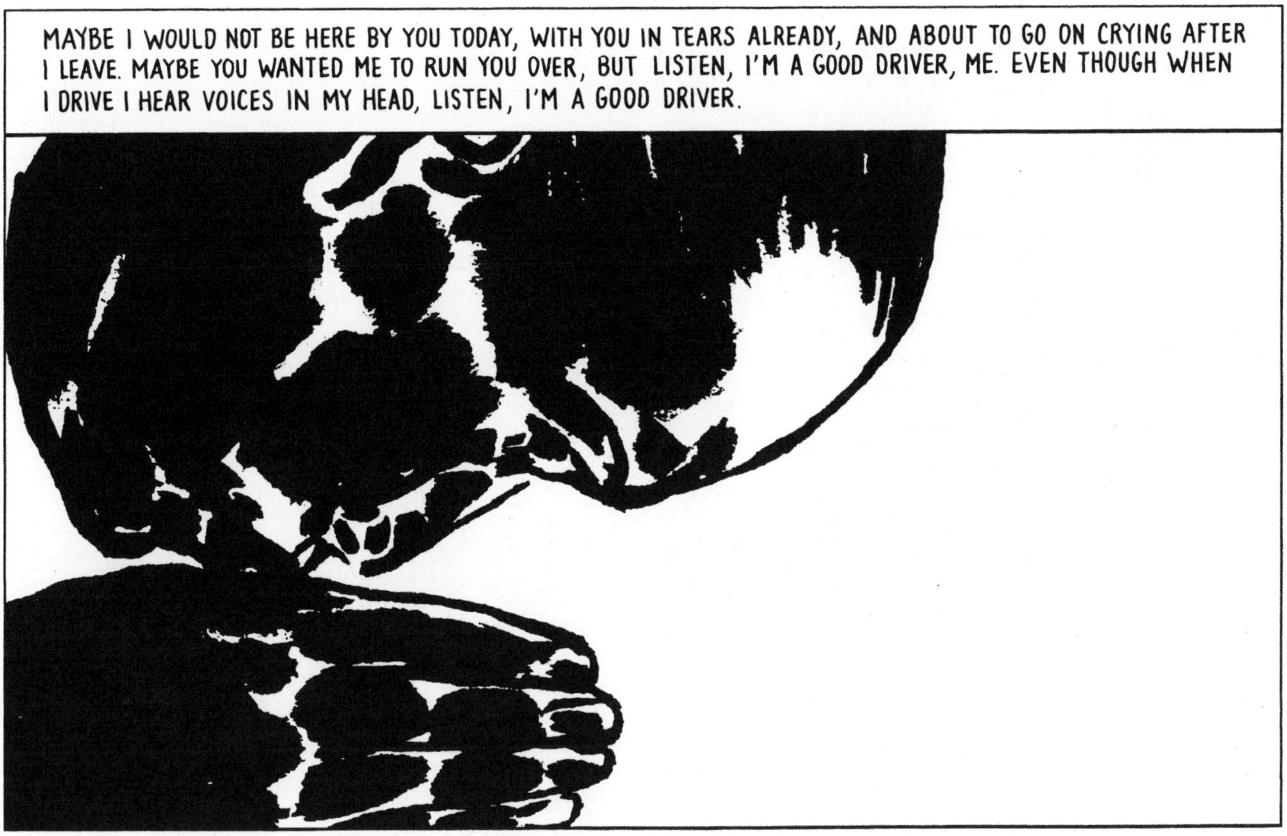
MAYBE I WOULD NOT BE HERE BY YOU TODAY, WITH YOU IN TEARS ALREADY, AND ABOUT TO GO ON CRYING AFTER I LEAVE. MAYBE YOU WANTED ME TO RUN YOU OVER, BUT LISTEN, I'M A GOOD DRIVER, ME. EVEN THOUGH WHEN I DRIVE I HEAR VOICES IN MY HEAD, LISTEN, I'M A GOOD DRIVER.

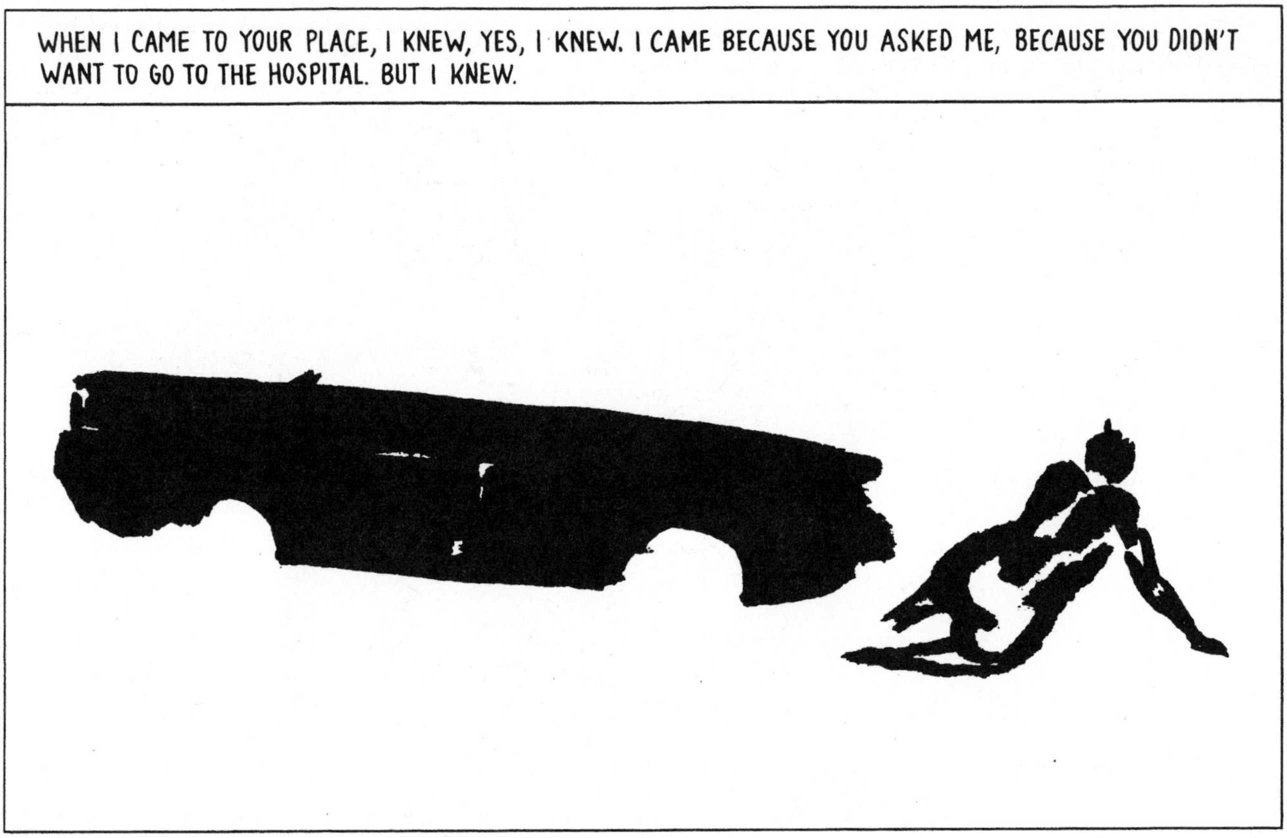
WHEN I CAME TO YOUR PLACE, I KNEW, YES, I KNEW. I CAME BECAUSE YOU ASKED ME, BECAUSE YOU DIDN'T WANT TO GO TO THE HOSPITAL. BUT I KNEW.

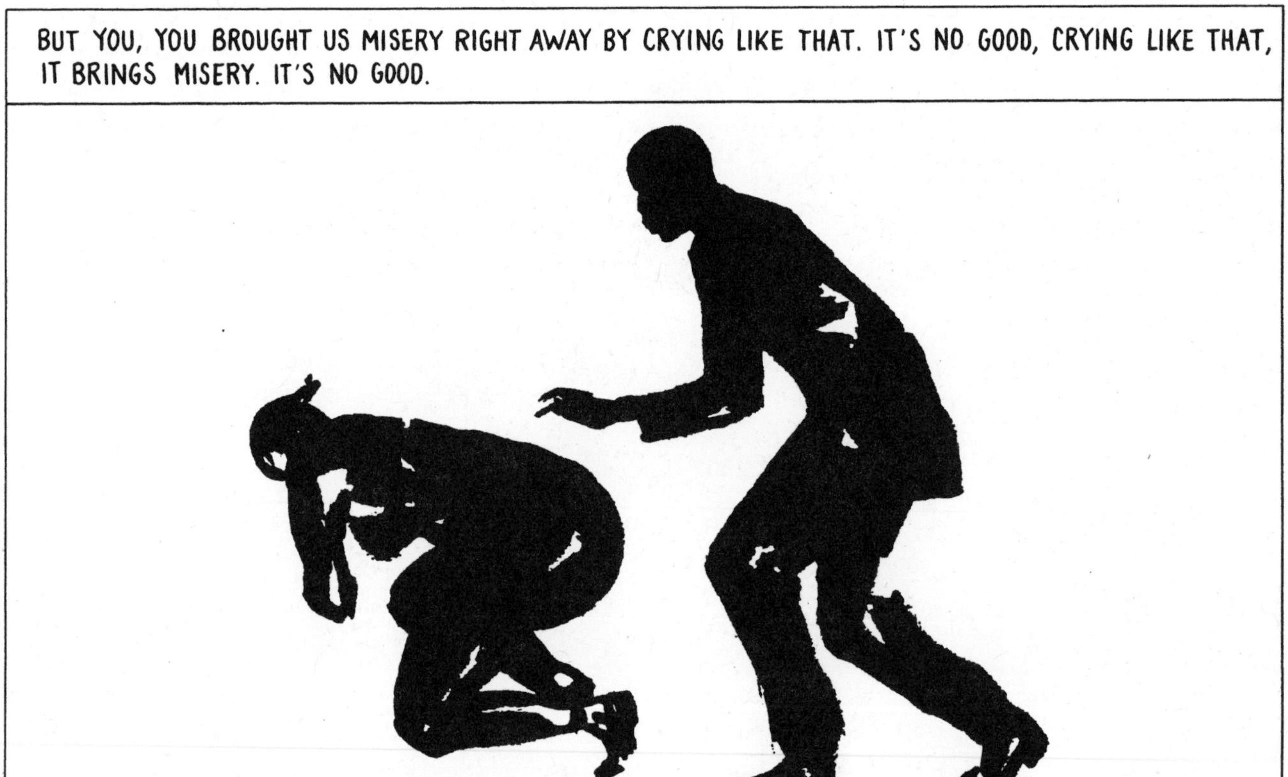
BUT YOU, YOU BROUGHT US MISERY RIGHT AWAY BY CRYING LIKE THAT. IT'S NO GOOD, CRYING LIKE THAT, IT BRINGS MISERY. IT'S NO GOOD.

GET UNDRESSED AGAIN NOW. I SAID UNDRESS. I WANT YOU TO SHOW HIM, SHOW HIM YOUR BREASTS AND YOUR ASS, I WANT YOU TO SHOW HIM EVERYTHING PLAIN.

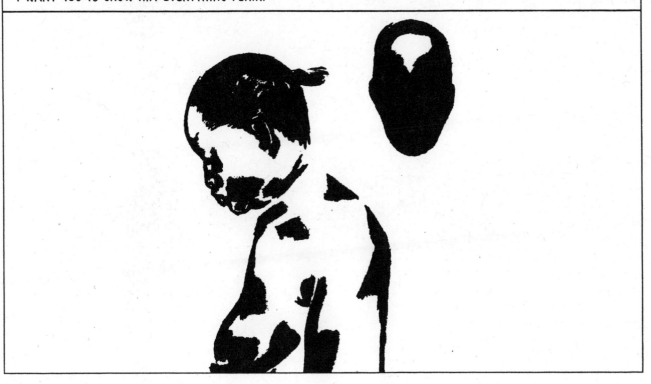

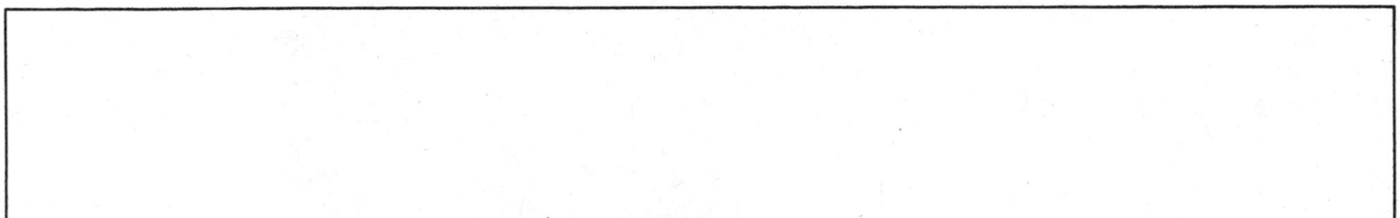

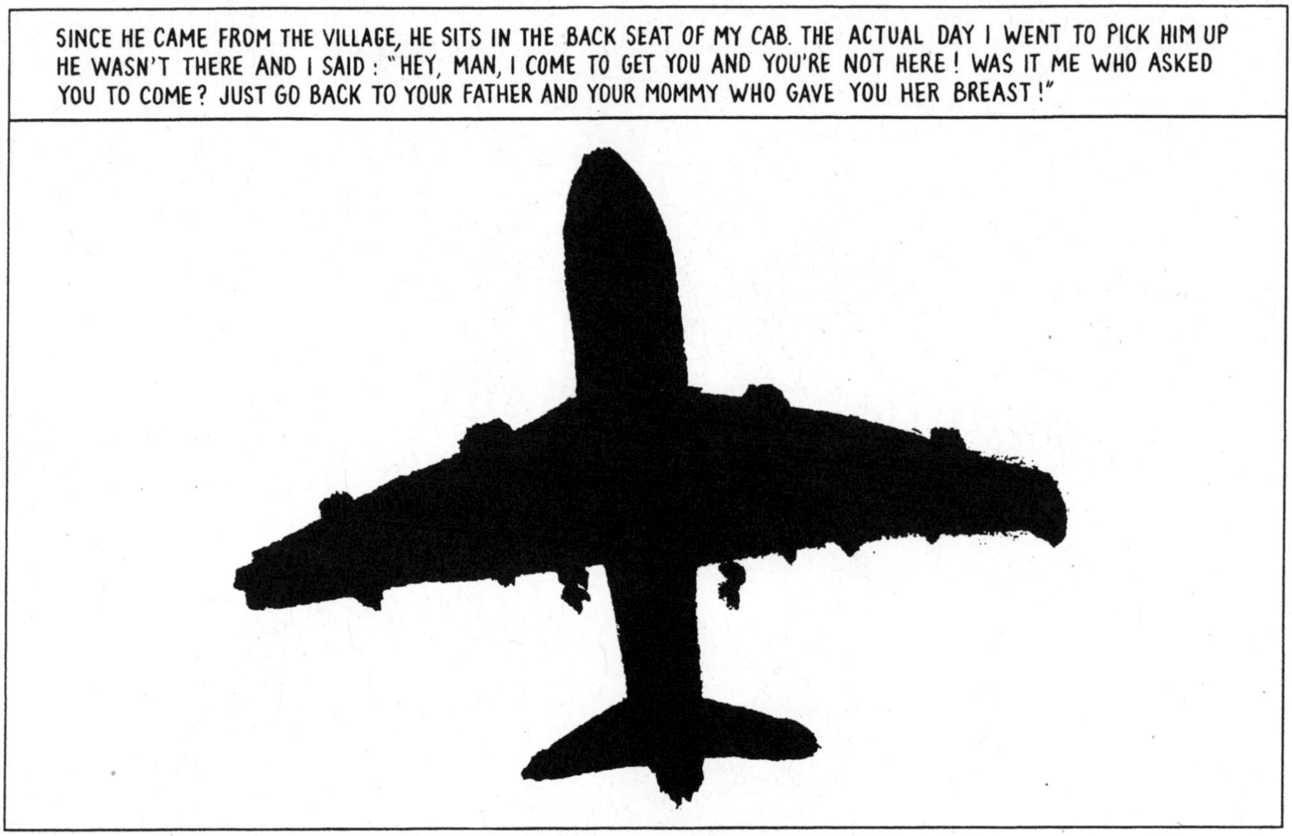
SINCE HE CAME FROM THE VILLAGE, HE SITS IN THE BACK SEAT OF MY CAB. THE ACTUAL DAY I WENT TO PICK HIM UP HE WASN'T THERE AND I SAID: "HEY, MAN, I COME TO GET YOU AND YOU'RE NOT HERE! WAS IT ME WHO ASKED YOU TO COME? JUST GO BACK TO YOUR FATHER AND YOUR MOMMY WHO GAVE YOU HER BREAST!"

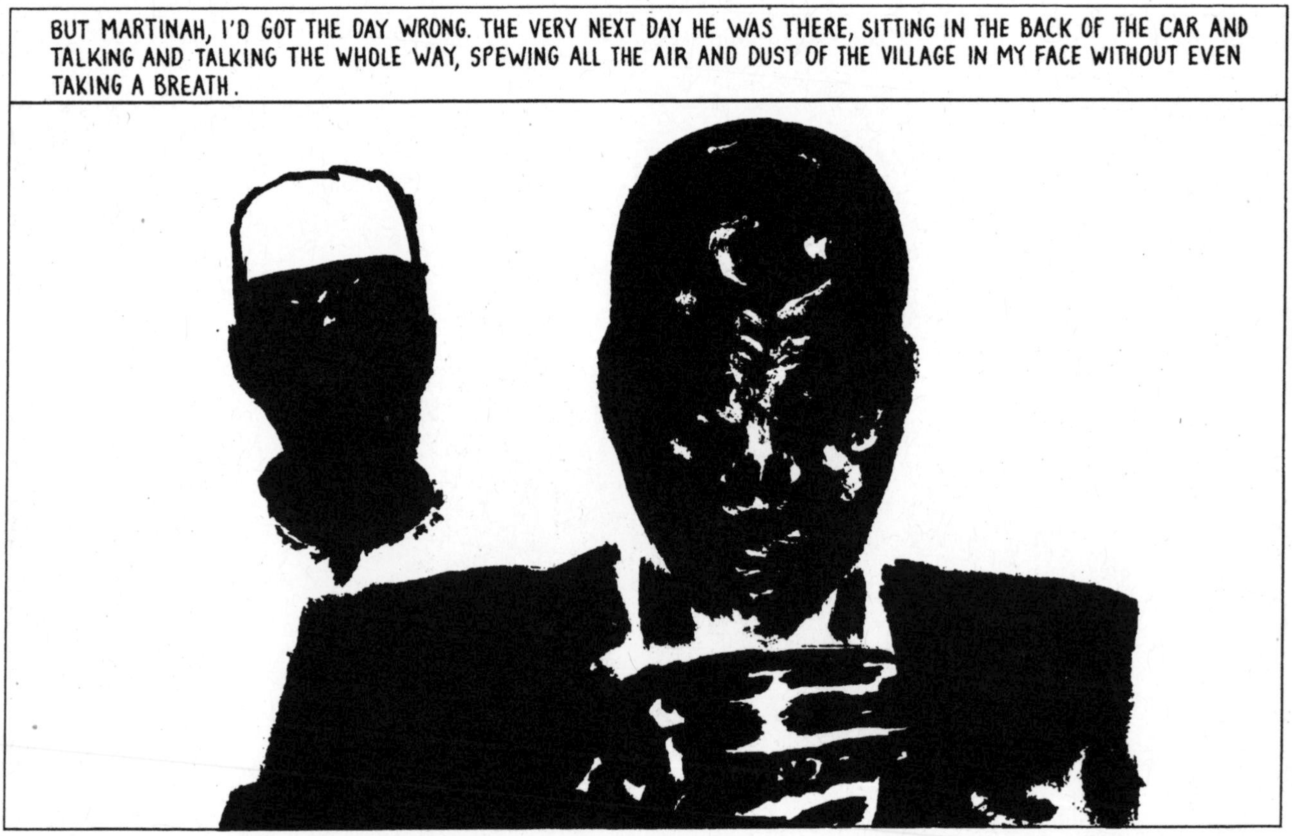
BUT MARTINAH, I'D GOT THE DAY WRONG. THE VERY NEXT DAY HE WAS THERE, SITTING IN THE BACK OF THE CAR AND TALKING AND TALKING THE WHOLE WAY, SPEWING ALL THE AIR AND DUST OF THE VILLAGE IN MY FACE WITHOUT EVEN TAKING A BREATH.

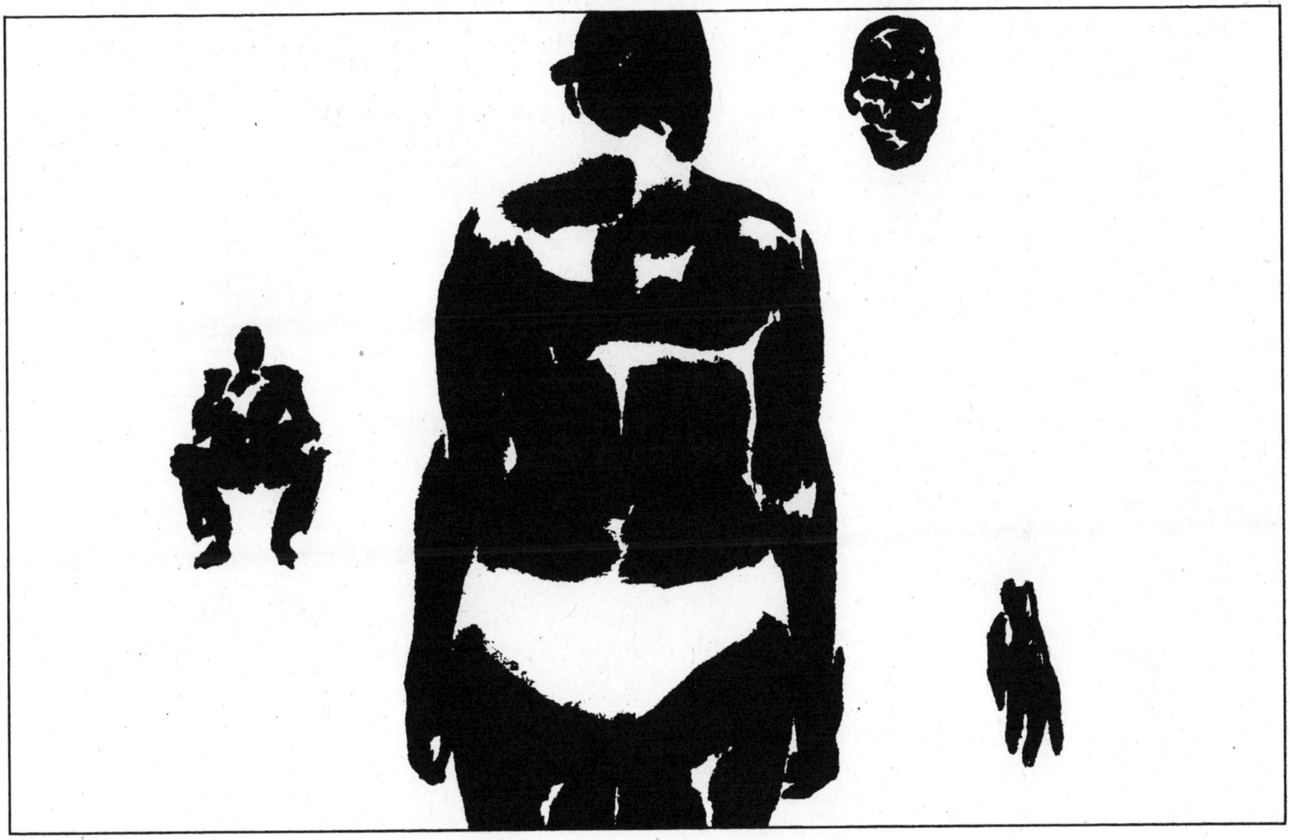

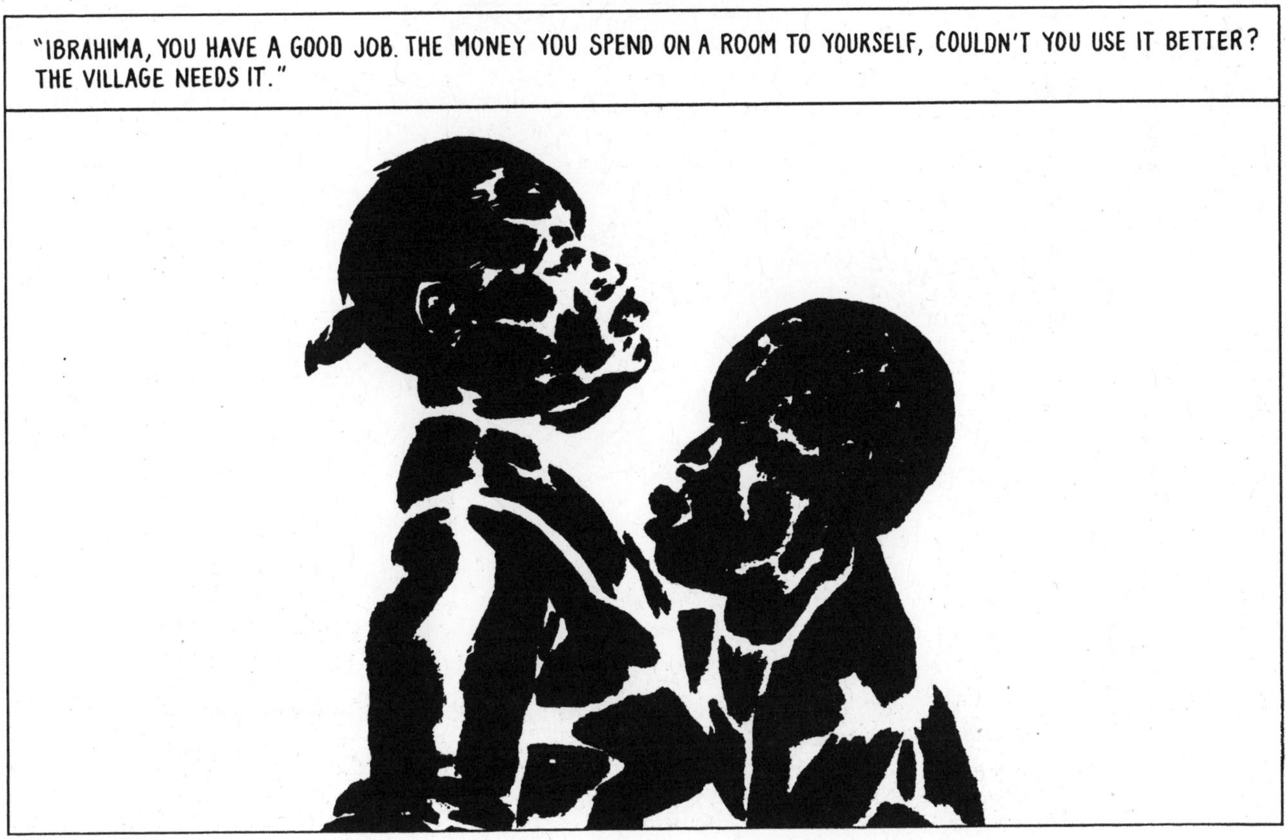
"IBRAHIMA, YOU HAVE A GOOD JOB. THE MONEY YOU SPEND ON A ROOM TO YOURSELF, COULDN'T YOU USE IT BETTER? THE VILLAGE NEEDS IT."

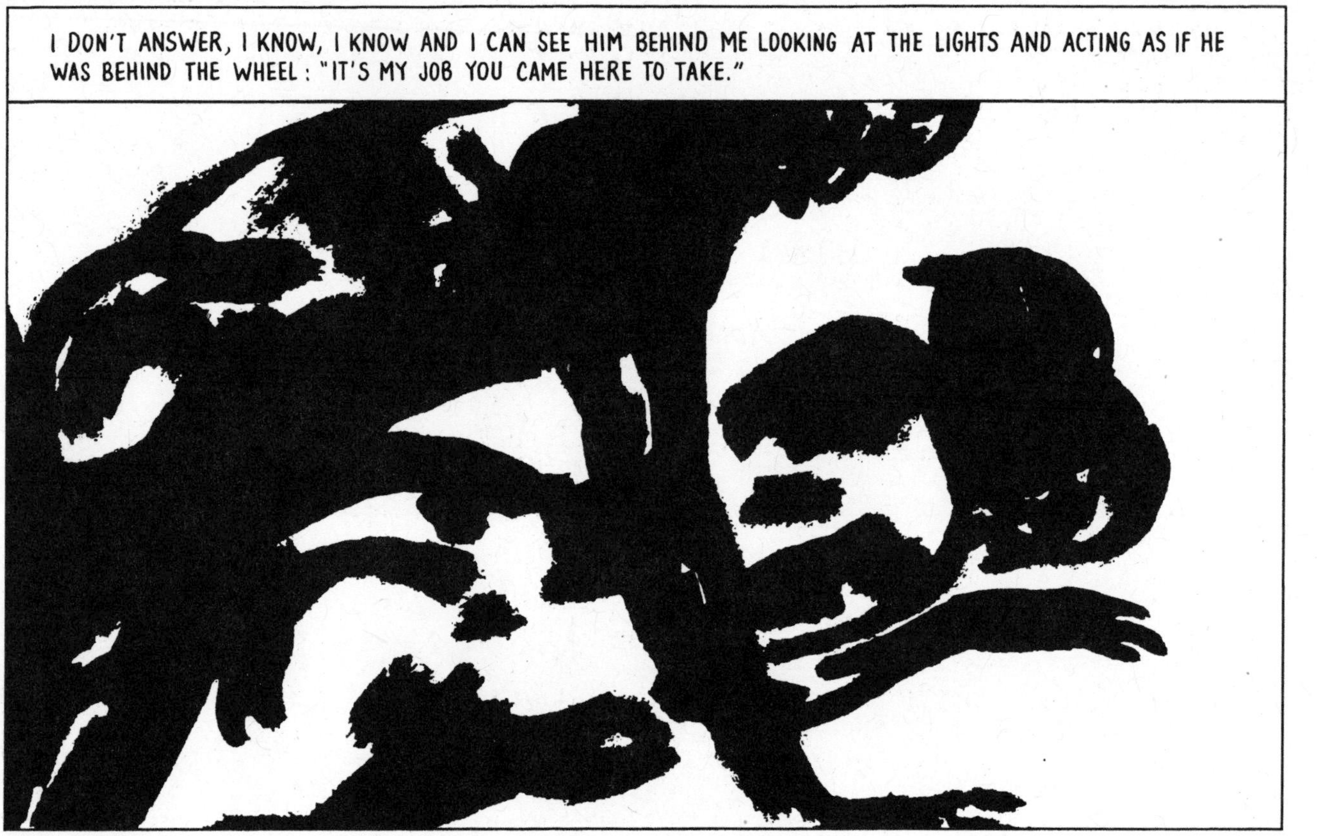
I DON'T ANSWER, I KNOW, I KNOW AND I CAN SEE HIM BEHIND ME LOOKING AT THE LIGHTS AND ACTING AS IF HE WAS BEHIND THE WHEEL: "IT'S MY JOB YOU CAME HERE TO TAKE."

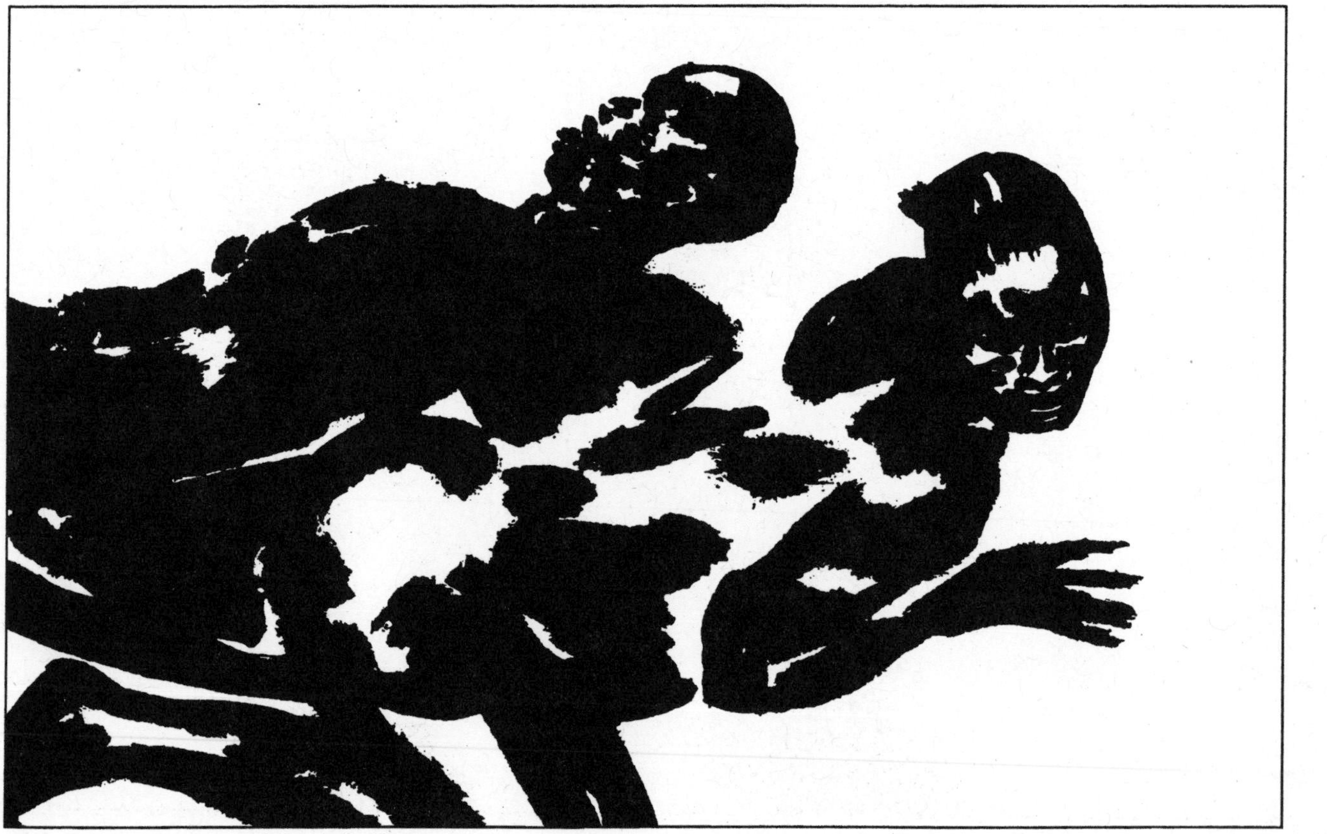

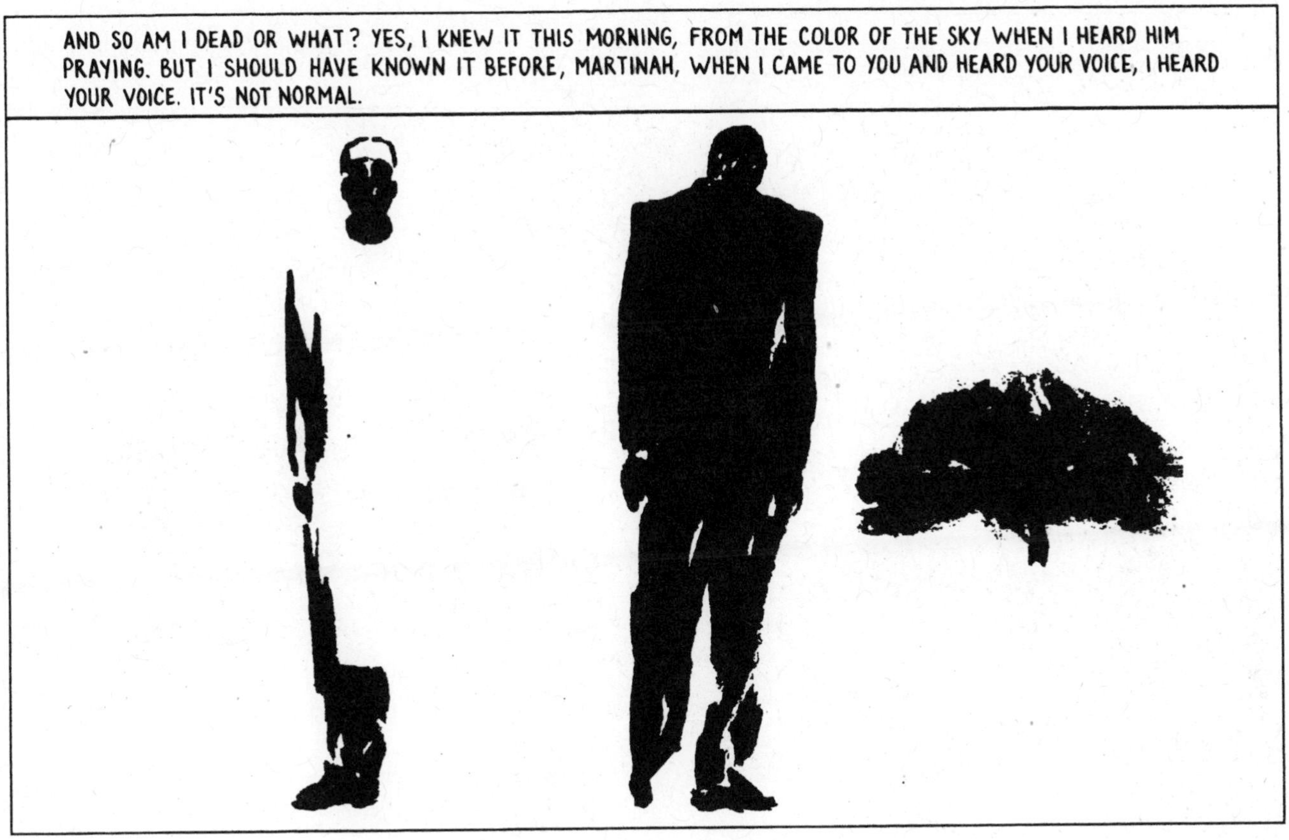
AND SO AM I DEAD OR WHAT? YES, I KNEW IT THIS MORNING, FROM THE COLOR OF THE SKY WHEN I HEARD HIM PRAYING. BUT I SHOULD HAVE KNOWN IT BEFORE, MARTINAH, WHEN I CAME TO YOU AND HEARD YOUR VOICE, I HEARD YOUR VOICE. IT'S NOT NORMAL.

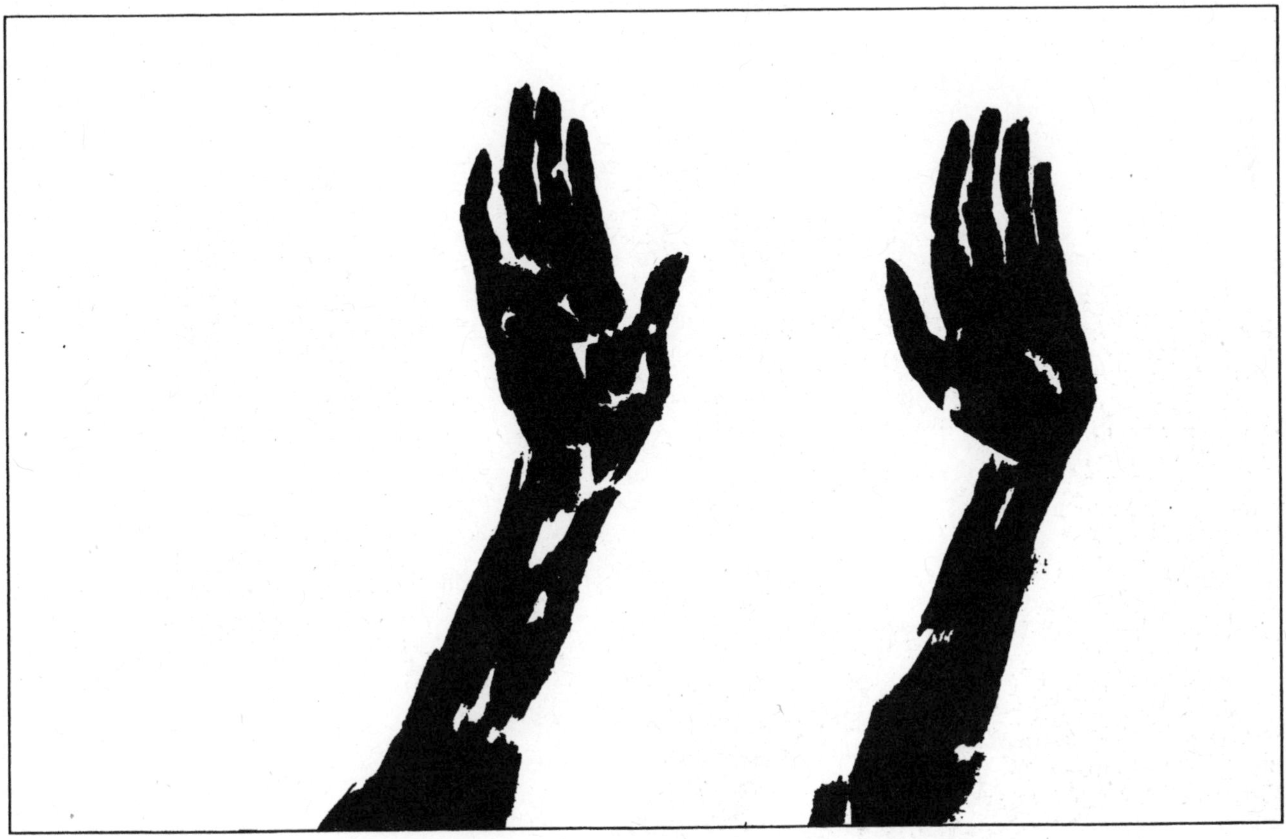

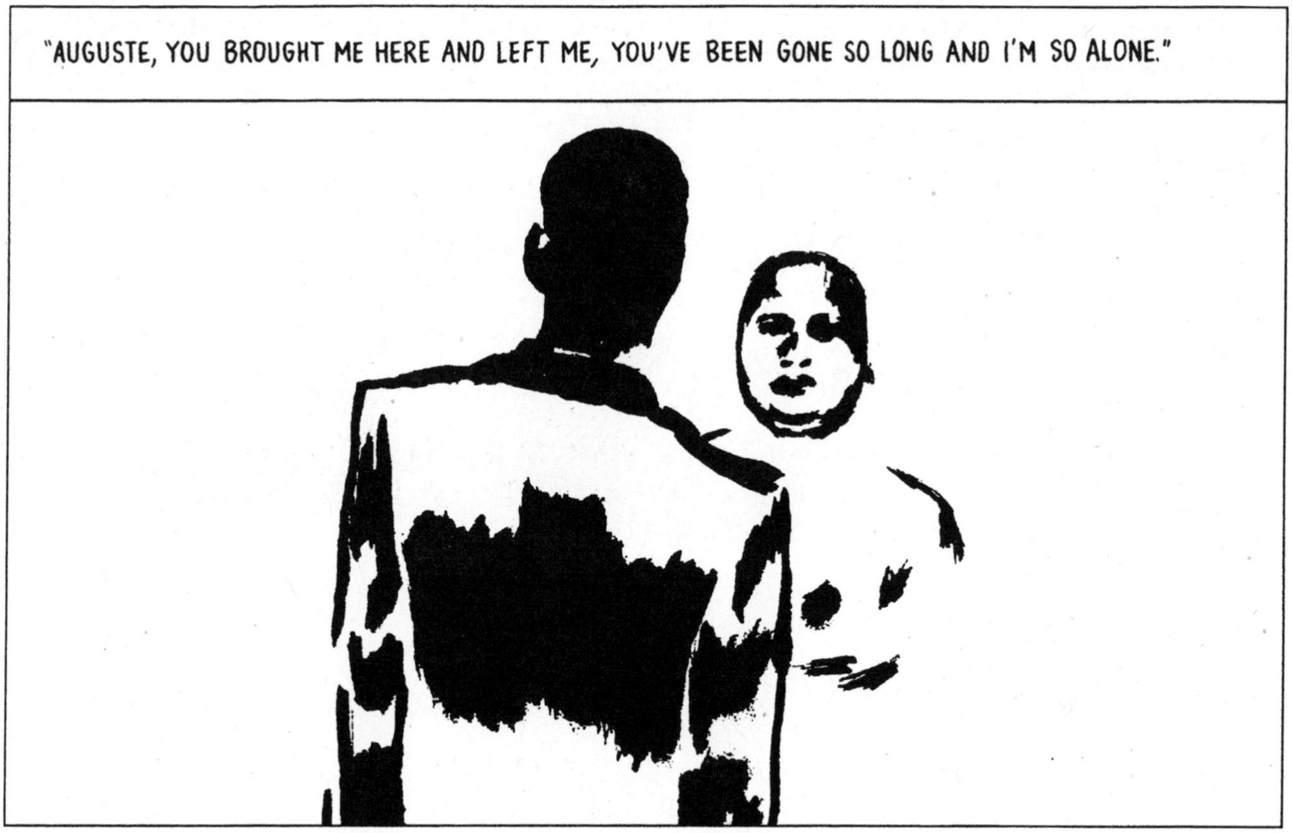
"AUGUSTE, YOU BROUGHT ME HERE AND LEFT ME, YOU'VE BEEN GONE SO LONG AND I'M SO ALONE."

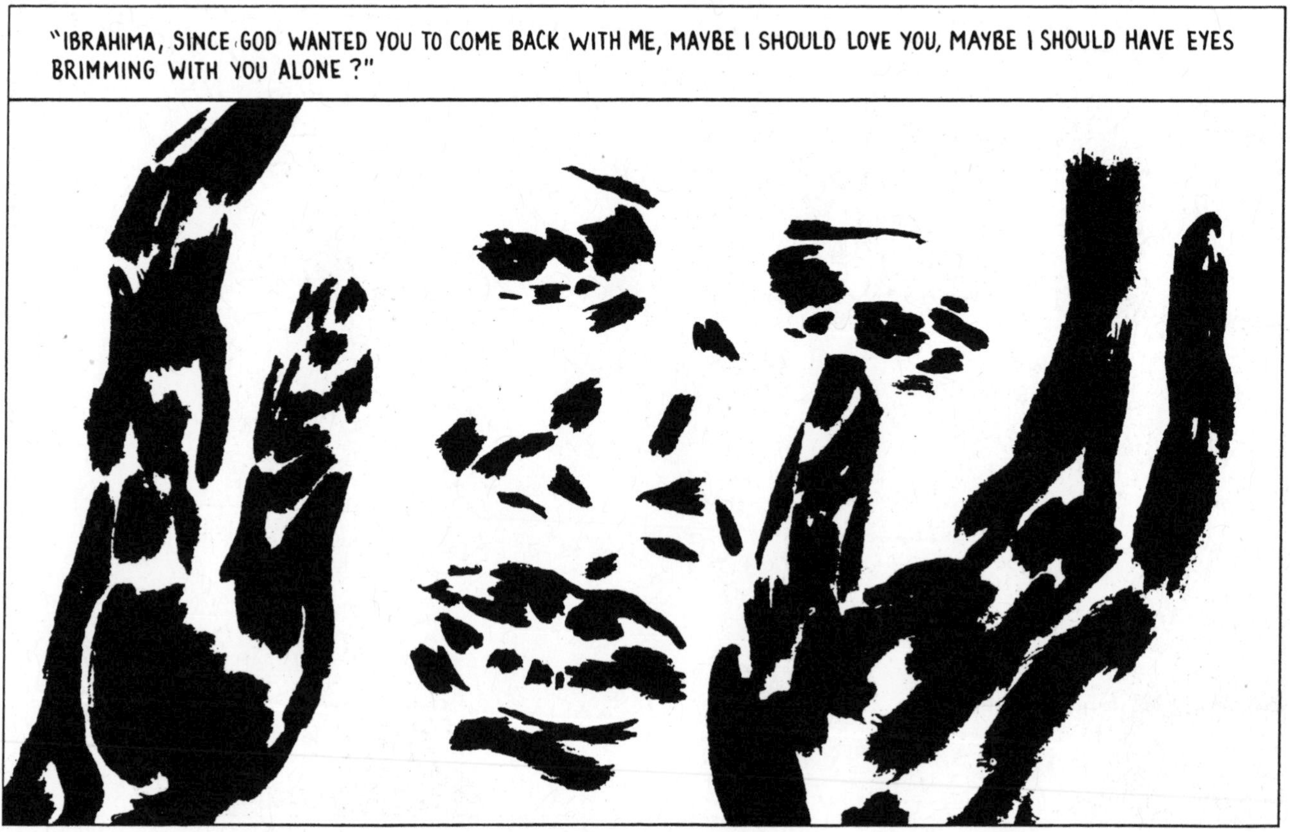
"IBRAHIMA, SINCE GOD WANTED YOU TO COME BACK WITH ME, MAYBE I SHOULD LOVE YOU, MAYBE I SHOULD HAVE EYES BRIMMING WITH YOU ALONE ?"

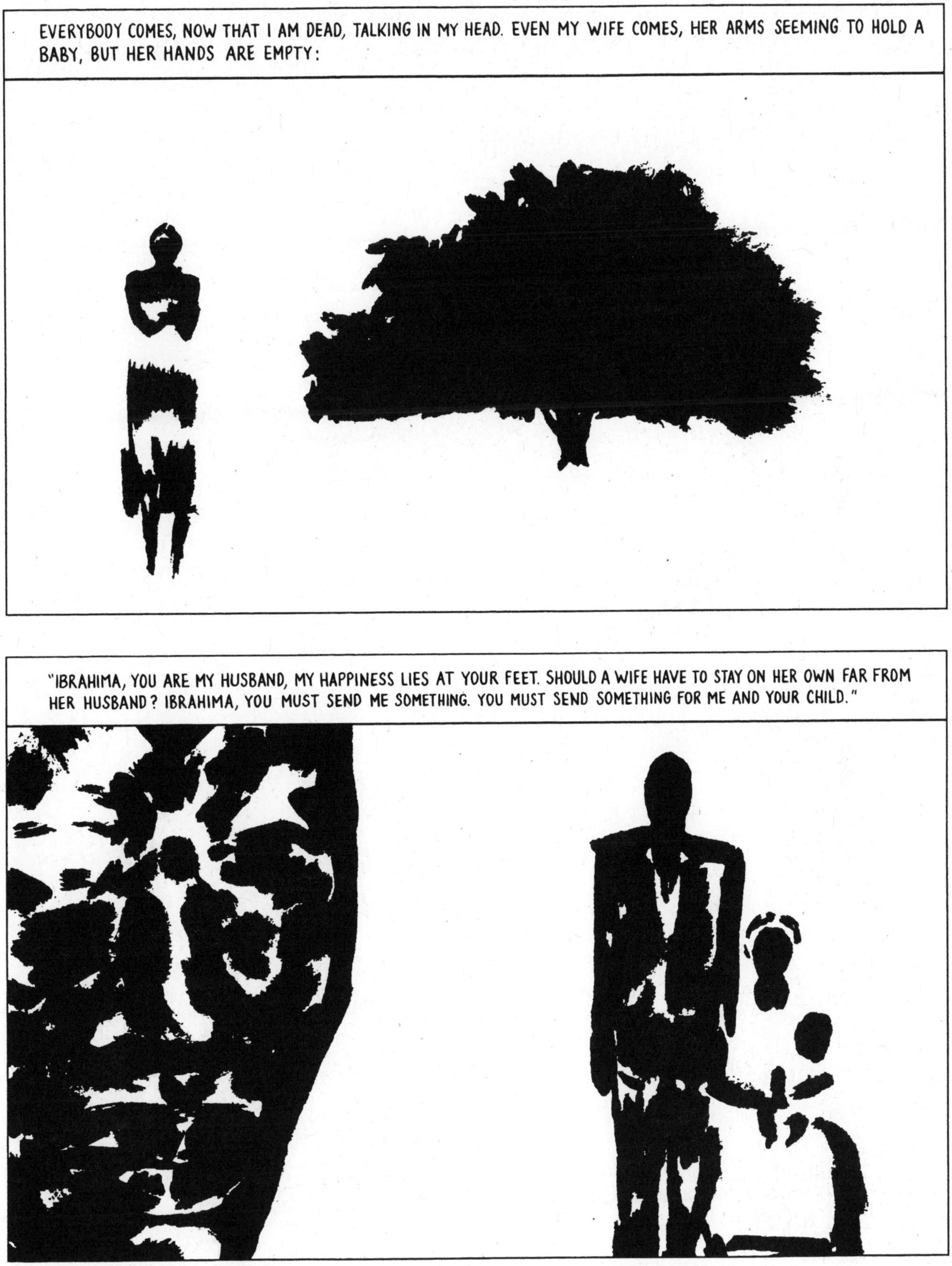
EVERYBODY COMES, NOW THAT I AM DEAD, TALKING IN MY HEAD. EVEN MY WIFE COMES, HER ARMS SEEMING TO HOLD A BABY, BUT HER HANDS ARE EMPTY:
"IBRAHIMA, YOU ARE MY HUSBAND, MY HAPPINESS LIES AT YOUR FEET. SHOULD A WIFE HAVE TO STAY ON HER OWN FAR FROM HER HUSBAND? IBRAHIMA, YOU MUST SEND ME SOMETHING. YOU MUST SEND SOMETHING FOR ME AND YOUR CHILD."

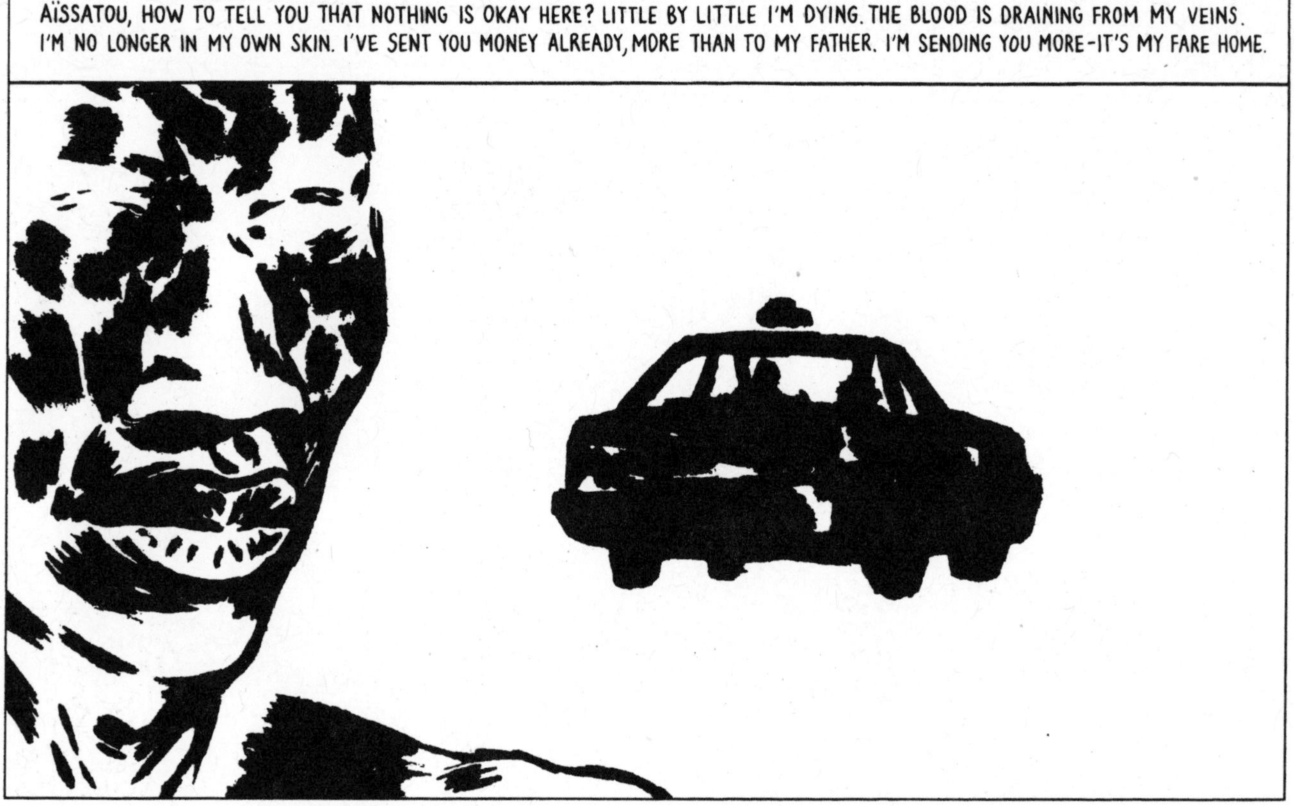
AÏSSATOU, HOW TO TELL YOU THAT NOTHING IS OKAY HERE? LITTLE BY LITTLE I'M DYING. THE BLOOD IS DRAINING FROM MY VEINS. I'M NO LONGER IN MY OWN SKIN. I'VE SENT YOU MONEY ALREADY, MORE THAN TO MY FATHER. I'M SENDING YOU MORE-IT'S MY FARE HOME.

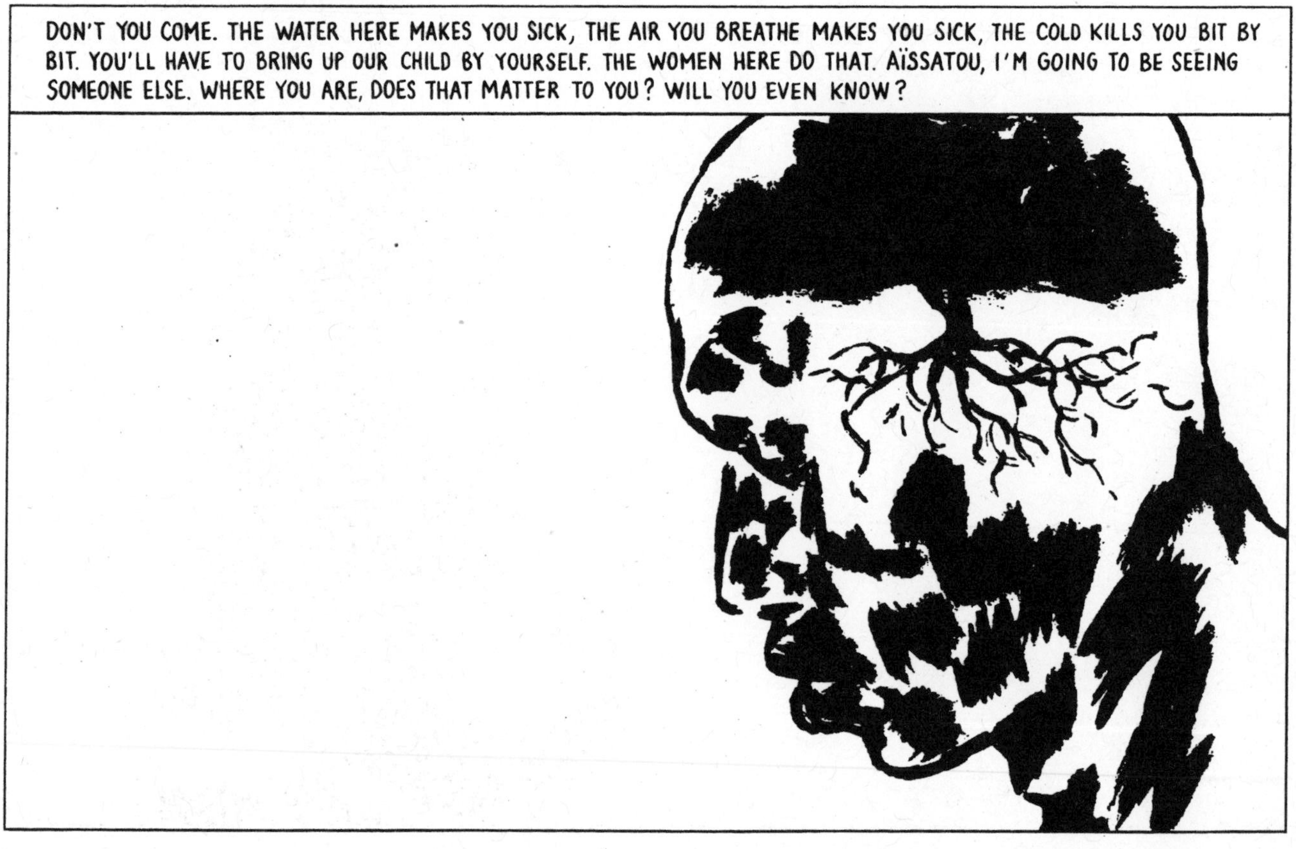
DON'T YOU COME. THE WATER HERE MAKES YOU SICK, THE AIR YOU BREATHE MAKES YOU SICK, THE COLD KILLS YOU BIT BY BIT. YOU'LL HAVE TO BRING UP OUR CHILD BY YOURSELF. THE WOMEN HERE DO THAT. AÏSSATOU, I'M GOING TO BE SEEING SOMEONE ELSE. WHERE YOU ARE, DOES THAT MATTER TO YOU? WILL YOU EVEN KNOW?

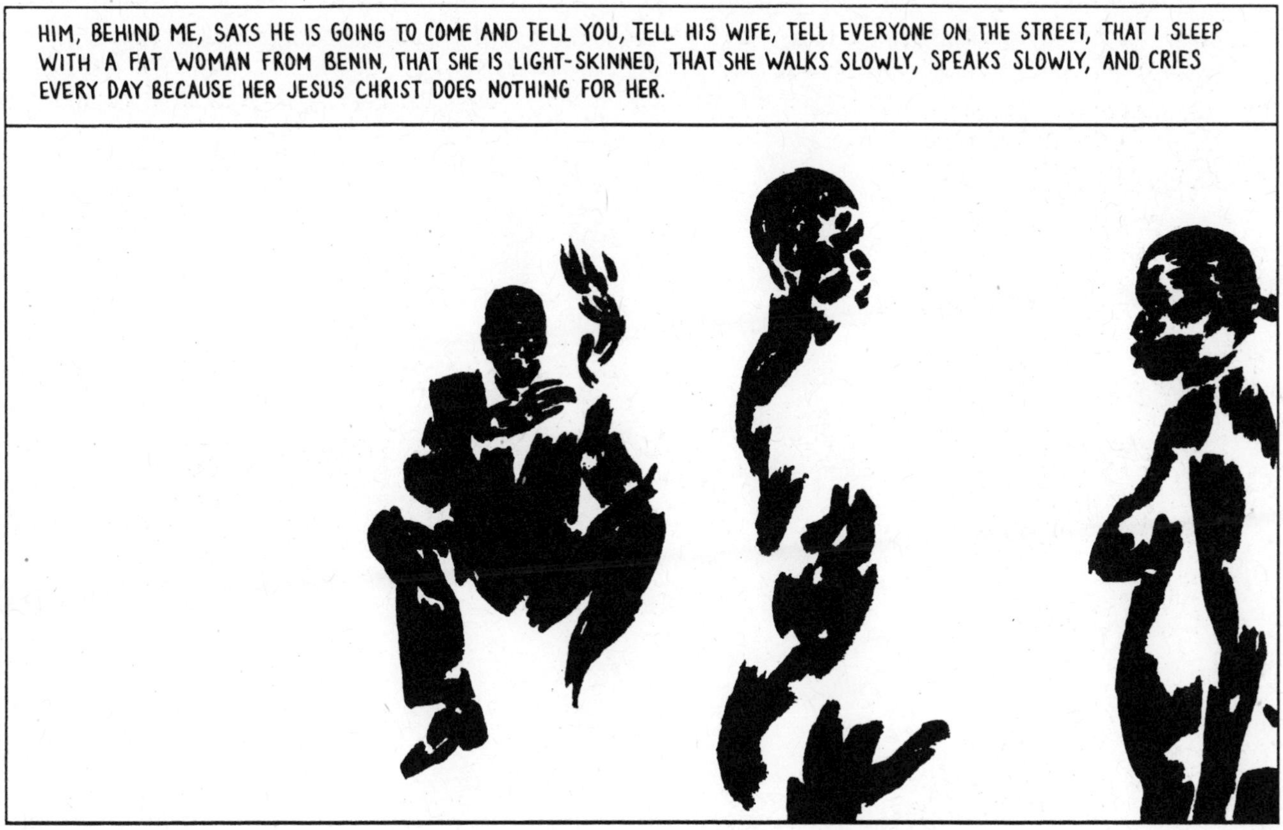
HIM, BEHIND ME, SAYS HE IS GOING TO COME AND TELL YOU, TELL HIS WIFE, TELL EVERYONE ON THE STREET, THAT I SLEEP WITH A FAT WOMAN FROM BENIN, THAT SHE IS LIGHT-SKINNED, THAT SHE WALKS SLOWLY, SPEAKS SLOWLY, AND CRIES EVERY DAY BECAUSE HER JESUS CHRIST DOES NOTHING FOR HER.

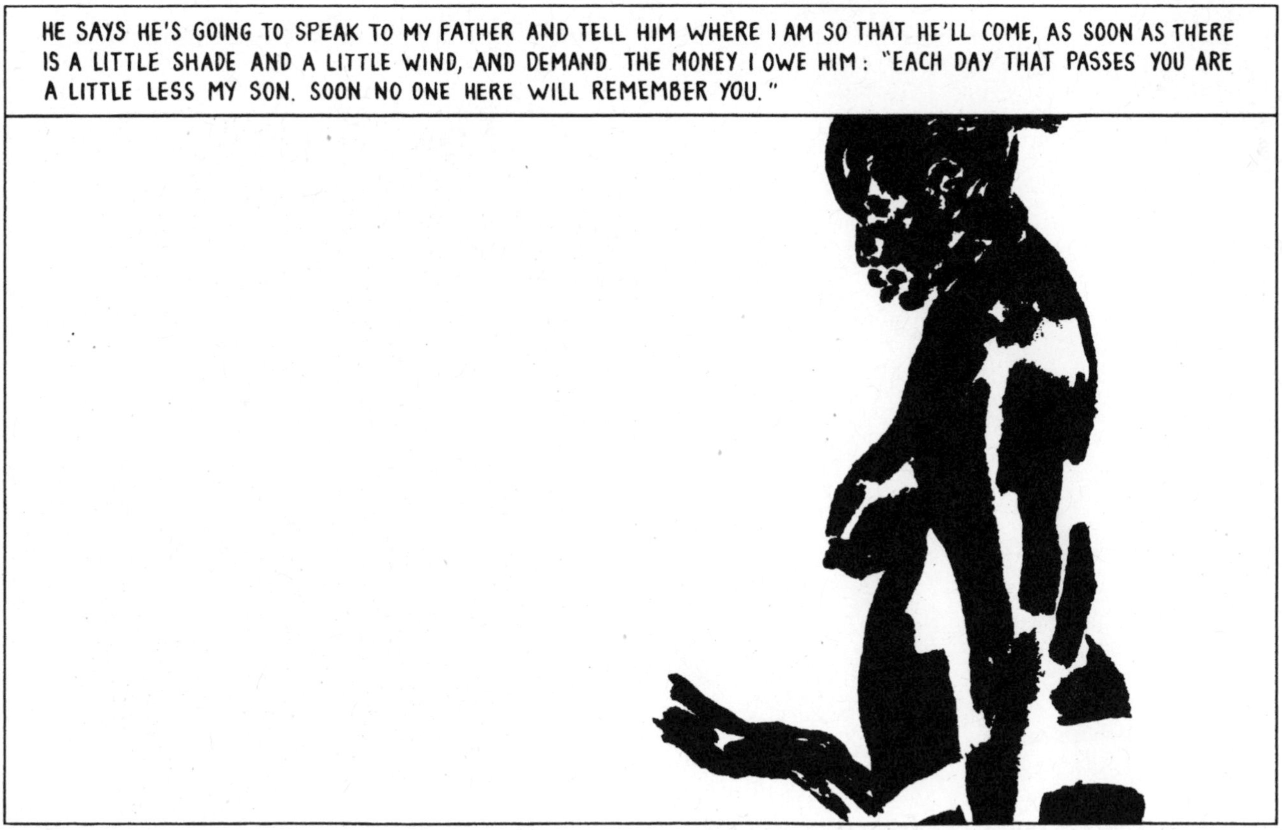
HE SAYS HE'S GOING TO SPEAK TO MY FATHER AND TELL HIM WHERE I AM SO THAT HE'LL COME, AS SOON AS THERE IS A LITTLE SHADE AND A LITTLE WIND, AND DEMAND THE MONEY I OWE HIM: "EACH DAY THAT PASSES YOU ARE A LITTLE LESS MY SON. SOON NO ONE HERE WILL REMEMBER YOU."

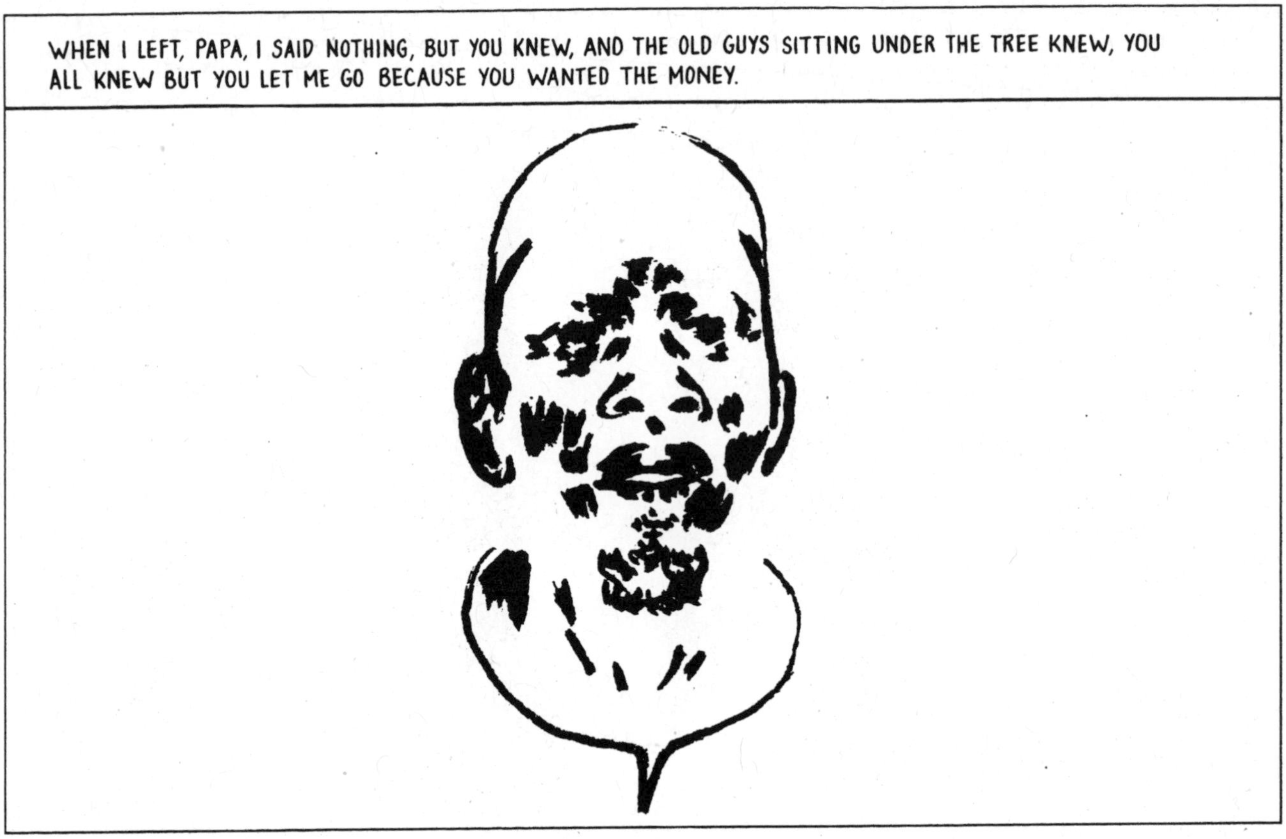
WHEN I LEFT, PAPA, I SAID NOTHING, BUT YOU KNEW, AND THE OLD GUYS SITTING UNDER THE TREE KNEW, YOU ALL KNEW BUT YOU LET ME GO BECAUSE YOU WANTED THE MONEY.

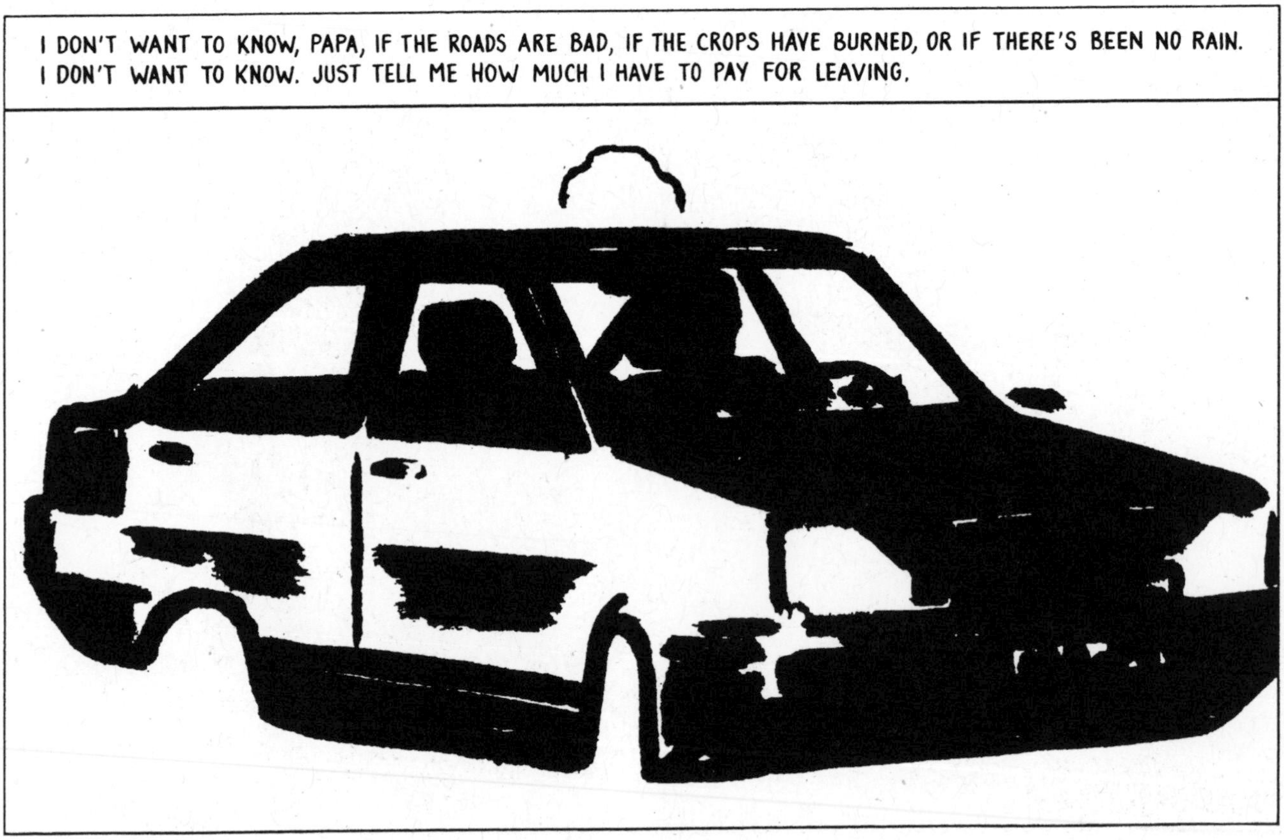
I DON'T WANT TO KNOW, PAPA, IF THE ROADS ARE BAD, IF THE CROPS HAVE BURNED, OR IF THERE'S BEEN NO RAIN. I DON'T WANT TO KNOW. JUST TELL ME HOW MUCH I HAVE TO PAY FOR LEAVING.

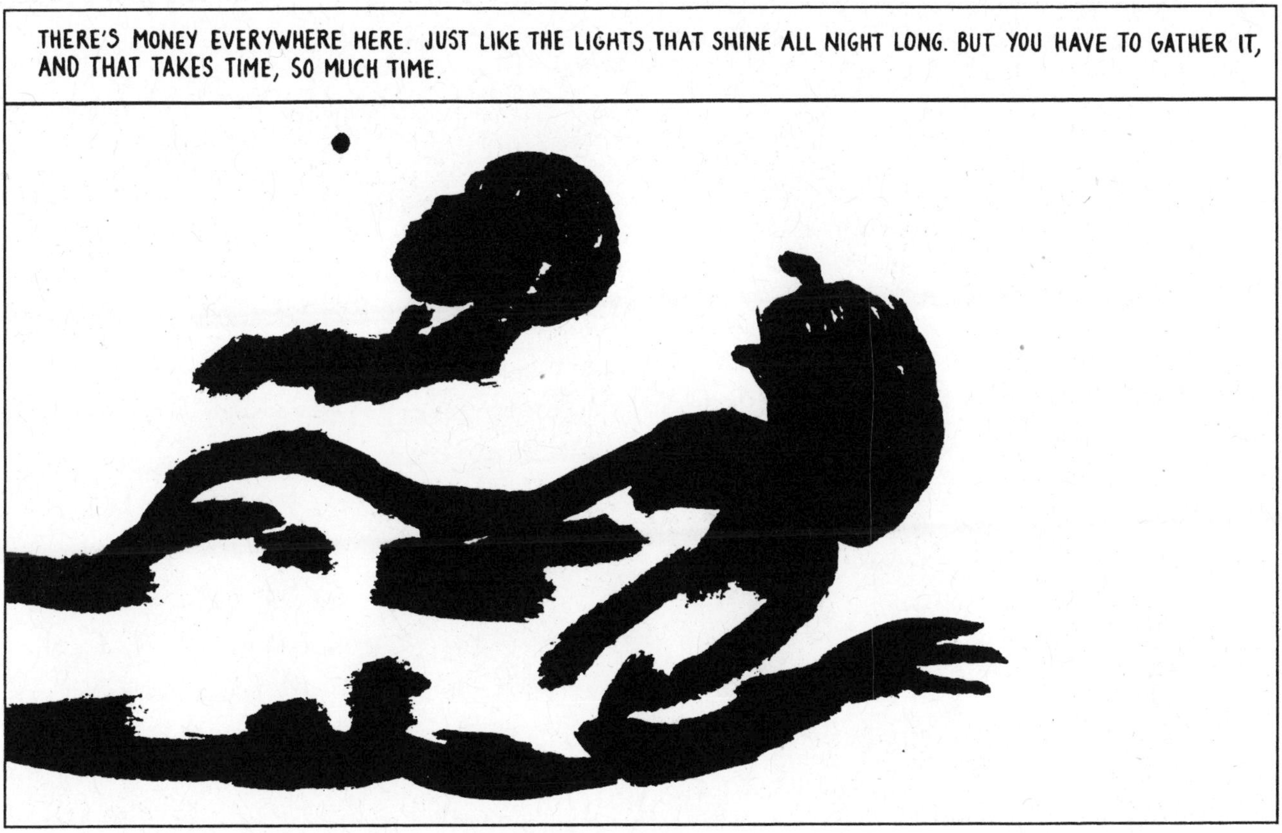
THERE'S MONEY EVERYWHERE HERE. JUST LIKE THE LIGHTS THAT SHINE ALL NIGHT LONG. BUT YOU HAVE TO GATHER IT, AND THAT TAKES TIME, SO MUCH TIME.

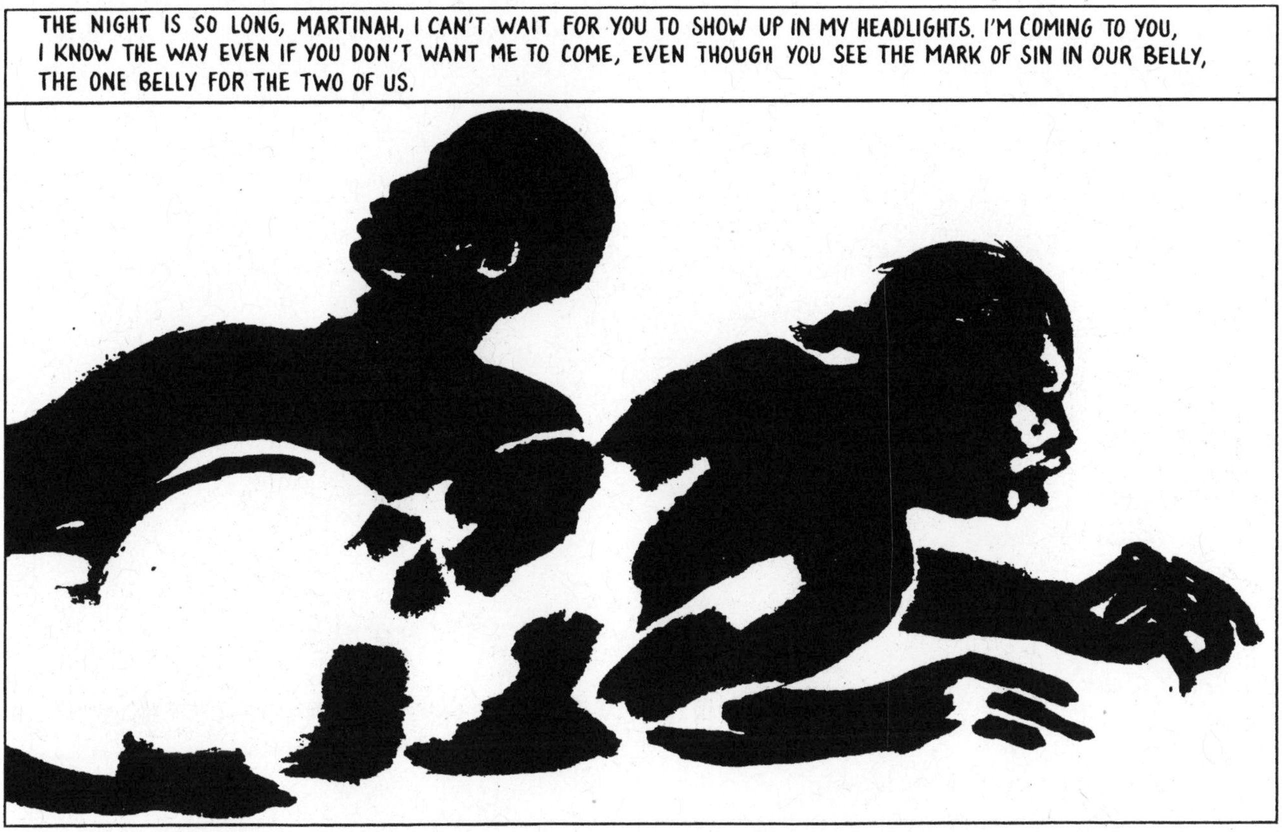
THE NIGHT IS SO LONG, MARTINAH, I CAN'T WAIT FOR YOU TO SHOW UP IN MY HEADLIGHTS. I'M COMING TO YOU, I KNOW THE WAY EVEN IF YOU DON'T WANT ME TO COME, EVEN THOUGH YOU SEE THE MARK OF SIN IN OUR BELLY, THE ONE BELLY FOR THE TWO OF US.

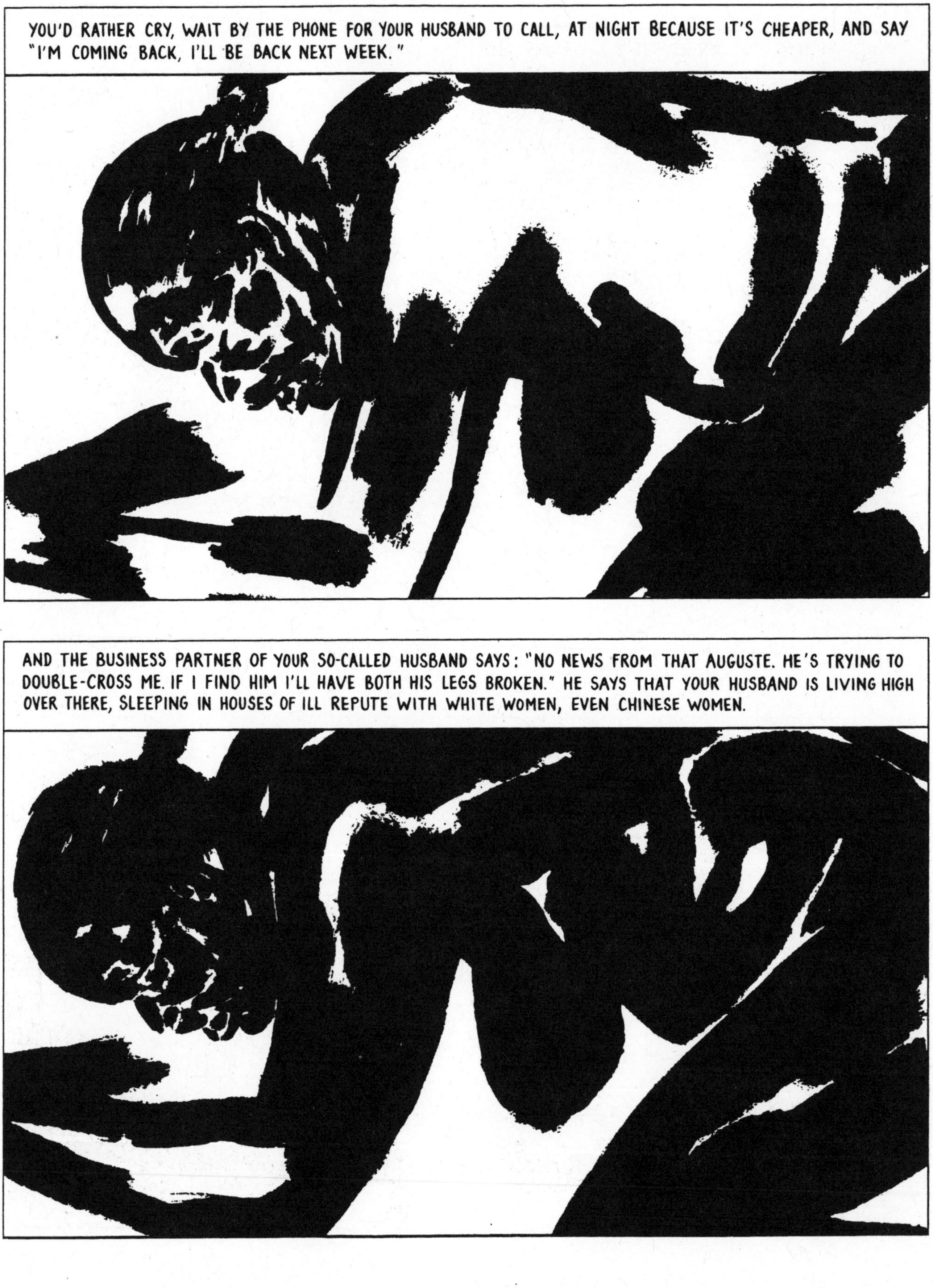
YOU'D RATHER CRY, WAIT BY THE PHONE FOR YOUR HUSBAND TO CALL, AT NIGHT BECAUSE IT'S CHEAPER, AND SAY "I'M COMING BACK, I'LL BE BACK NEXT WEEK."
AND THE BUSINESS PARTNER OF YOUR SO-CALLED HUSBAND SAYS: "NO NEWS FROM THAT AUGUSTE. HE'S TRYING TO DOUBLE-CROSS ME. IF I FIND HIM I'LL HAVE BOTH HIS LEGS BROKEN." HE SAYS THAT YOUR HUSBAND IS LIVING HIGH OVER THERE, SLEEPING IN HOUSES OF ILL REPUTE WITH WHITE WOMEN, EVEN CHINESE WOMEN.

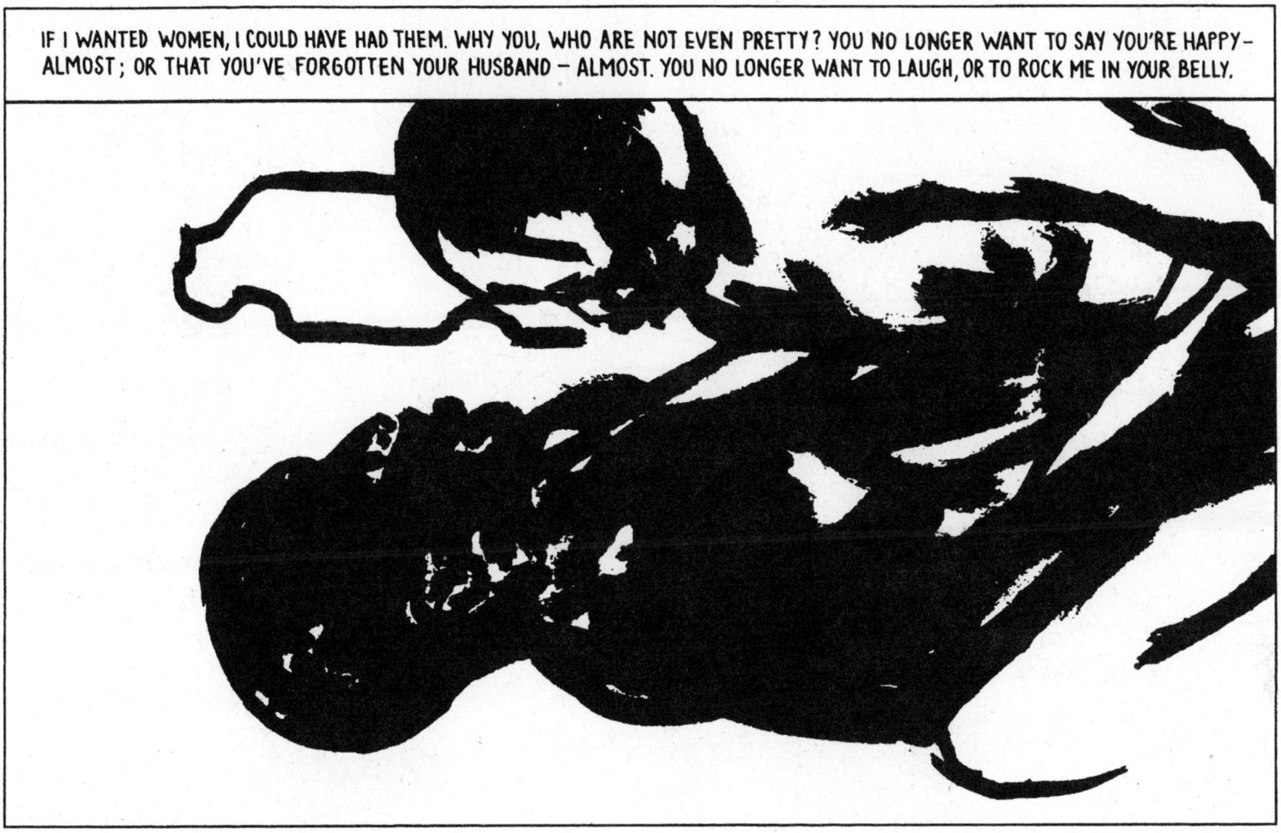
IF I WANTED WOMEN, I COULD HAVE HAD THEM. WHY YOU, WHO ARE NOT EVEN PRETTY? YOU NO LONGER WANT TO SAY YOU'RE HAPPY - ALMOST; OR THAT YOU'VE FORGOTTEN YOUR HUSBAND - ALMOST. YOU NO LONGER WANT TO LAUGH, OR TO ROCK ME IN YOUR BELLY.

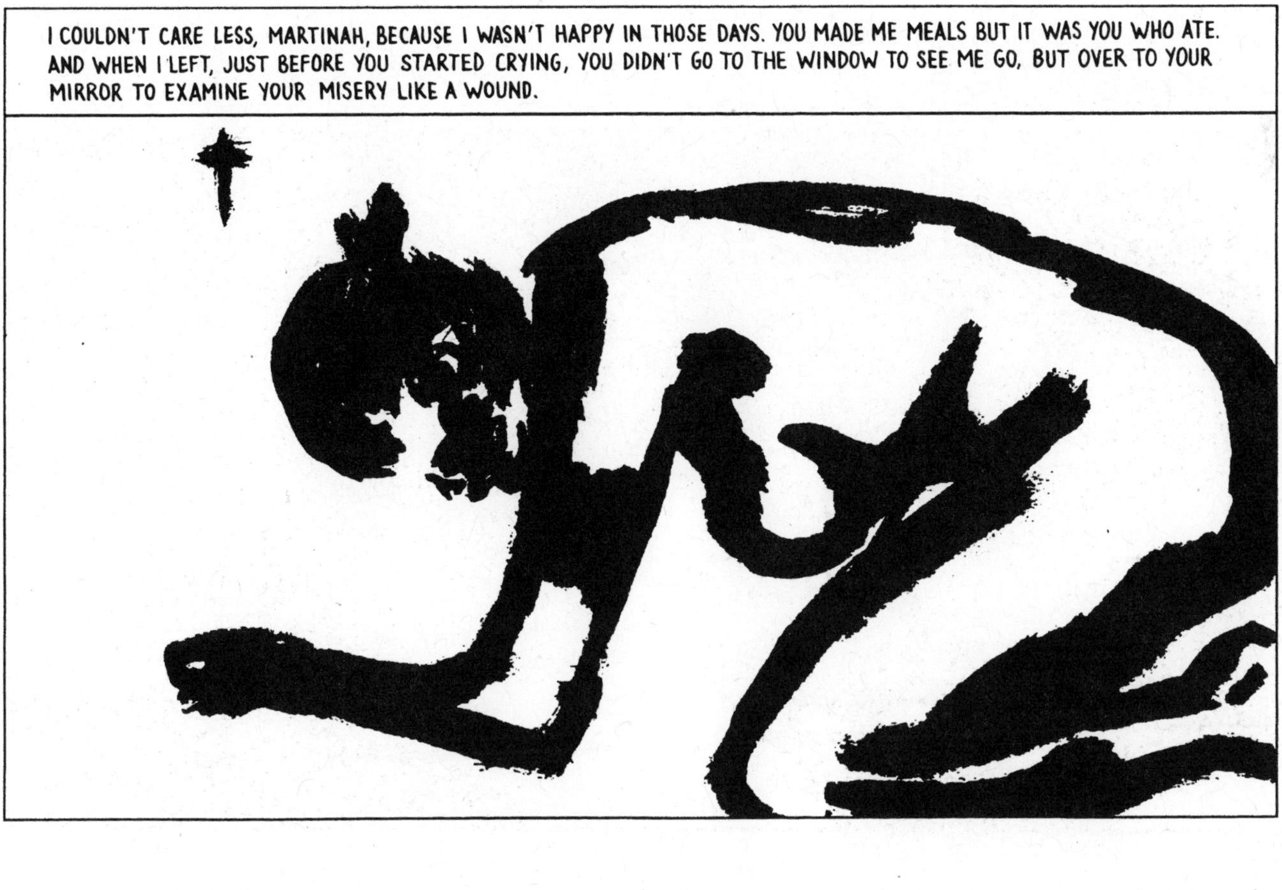
I COULDN'T CARE LESS, MARTINAH, BECAUSE I WASN'T HAPPY IN THOSE DAYS. YOU MADE ME MEALS BUT IT WAS YOU WHO ATE. AND WHEN I LEFT, JUST BEFORE YOU STARTED CRYING, YOU DIDN'T GO TO THE WINDOW TO SEE ME GO, BUT OVER TO YOUR MIRROR TO EXAMINE YOUR MISERY LIKE A WOUND.

THE NIGHT IS LONG AND I'M NOT WAITING FOR YOU TO APPEAR IN MY HEADLIGHTS. I'M COMING OVER, GET UNDRESSED. I'M GOING TO SHOW HIM. YOU DON'T WANT TO BELIEVE YOU ARE DEAD, YOU DON'T WANT TO SEE ANYTHING, JUST LIKE YOUR JESUS WITH HIS BEARD ON HIS WOMAN'S FACE. YOU WERE DEAD BEFORE I SHONE MY LIGHTS IN YOUR EYES.

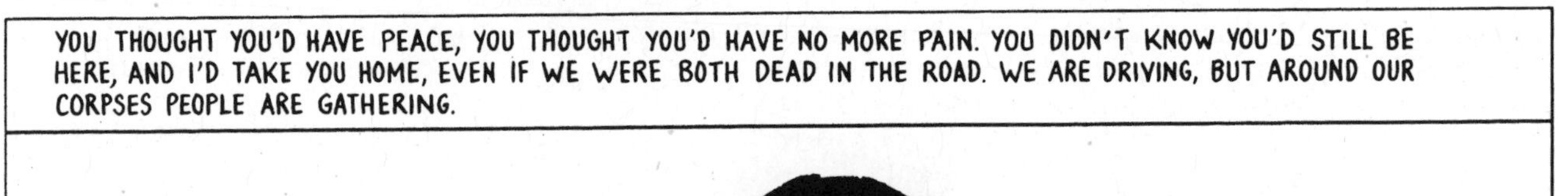

YOU THOUGHT YOU'D HAVE PEACE, YOU THOUGHT YOU'D HAVE NO MORE PAIN. YOU DIDN'T KNOW YOU'D STILL BE HERE, AND I'D TAKE YOU HOME, EVEN IF WE WERE BOTH DEAD IN THE ROAD. WE ARE DRIVING, BUT AROUND OUR CORPSES PEOPLE ARE GATHERING.

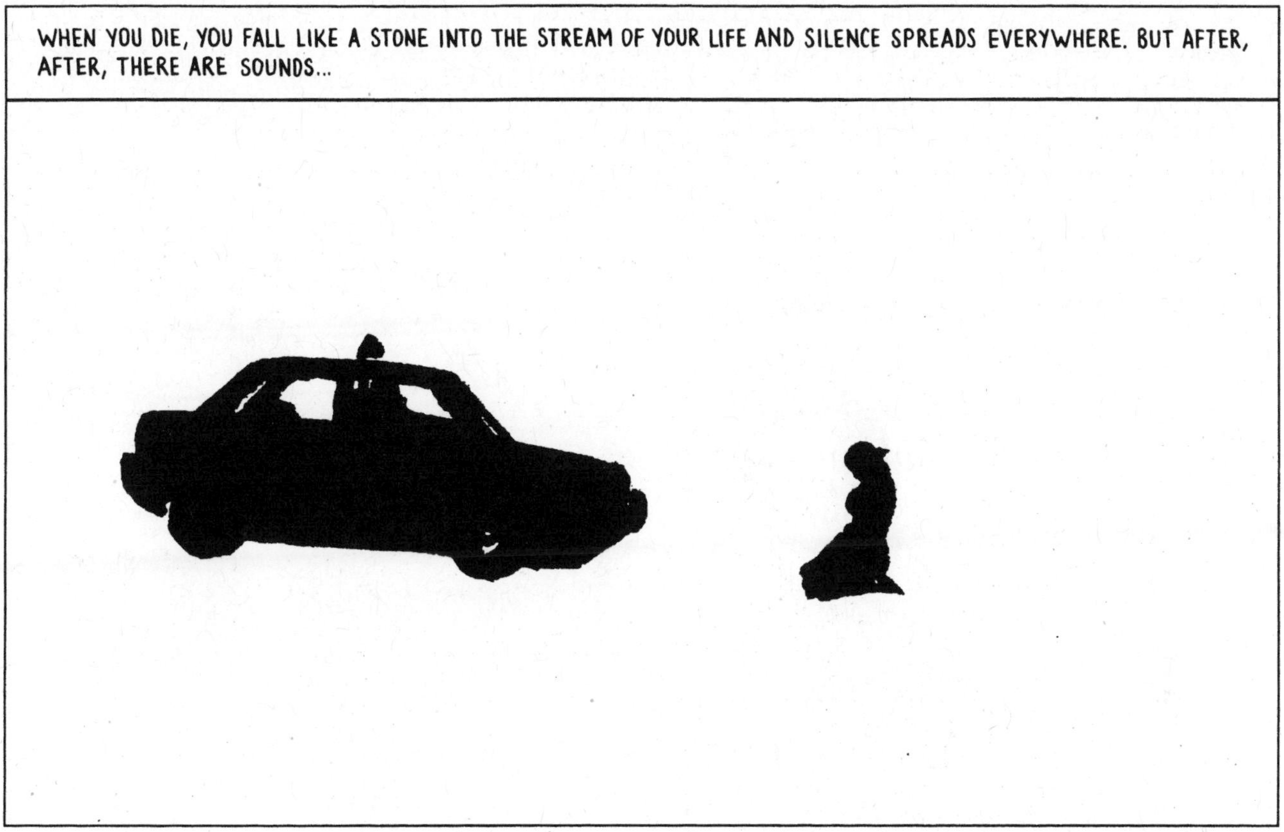
WHEN YOU DIE, YOU FALL LIKE A STONE INTO THE STREAM OF YOUR LIFE AND SILENCE SPREADS EVERYWHERE. BUT AFTER, AFTER, THERE ARE SOUNDS...

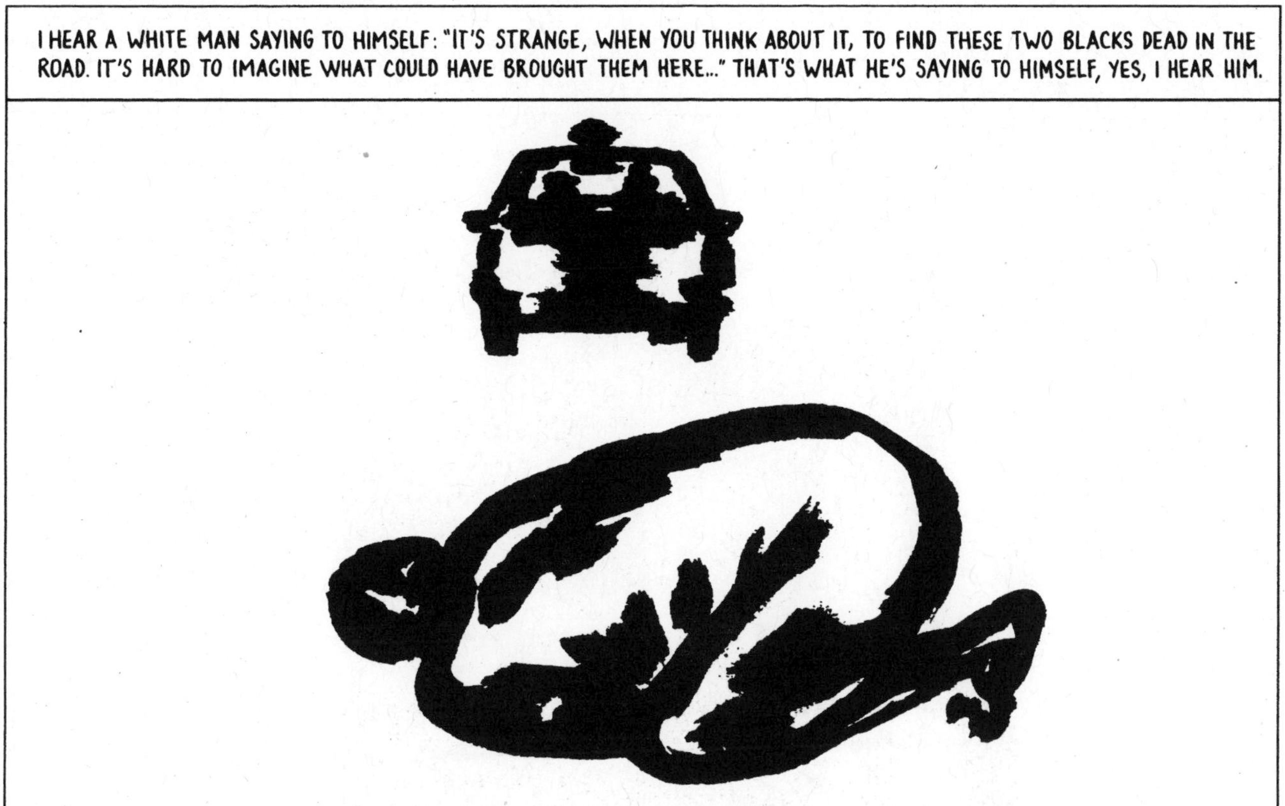
I HEAR A WHITE MAN SAYING TO HIMSELF: "IT'S STRANGE, WHEN YOU THINK ABOUT IT, TO FIND THESE TWO BLACKS DEAD IN THE ROAD. IT'S HARD TO IMAGINE WHAT COULD HAVE BROUGHT THEM HERE..." THAT'S WHAT HE'S SAYING TO HIMSELF, YES, I HEAR HIM.

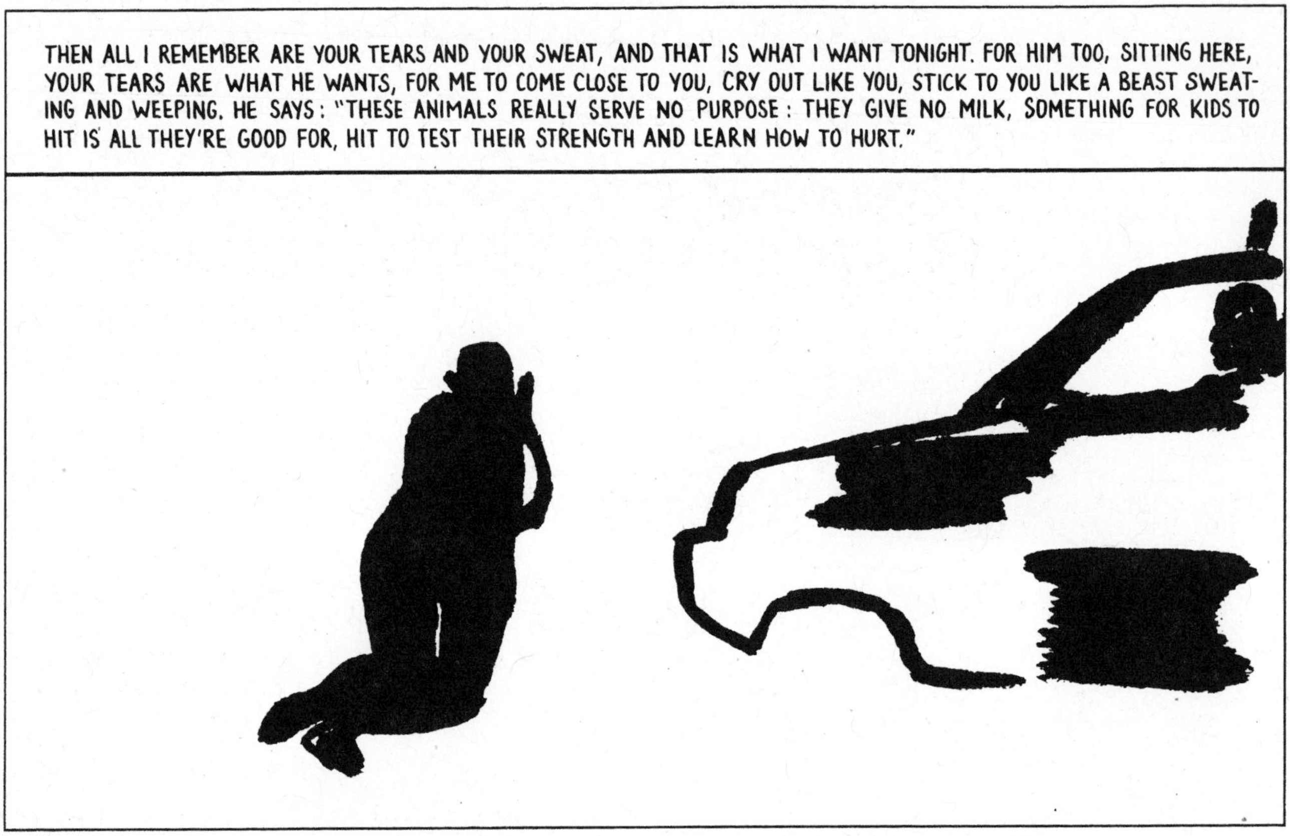
THEN ALL I REMEMBER ARE YOUR TEARS AND YOUR SWEAT, AND THAT IS WHAT I WANT TONIGHT. FOR HIM TOO, SITTING HERE, YOUR TEARS ARE WHAT HE WANTS, FOR ME TO COME CLOSE TO YOU, CRY OUT LIKE YOU, STICK TO YOU LIKE A BEAST SWEATING AND WEEPING. HE SAYS: "THESE ANIMALS REALLY SERVE NO PURPOSE: THEY GIVE NO MILK, SOMETHING FOR KIDS TO HIT IS ALL THEY'RE GOOD FOR, HIT TO TEST THEIR STRENGTH AND LEARN HOW TO HURT."

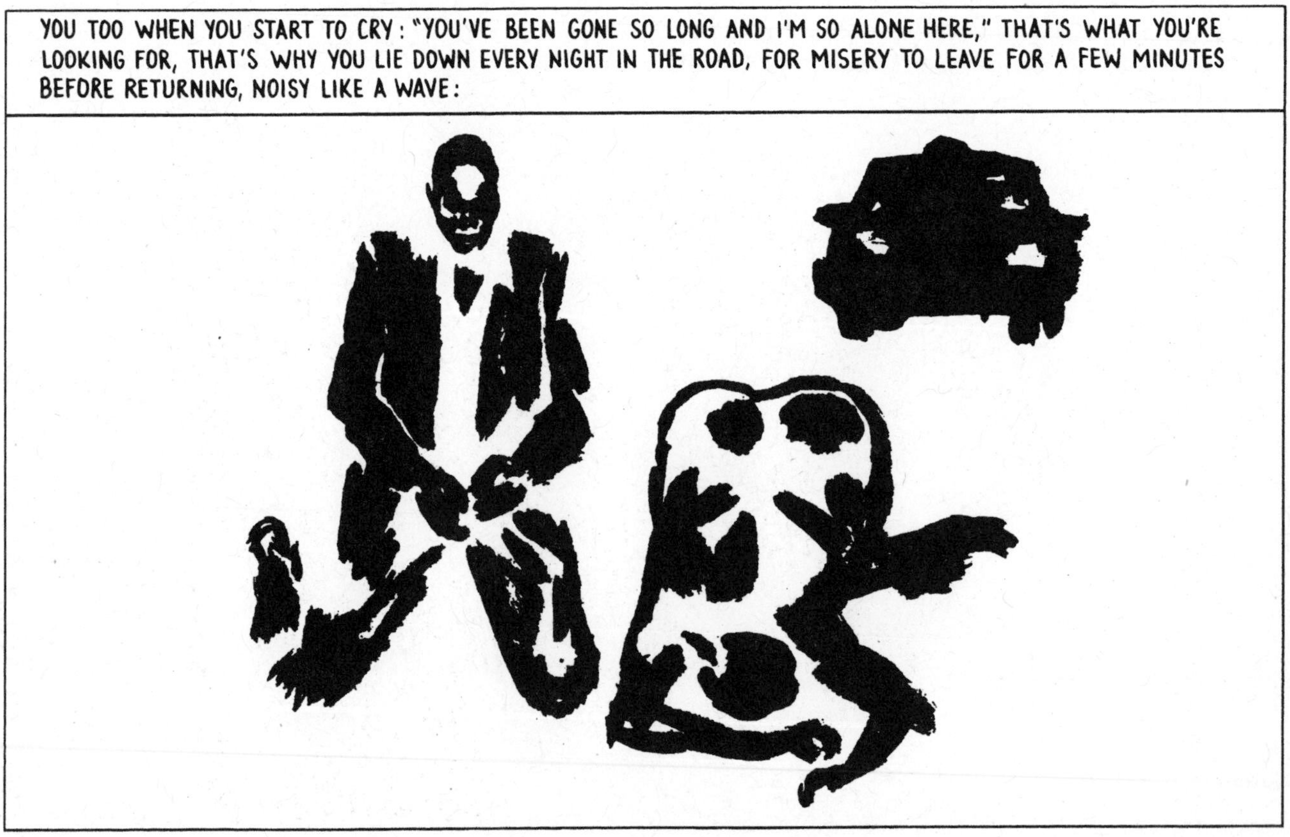
YOU TOO WHEN YOU START TO CRY: "YOU'VE BEEN GONE SO LONG AND I'M SO ALONE HERE," THAT'S WHAT YOU'RE LOOKING FOR, THAT'S WHY YOU LIE DOWN EVERY NIGHT IN THE ROAD, FOR MISERY TO LEAVE FOR A FEW MINUTES BEFORE RETURNING, NOISY LIKE A WAVE:

"THIS IS WHERE YOU'VE LEFT ME, AUGUSTE, HERE IN THE MIDDLE OF THE STREET WHERE EVERYONE CAN SEE ME GENTLY CLOSING MY WRAP AROUND ME AND CRYING..."

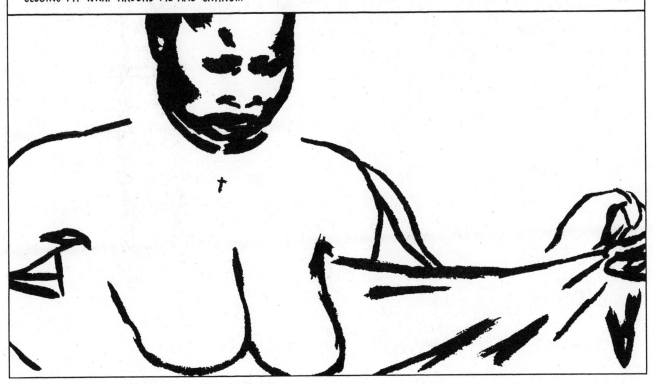

"WHEN WILL YOU DECIDE TO COME BACK, AND TURN MY HOPE INTO LOVE, WHEN, OH WHEN, MY DREAM, MY LORD?..." FERNANDO PESSOA, *MESSAGE*.

THE SUITCASE

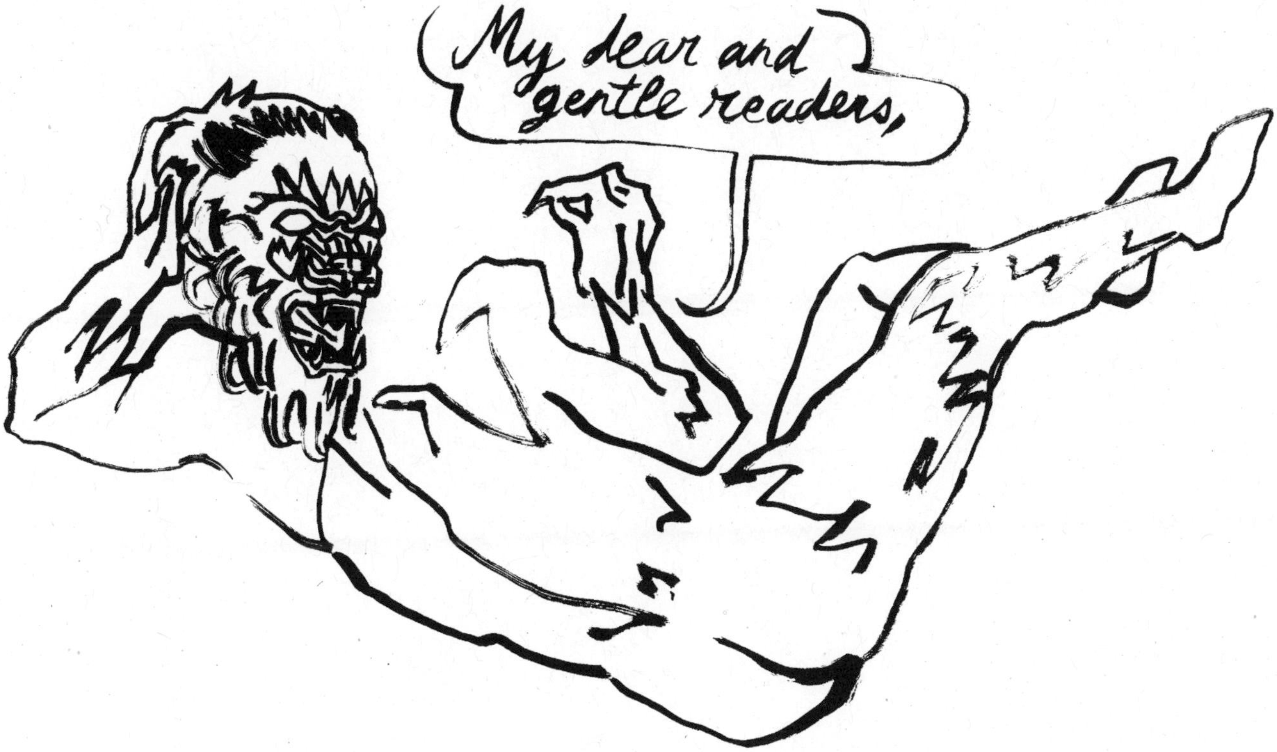
My dear and gentle readers,

Allow me to invite you to a conventional journey, as recounted by Jeanne Martine Eglo on returning from her native land to France/Hollywood.

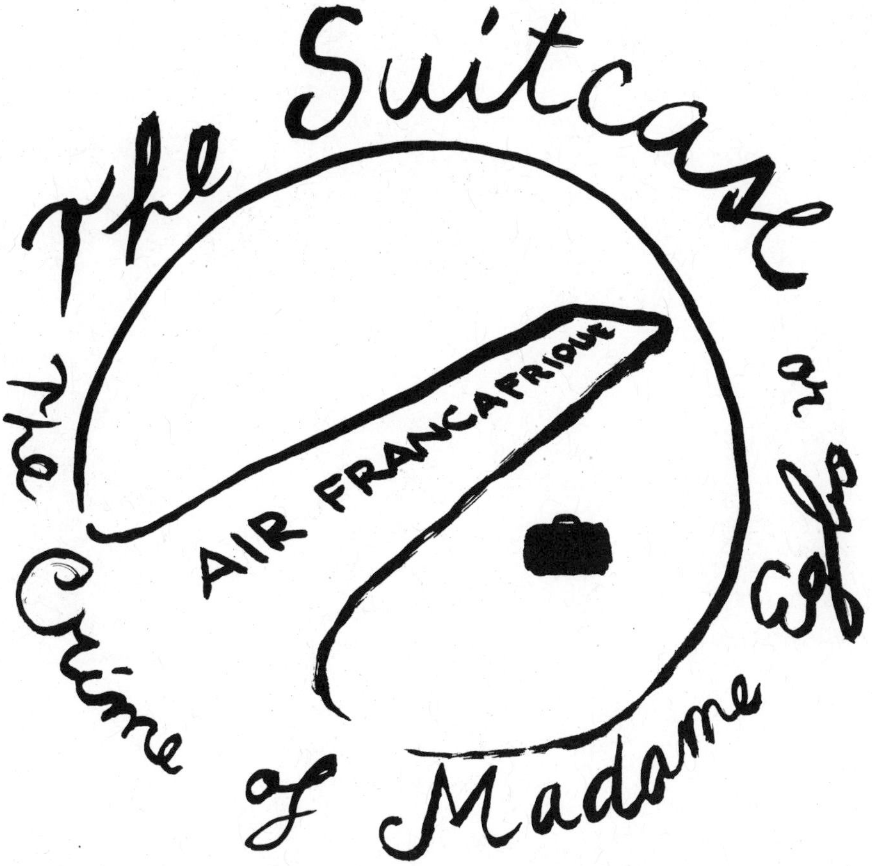
The Suitcase or The Crime of Madame Eglo
AIR FRANCAFRIQUE

Back there I didn't see Auguste but I ate. Let me tell you! I ate and ate. Ate well even. I showed the money. They called me Jeannie or Titine but I didn't reply. To all their salamalekums I didn't reply.

Oh! How furious the old men got!

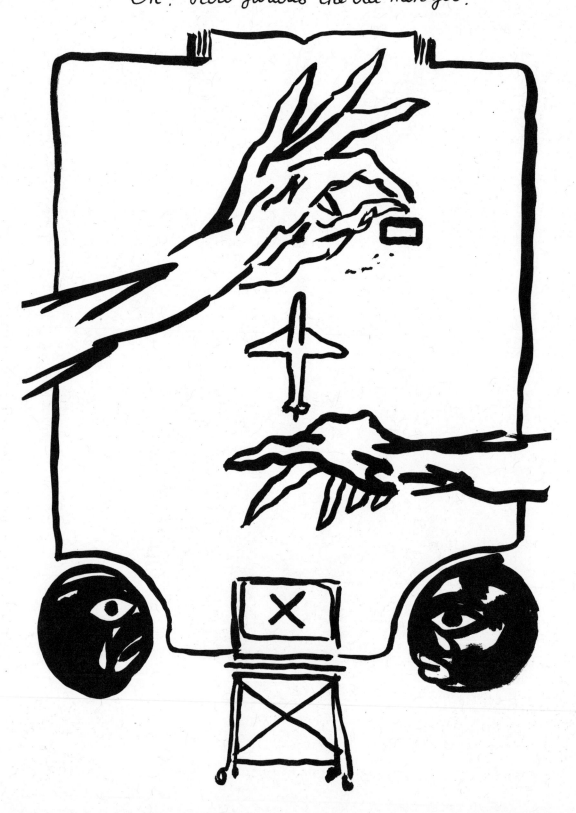

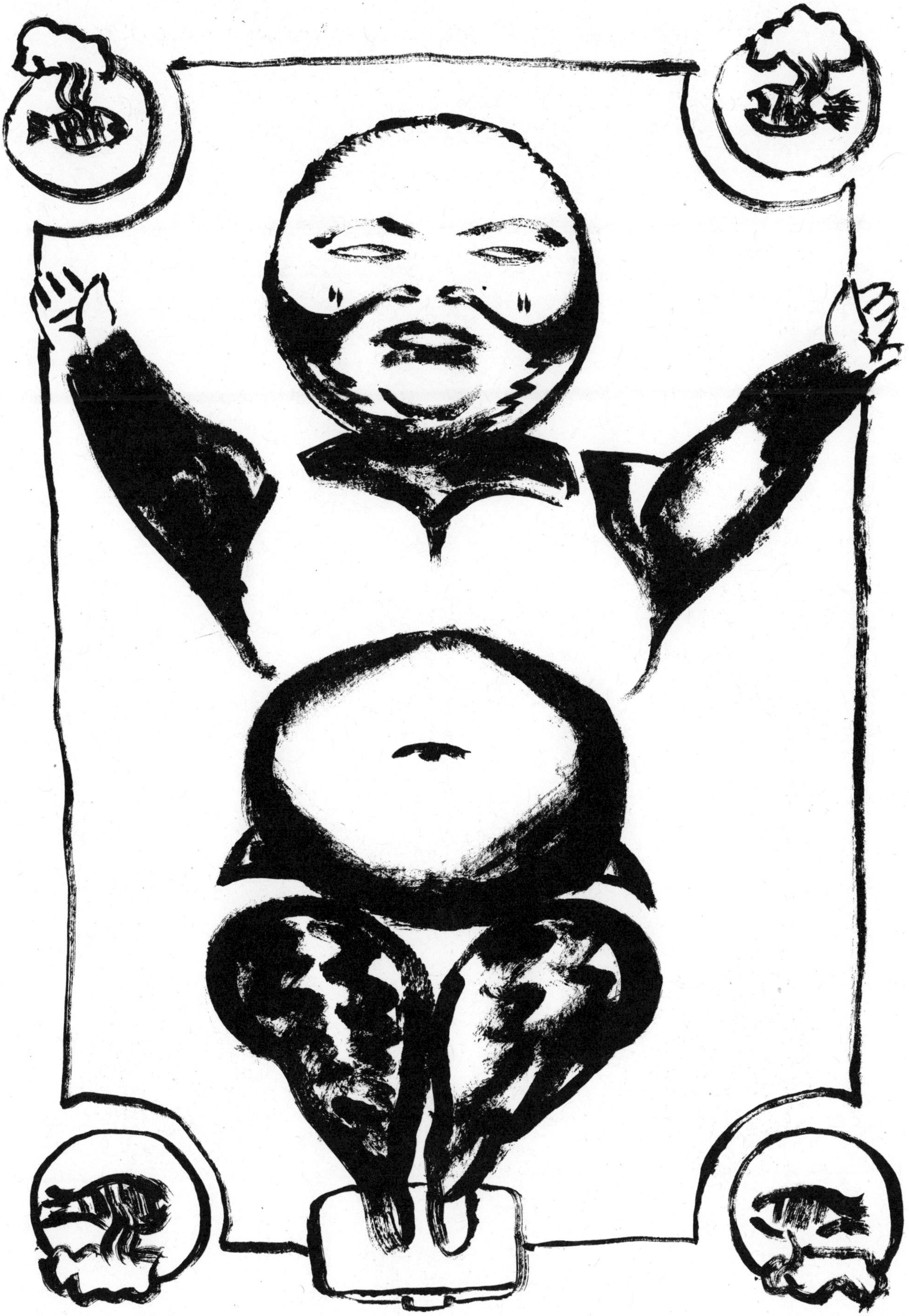

All the ones who wept over me, poor Jeannie this, poor Titine that, well, when they saw the money they wept even more! If they call me Tina, I reply. Eléonora, I reply. Cassandra, I reply.

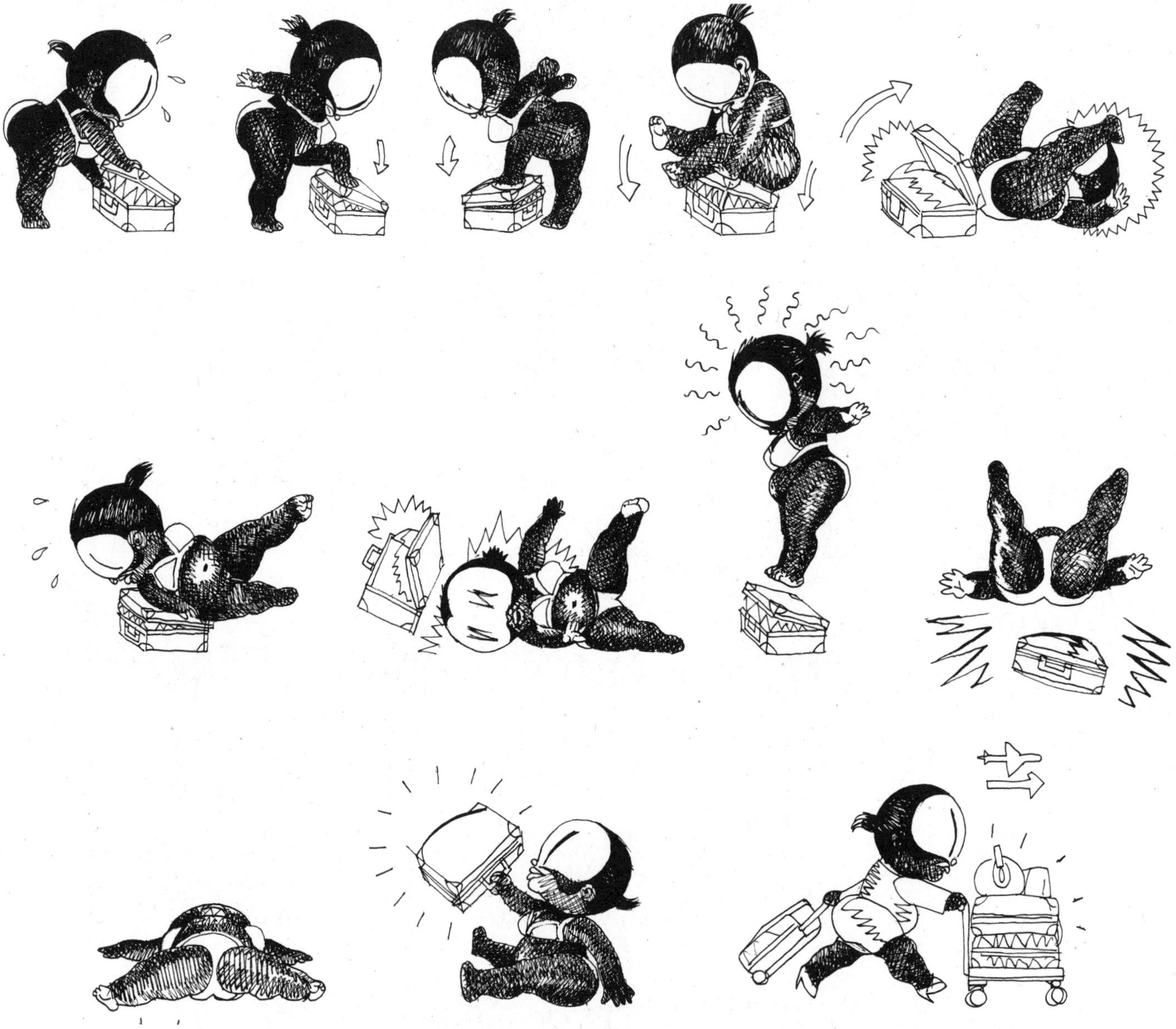

Before leaving I stuffed the suitcase with grilled fish, agouti, monkey nuts, stuck in everything everything everything! But at the airport, too many kilos. So I give the case to this gentleman. Just in front of me is a sign saying forbidden. The gentleman sees it too, but I say please, please, you don't have much baggage. He says okay but I don't want any problem. And my belly says: no problem!

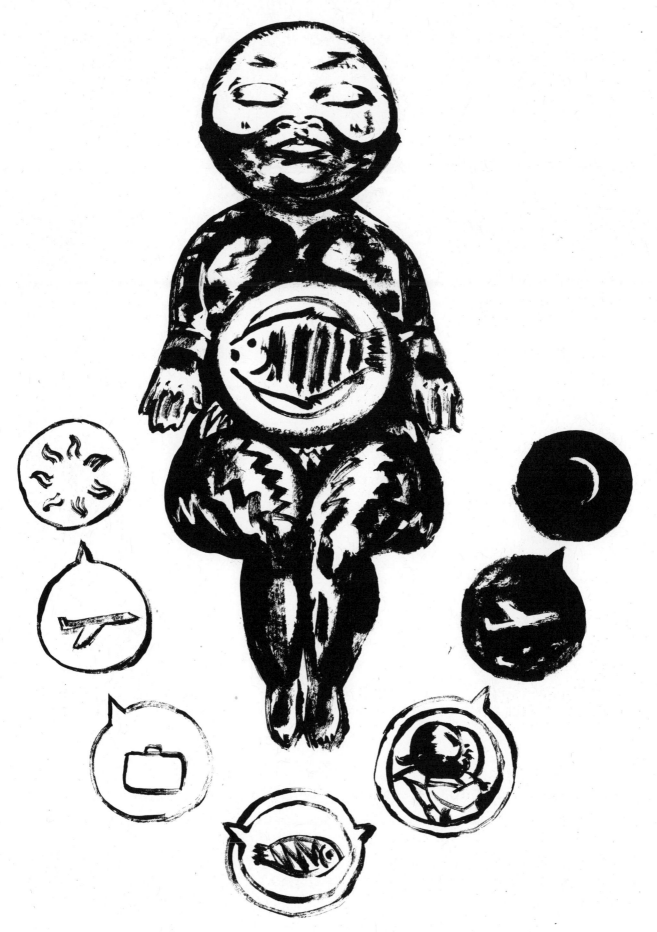

When we land, we're waiting for our bags but that suitcase doesn't come out. All the others come out but not the one with the food. The gentleman says he doesn't want any trouble and leaves. My bag doesn't have my name on it but I keep waiting. I wait but no bag arrives. No suitcase, no fish, no nothing.

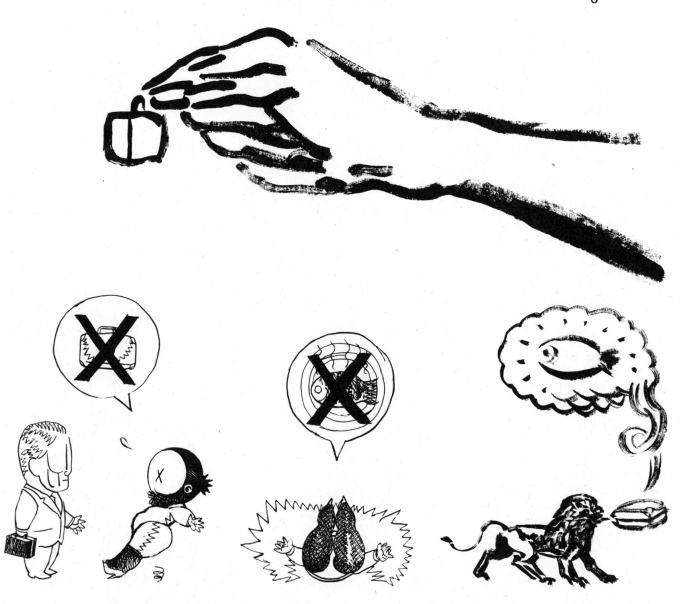

Two hours I wait, then I go home. I turn the TV on, and there I see him. By my lord Jesus Christ, there he was! I'm telling you, the gentleman I gave the suitcase to, it was him, Moses! Oh dear God in Heaven, crime doesn't pay. We must eat to live, not live to eat!

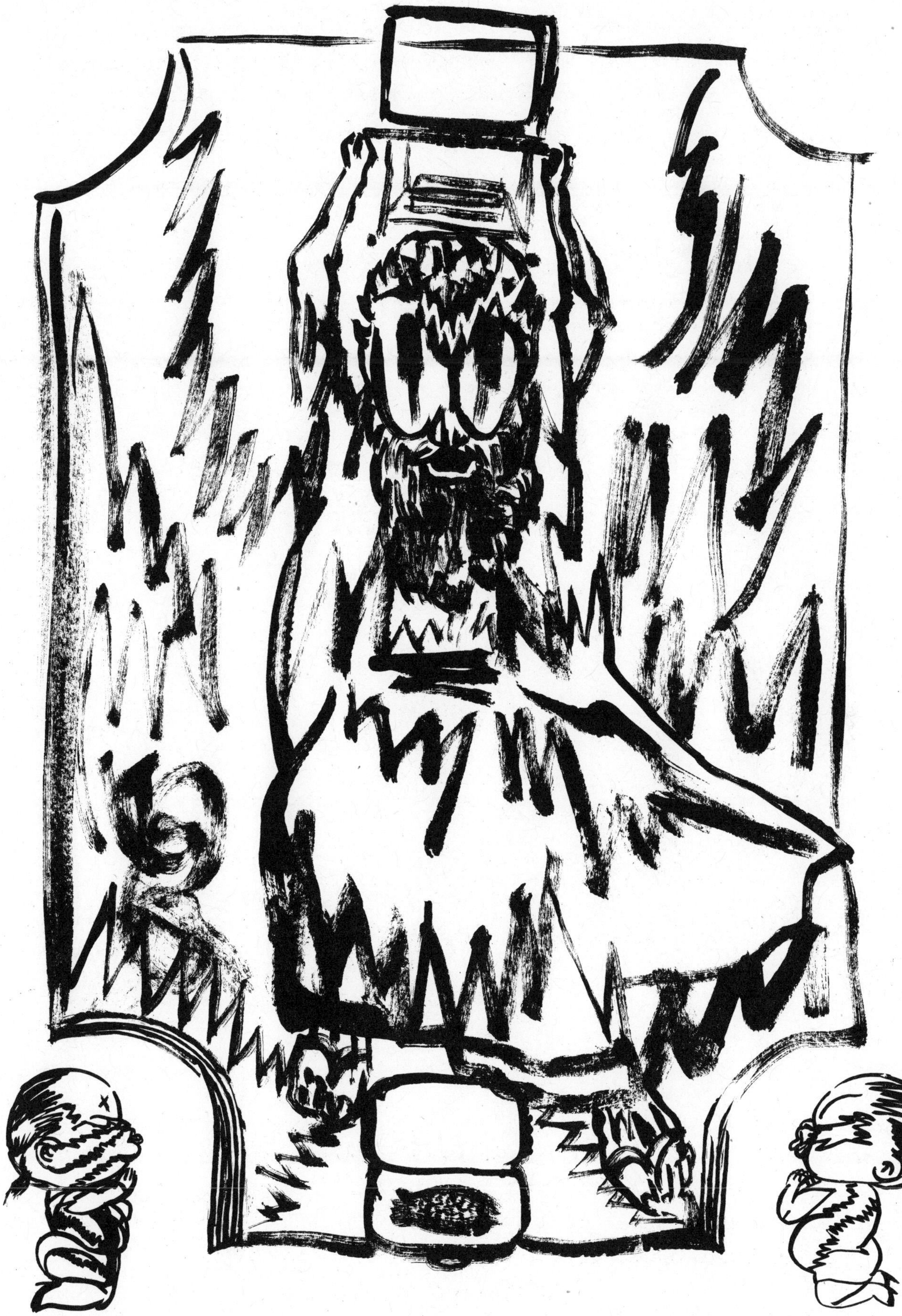

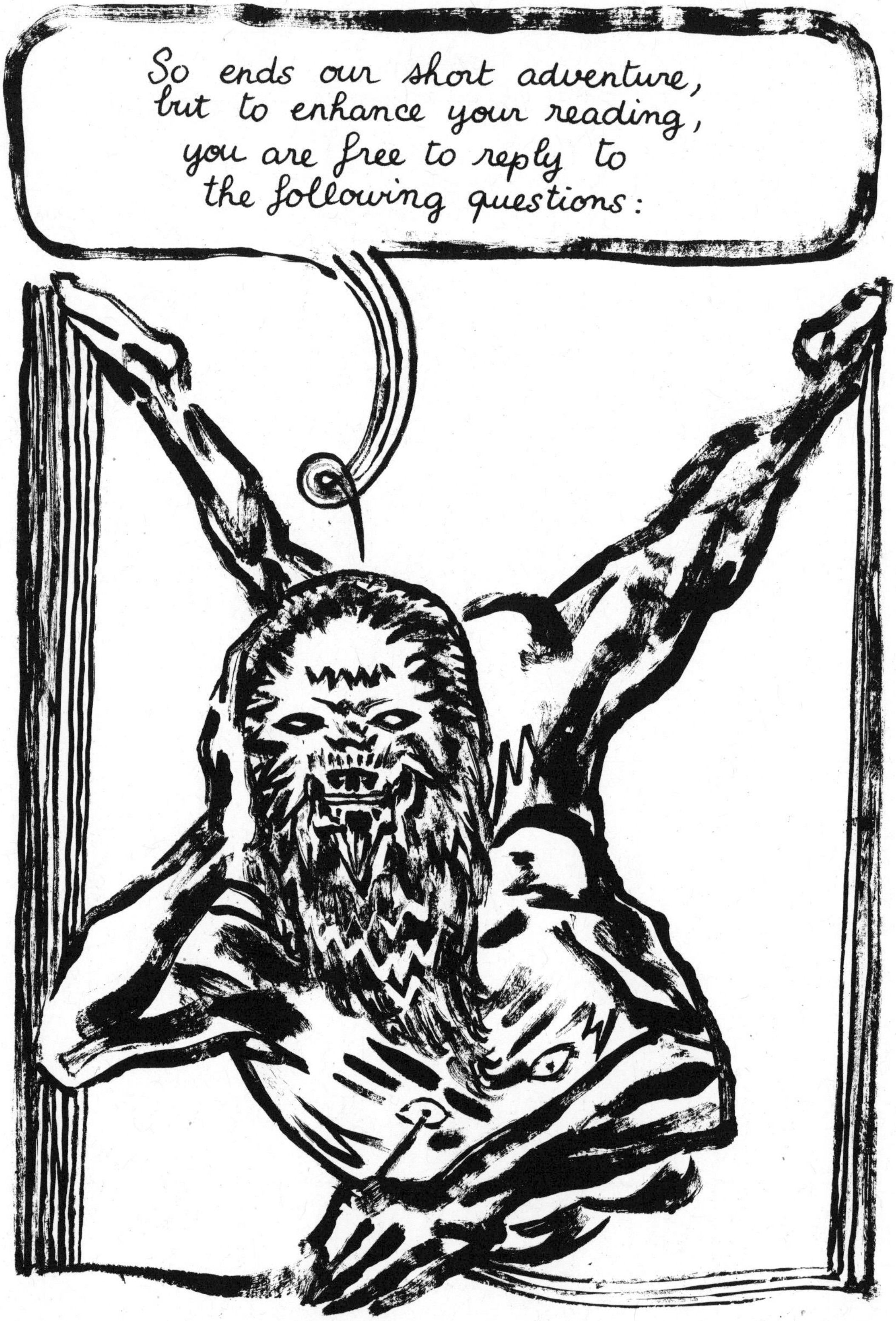
So ends our short adventure, but to enhance your reading, you are free to reply to the following questions:

What item in this story represents the Golden Calf?

☐ the grilled fish ☐ Charlton Heston

Is Jeanne Martine Egbo a grilled fish rotting in a suitcase?

☐ yes ☐ no

POSTCARD FROM MONTREUIL

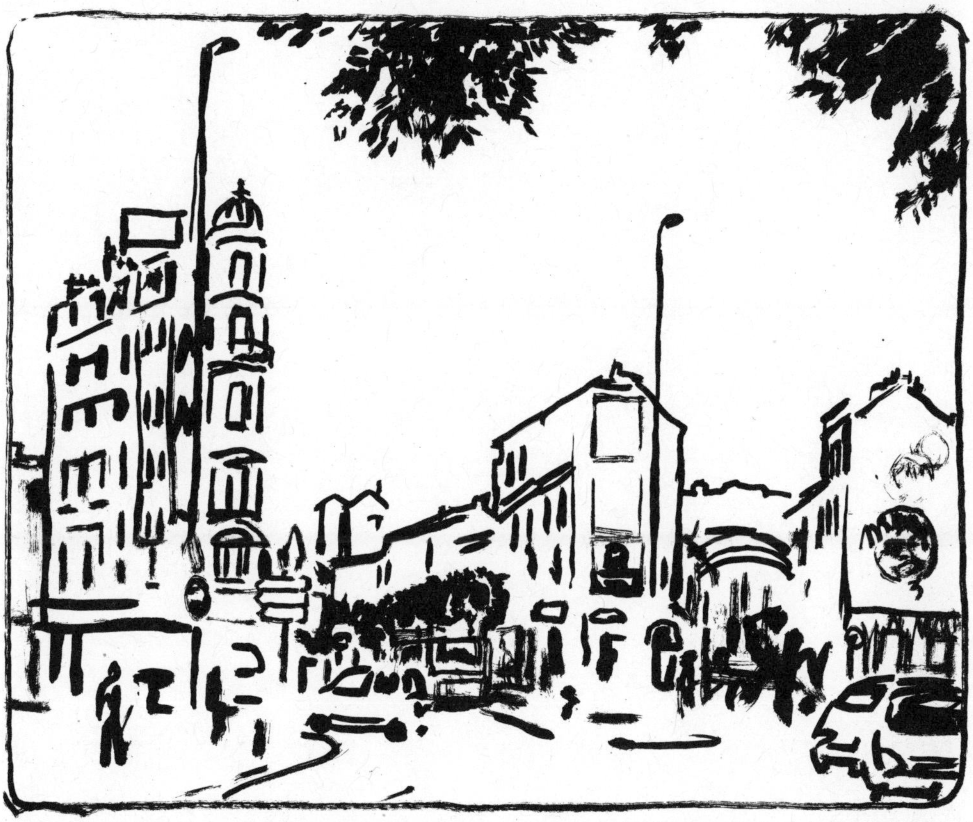

A FEW METERS FROM THE CROIX-DE-CHAVAUX METRO STATION, AT THE CORNER OF A PEDESTRIAN SHOPPING AREA AND A BUS-ONLY STREET, IS A TEMPORARY-EMPLOYMENT AGENCY.

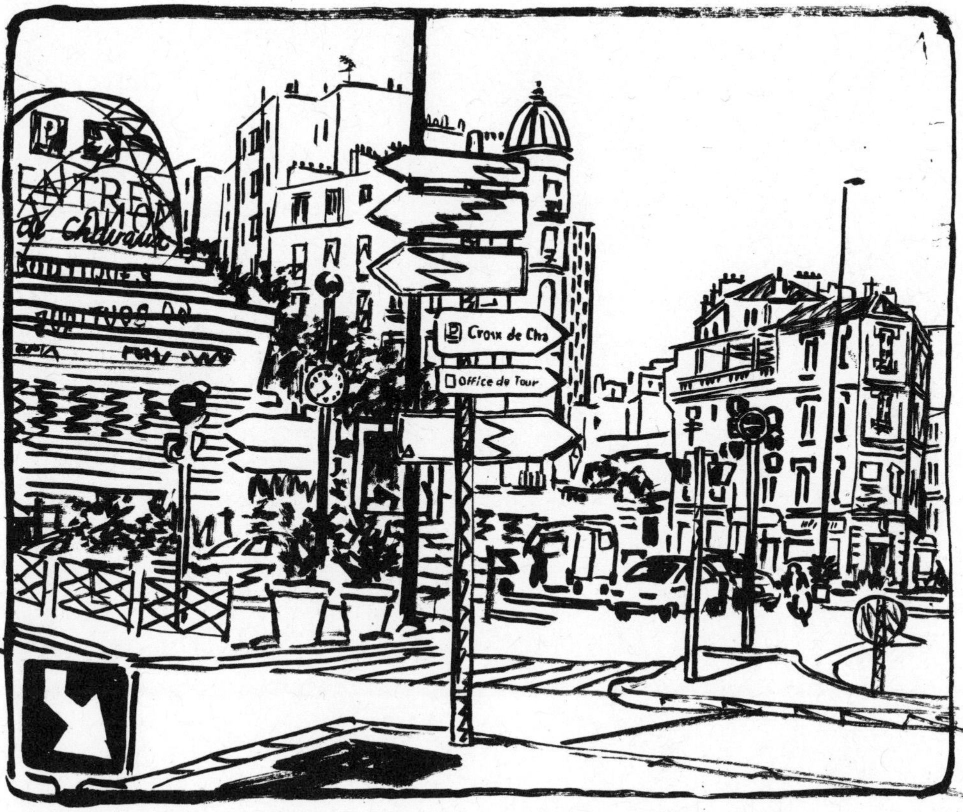
Croix de Cha
Office de Tour

SINCE THE WINTER OF 2009, IT HAS BEEN OCCUPIED BY A GROUP OF UNDOCUMENTED WORKERS, MAINLY MALIANS, DEMANDING REGULAR STATUS AND RESIDENCE PERMITS.

THEY ARE FUNDED BY A MAJOR FRENCH TRADE UNION AND THE SPARE CHANGE OF THE ODD PASSERBY.

THEY CAN BE SEEN IN THE DAYTIME TRYING TO INTEREST PEOPLE ON THE STREET IN THEIR PRECARIOUS SITUATION, AND SOMETIMES LATE AT NIGHT HAVING A COFFEE WHILE HOLDING INFORMATIONAL AND PLANNING MEETINGS.

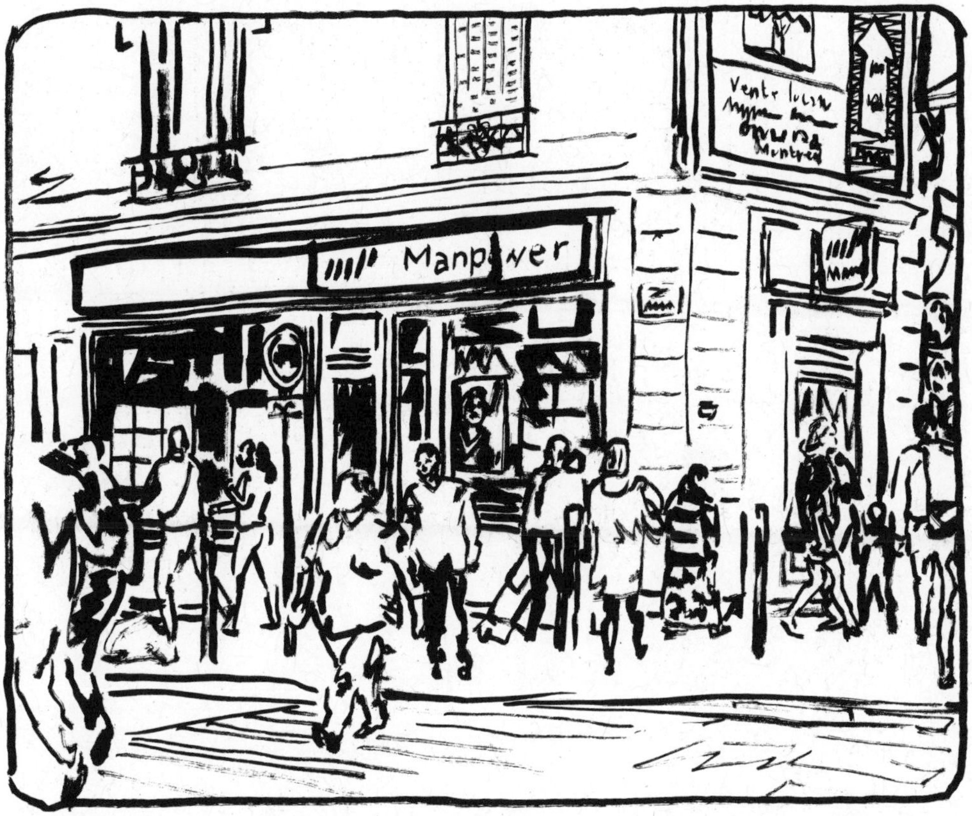
Manpower

AT THIS STRATEGIC INTERSECTION THEY ARE SOMETIMES JOINED, OUT OF SOLIDARITY OR BY CHANCE, BY OTHER GROUPS OF DEMONSTRATORS: MEMBERS OF ORGANIZATIONS OF THE UNEMPLOYED,

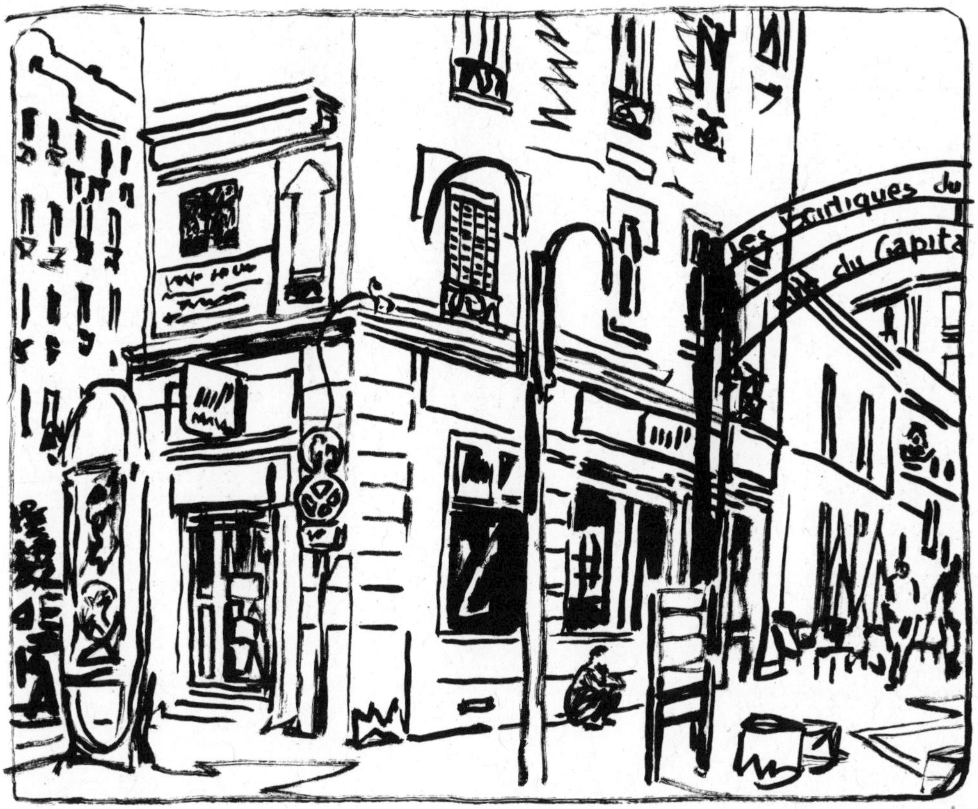

EVICTED ROMA, ROMANIANS AND BULGARIANS, ANGRY ENTERTAINMENT-INDUSTRY CONTRACT WORKERS, OTHER TEMPS, AND VARIOUS ANTI-CAPITALIST MILITANTS, REVOLUTIONARIES OR ANARCHISTS...

THEY HAVE BEEN OCCUPYING THIS AGENCY FOR ALMOST A YEAR AND IT FEELS LIKE A PERMANENT THING... THIS MORNING, THOUGH, ON GETTING OFF THE BUS I NOTICED A SLIGHT CHANGE: NOT A SINGLE MALIAN HOLDING A CUP OR A SIGN.

THE AGENCY HAS BEEN EMPTIED AND THE BUSINESS TRANSFERRED ELSEWHERE WITHOUT NOISE OR PROTEST, SURREPTITIOUSLY, THIS ACCORDING TO A SCRAWLED NOTE TAPED TO THE DOOR.

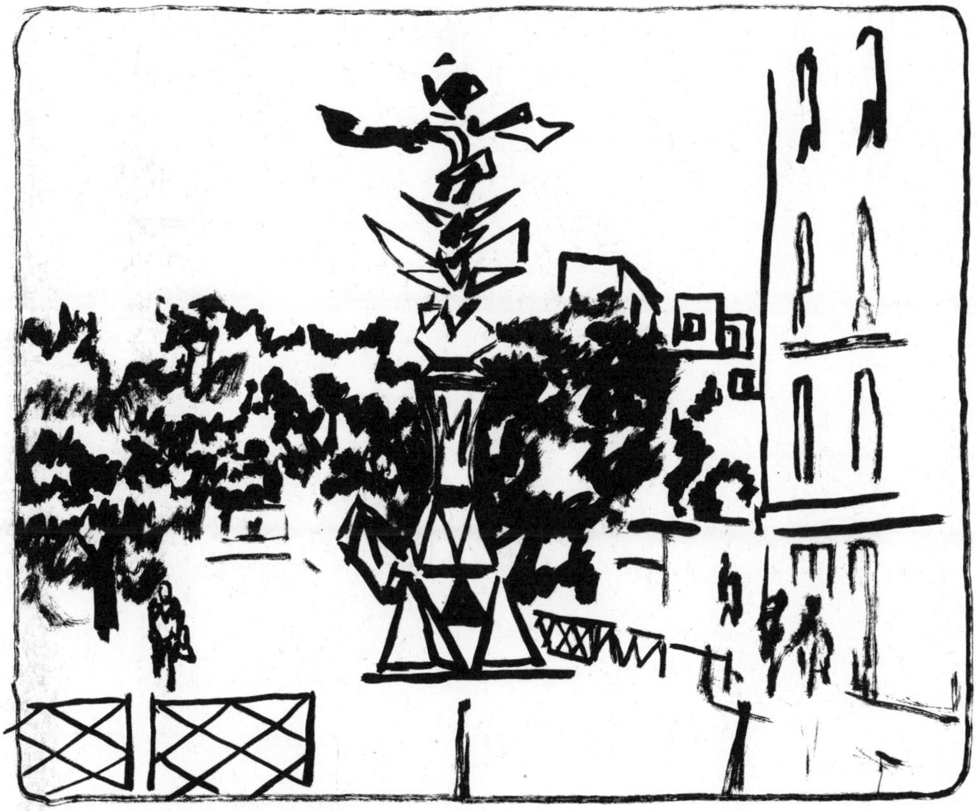

ALL THAT REMAIN ARE THE USUAL PASSERSBY, THE REGULARS IN THE CAFÉ ACROSS THE STREET, AND, REIGNING OVER THE SQUARE, THE IMPRESSIVE AND UNMOVABLE MONUMENT TO THE FRENCH RESISTANCE TO NAZI BARBARITY.

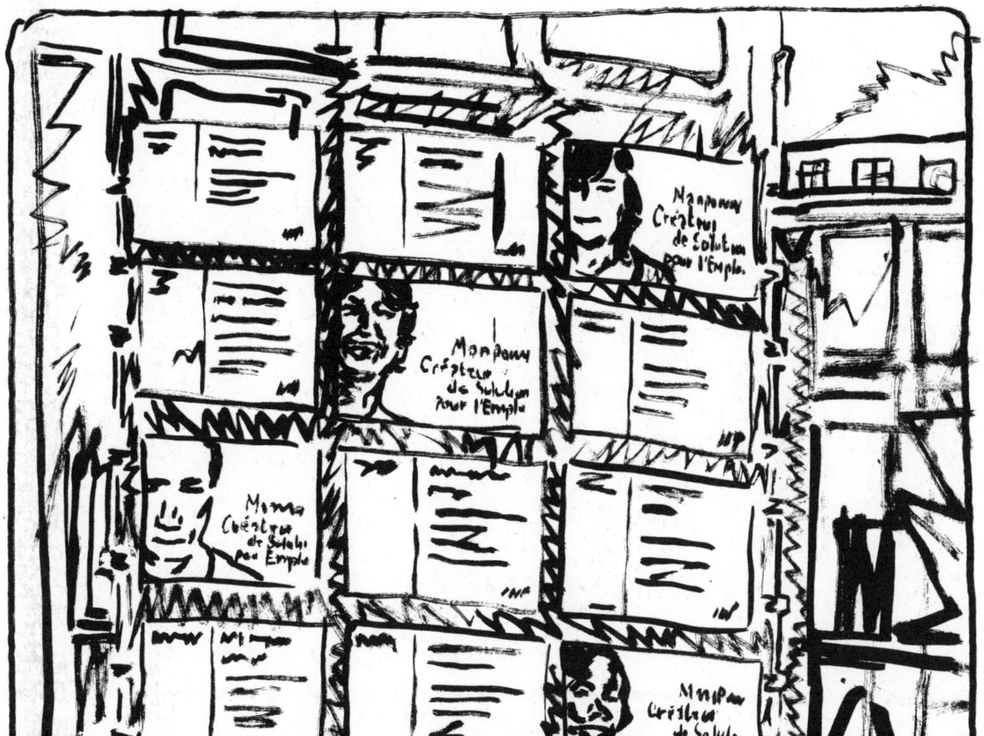

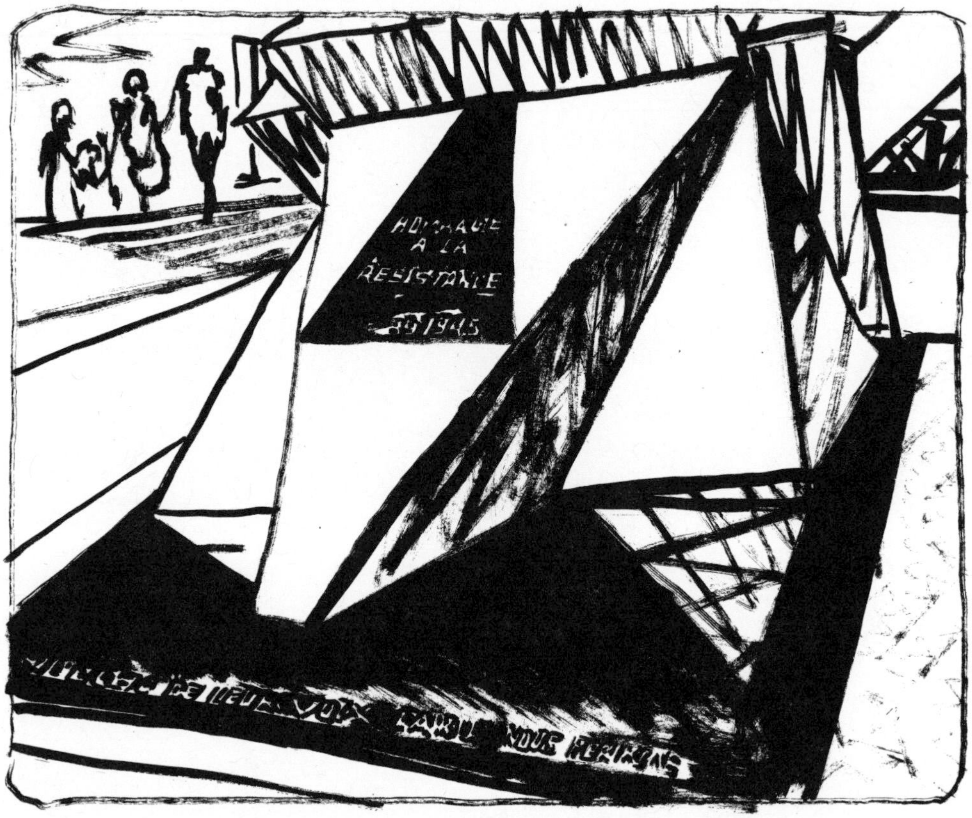

AT THE BASE OF THIS CURIOUS SCULPTURE, ENGRAVED ON THE MARBLE, ARE WORDS ATTRIBUTED TO PAUL ÉLUARD WHICH SPEAK TO ME: "IF THE ECHO OF THEIR VOICES WEAKENS, WE SHALL PERISH."

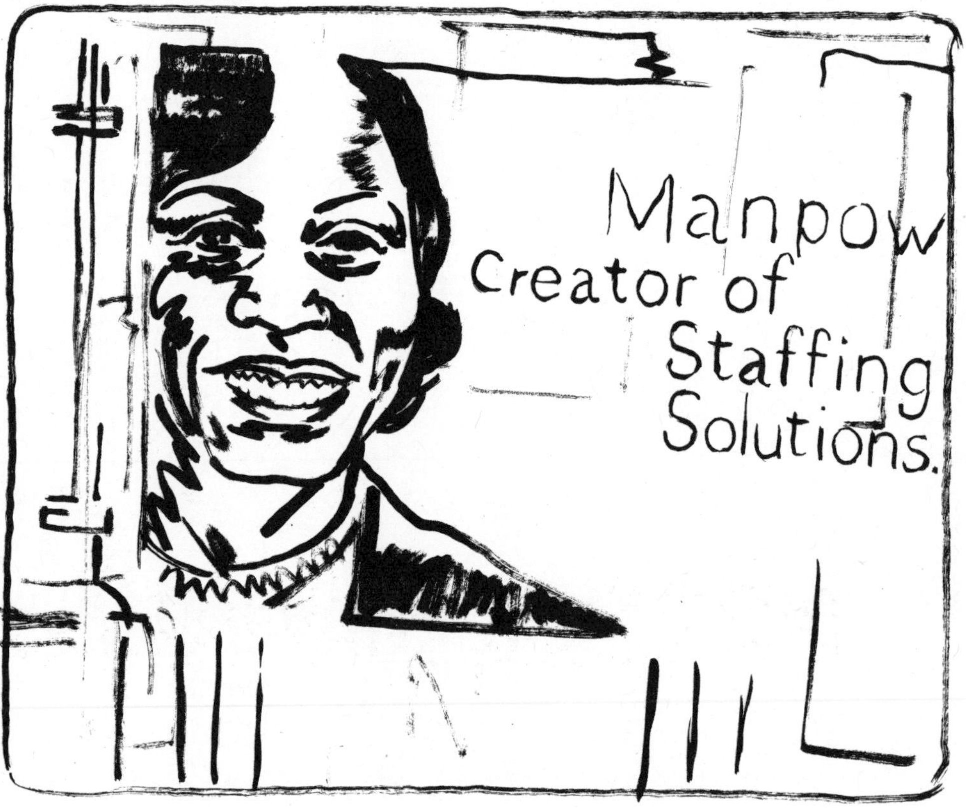
Manpow
Creator of
Staffing
Solutions.

POSTSCRIIPTUM

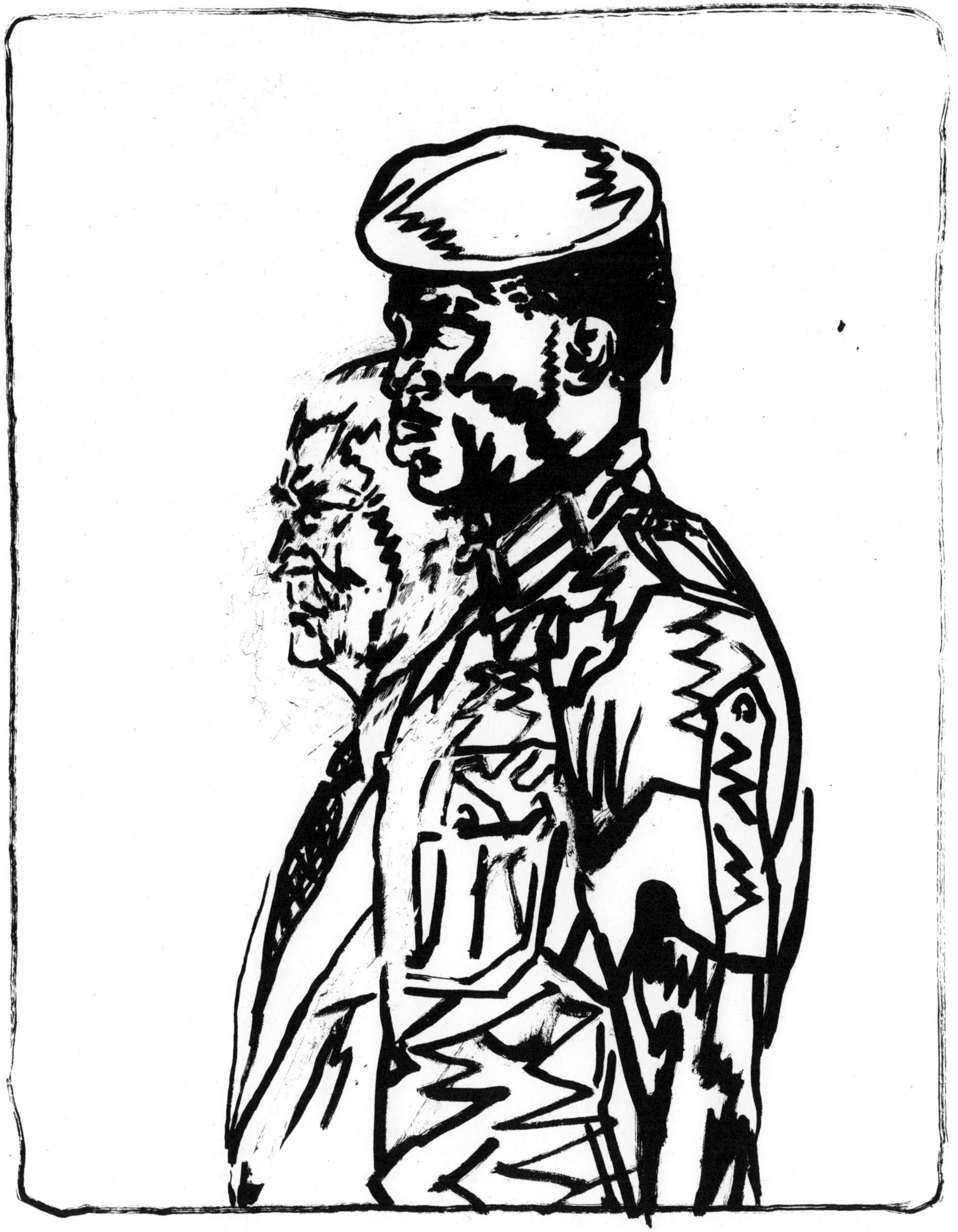

IN THE WINDOW OF THE UNDOCUMENTED STRIKERS OF MONTREUIL IS A PHOTOGRAPH. A PHOTOGRAPH OF THOMAS SANKARA. TO FIND OUT WHO THOMAS SANKARA IS, DON'T BOTHER LOOKING HIM UP IN LAROUSSE.

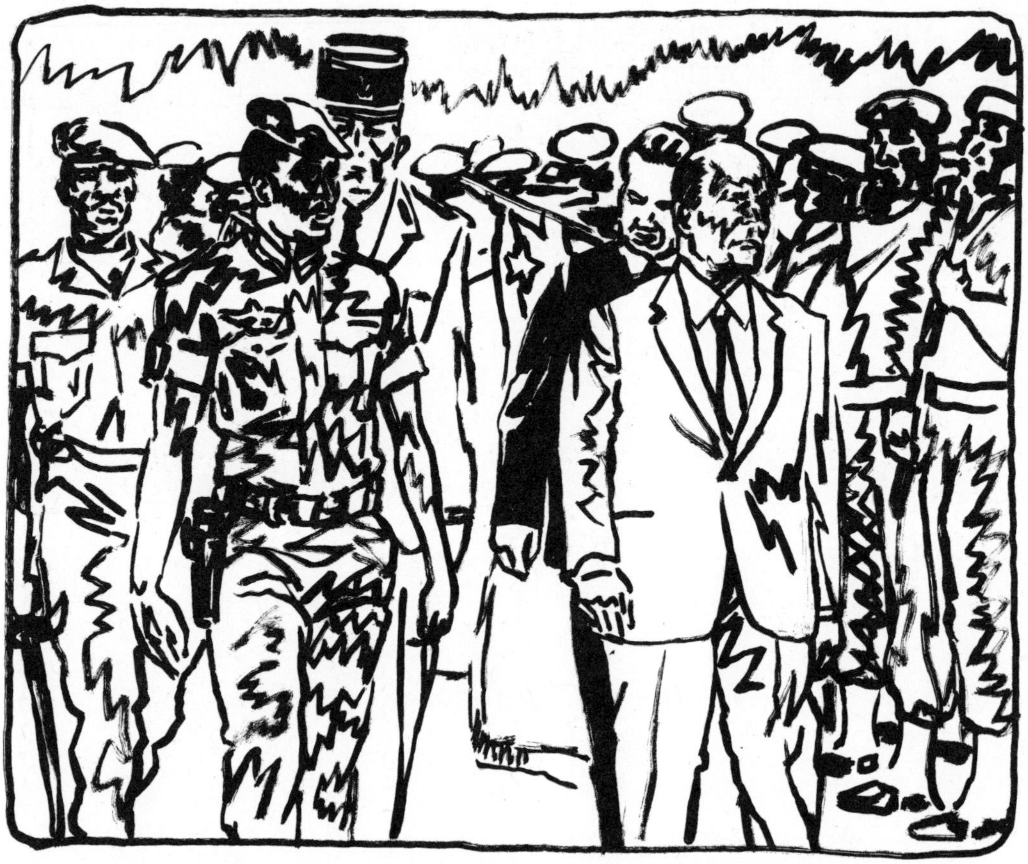

THERE IS NO ENTRY FOR HIM IN THAT STAR DICTIONARY OF THE LAGARDÈRE GROUP. HE MUST FALL UNDER THE HEADING "WITHOUT A SIGNIFICANT ENOUGH ROLE IN HISTORY."

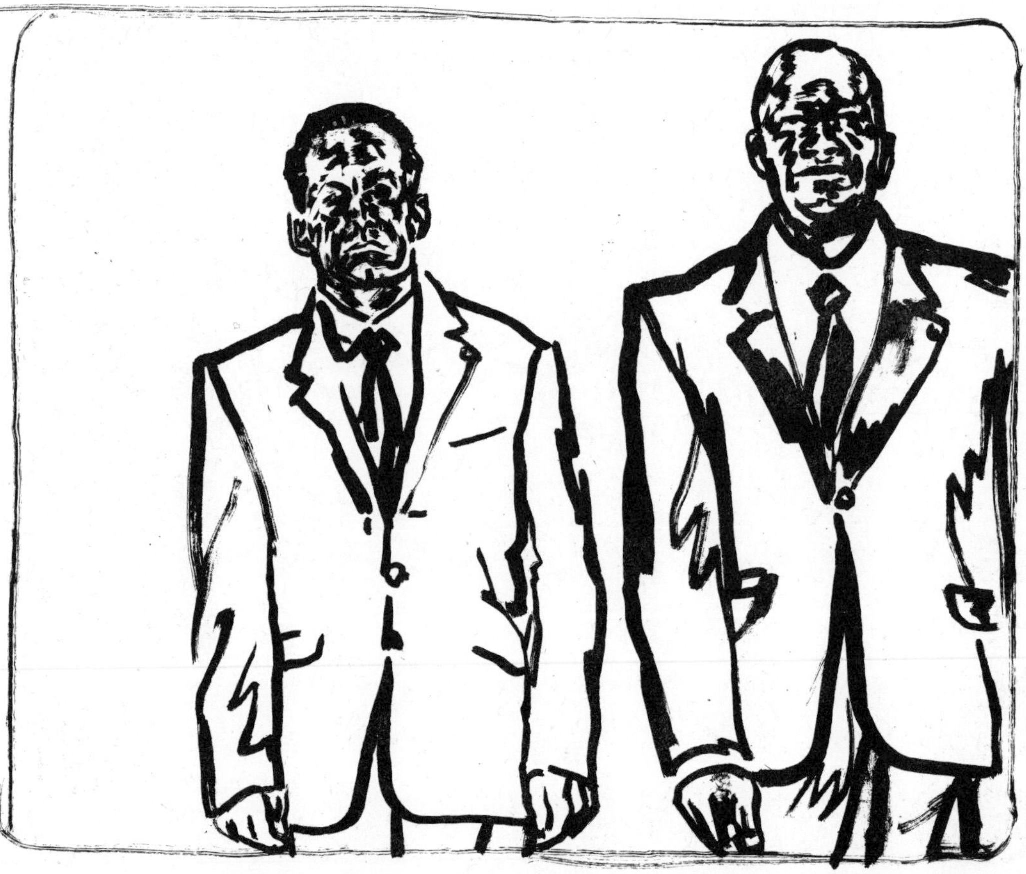

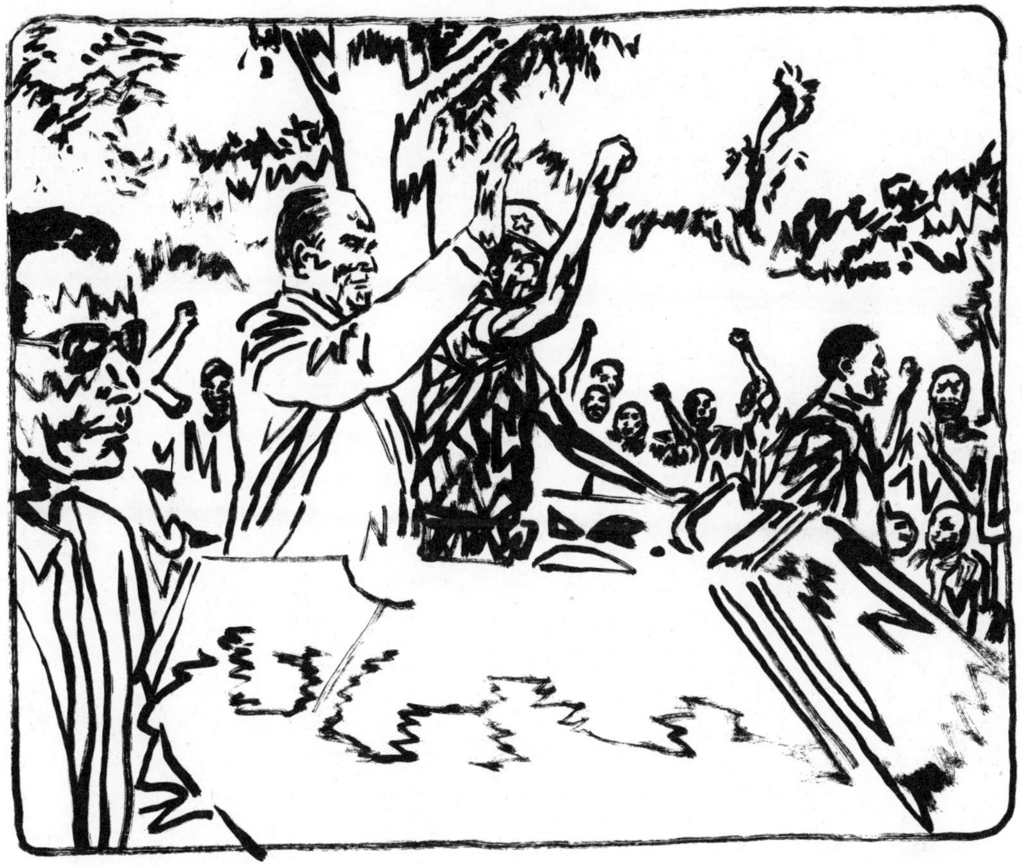

AS FOR MONSIEUR BLAISE COMPAORÉ, HE HAS WON A SURE PLACE UNDER "GOOD FRIENDS OF FRANCE." FURTHERMORE, HE HAS THE GOOD TASTE NOT TO GO ABOUT IN MILITARY UNIFORM.

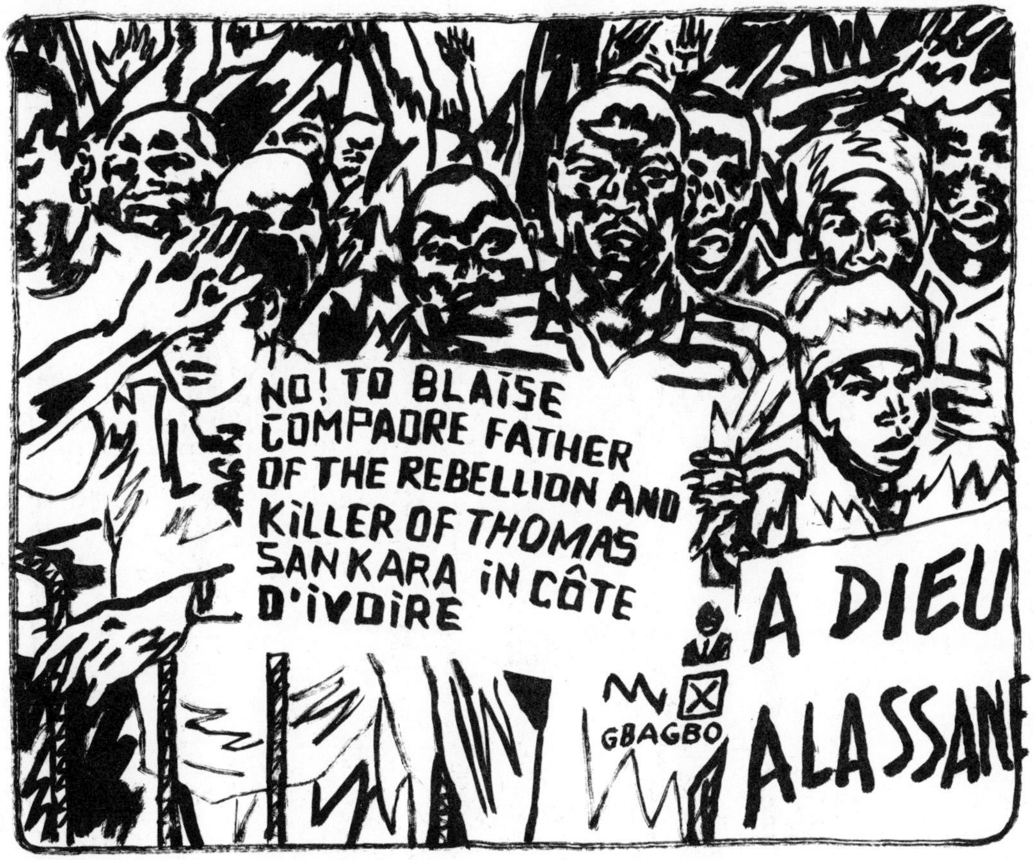
NO! TO BLAISE COMPAORE FATHER OF THE REBELLION AND KILLER OF THOMAS SANKARA IN CÔTE D'IVOIRE
A DIEU ALASSANE
GBAGBO

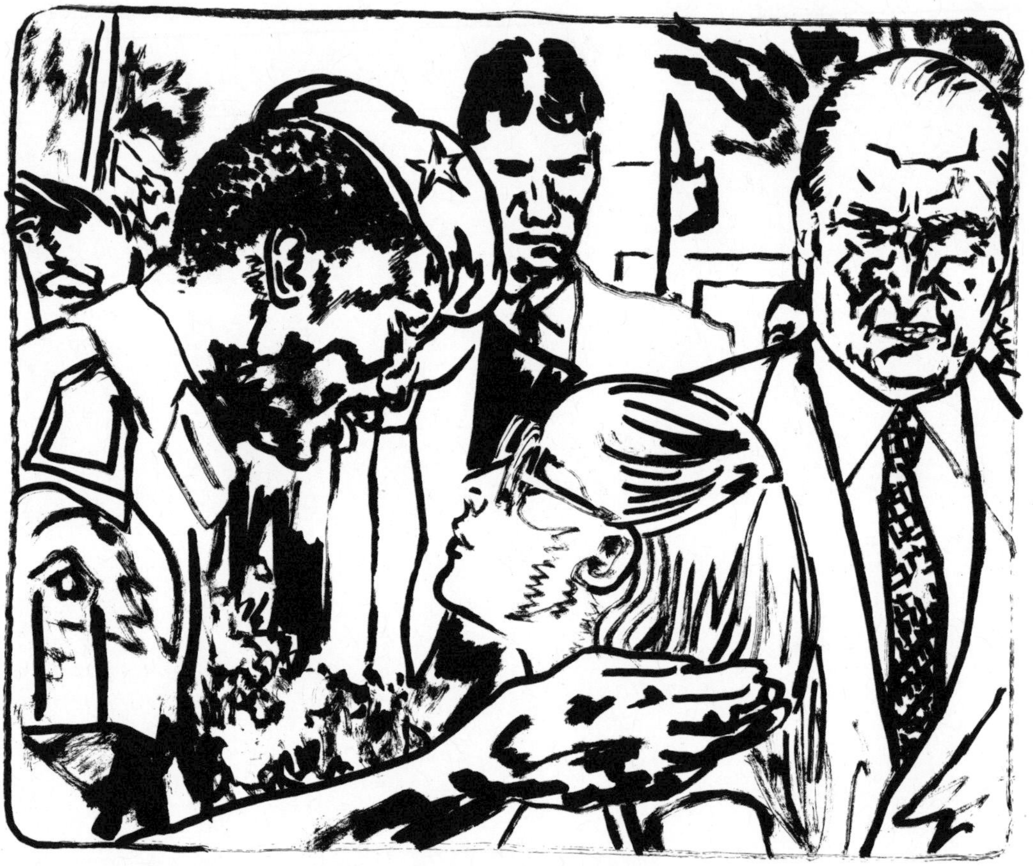

AND YET, DESPITE THE GOVERNORS, EMPERORS, AND WHITE-COLLAR KILLERS, IN THE WINDOW OF THE STRIKING TEMPS OF MONTREUIL, AS IN THE HEART OF AFRICA, THE MEMORY OF THOMAS SANKARA LIVES ON. THAT'S THE STORY, MISTER PRESIDENT. THAT'S HISTORY.

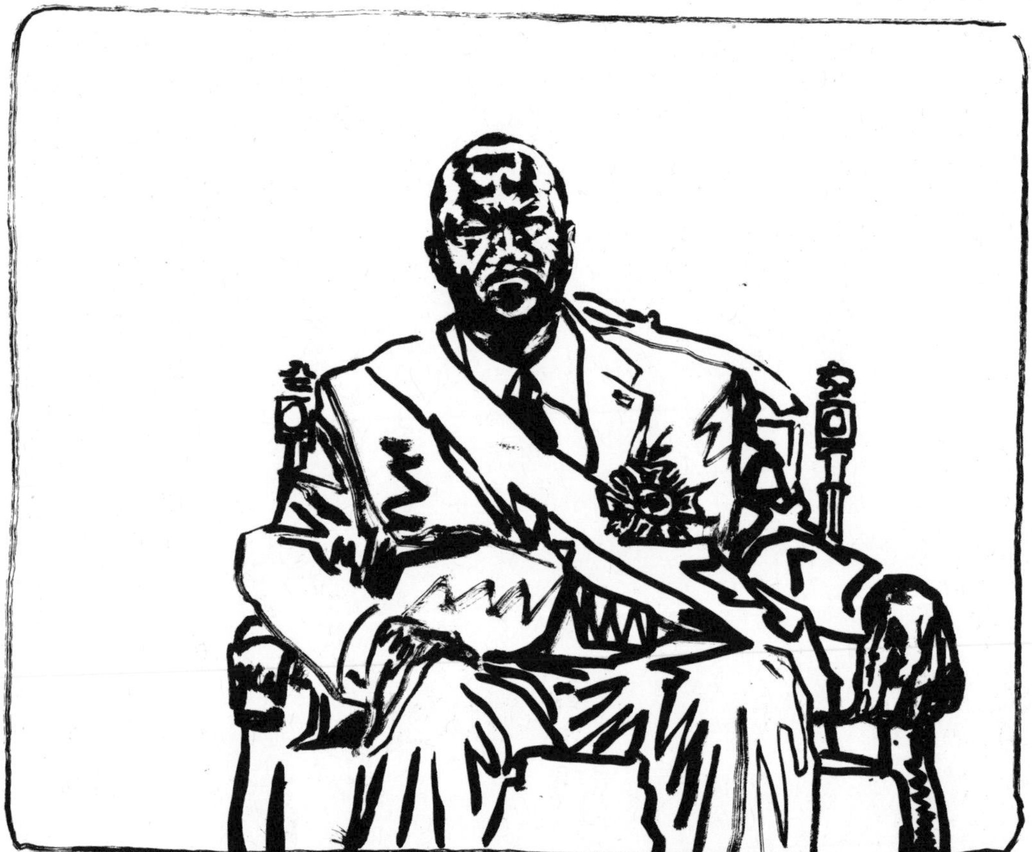

SAND NIIGGERS

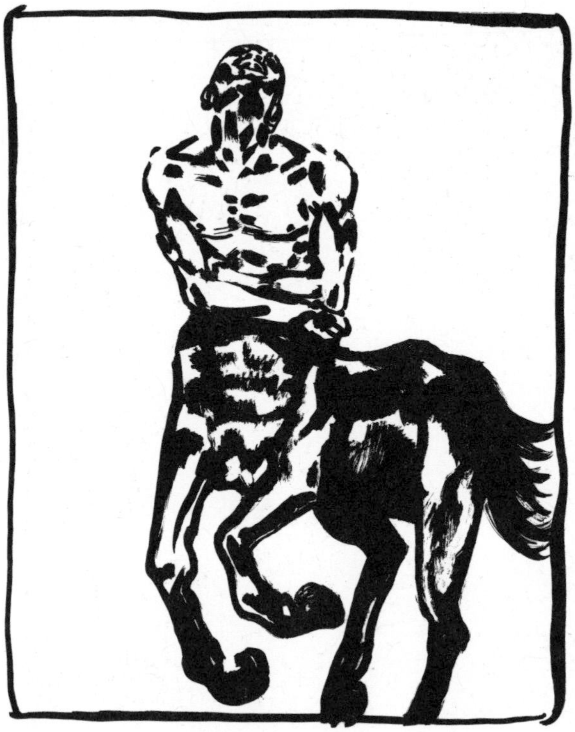

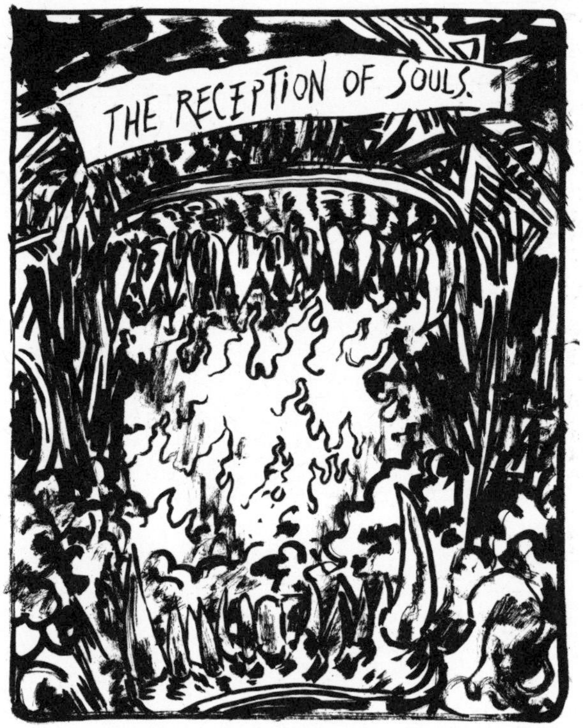
THE RECEPTION OF SOULS.

ARE YELLOW NEGROES CENTAURS CROSSING THE DESERT? PROBABLY NOT. NOR ARE THEY SHE-CAMEL MEN ACCUSTOMED TO THIRST. MY LOVE. YOU ARE THE MISERY OF THE WORLD. YOU ARE THE BURIED TREASURE. MY JOSEPH DOWN IN THE PIT.

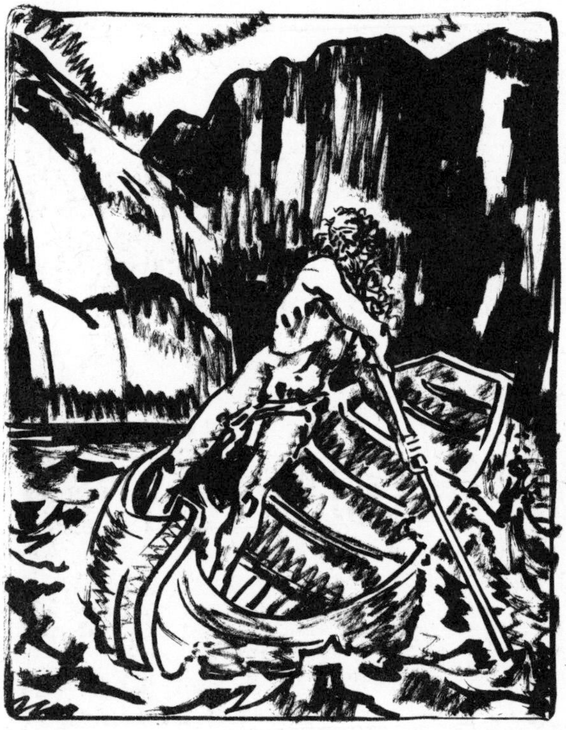

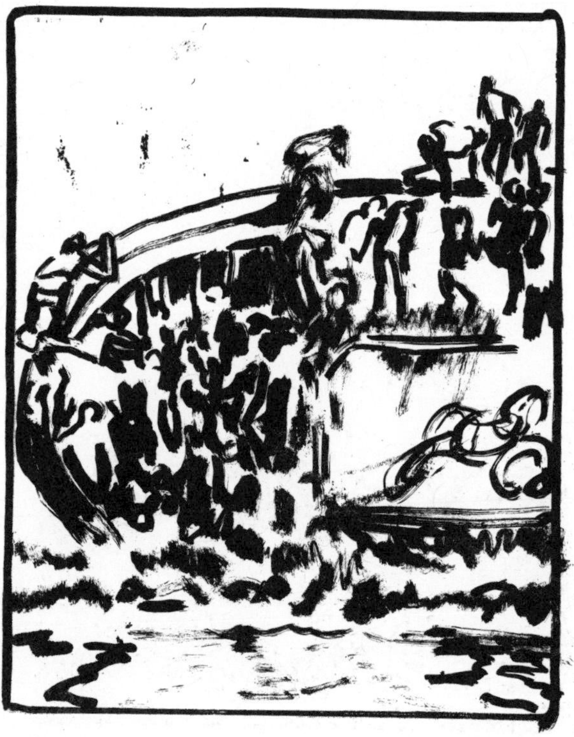

SAND NIGGER ON THE BEACH, THE MOMENT YOUR WORLD BECOMES INHABITABLE ONCE MORE, SELL YOUR SOUL TO THE WIND. DRINK THE SEA. I HAVE READ: TELLING TALES IS THE BUSINESS OF SURVIVORS. GHOST STORIES. I HAVE RECEIVED THE TRANSLATION OF *YELLOW NEGROES AND OTHER IMAGINARY CREATURES*. SIGNED BY DONALD NICHOLSON-SMITH. LET ME REPLY TO HIS QUESTIONS. AND THEN TOO LET ME REMEMBER YOU, SAND NIGGER.

WITH ALL THE TALK OF "MIGRANTS," OR IN OTHER WORDS EVER SINCE PEOPLE STARTED FLEEING AND DYING IN SUCH NUMBERS AND WASHING UP IN SUCH NUMBERS ON BEACHES, I KEEP THINKING OF THE FIRST PAGES OF ARISTOPHANE'S *DEMONIC TALE*. HAVE THOSE WHO REACH THE SHORES OF EUROPE REALLY ESCAPED FROM HELL?

PARIS SCENE. THE MASSACRES OF ALGERIANS THROWN INTO THE SEINE IN OCTOBER 1961. PARIS SCENE. IN JANUARY 2017, AN ARTIST NAMED PIERRE DELAVIE HUNG A TARP BY THE QUAYSIDE OF THE SEINE BEARING THE IMAGE OF A CAPSIZING BOAT OF "MIGRANTS." WHENCE "THE UNIVERSES OF BLOOD AND STONE MIXED" (PAGE 40): STONES WHERE NO DISTINCTION CAN BE MADE BETWEEN THE STONE OF 1961 AND THE STONE OF 2017, THE STONE PRINTED ON THE PAGE AND THE STONE HIDDEN BEHIND THE TARP.

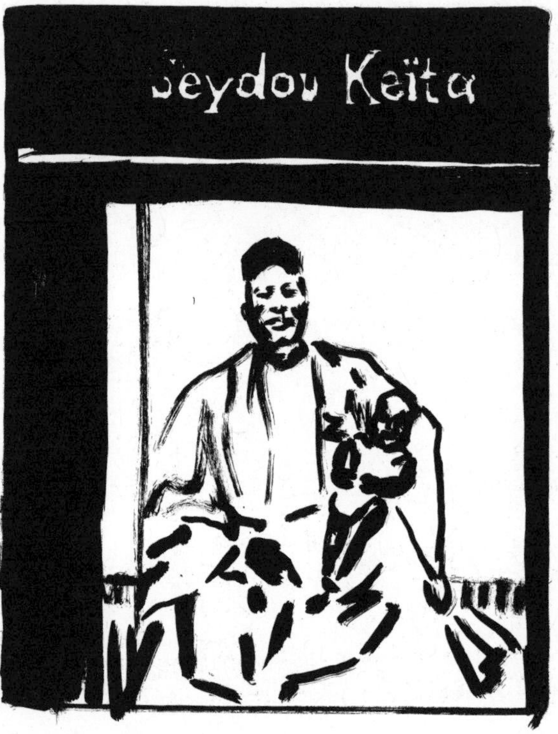
Seydou Keïta

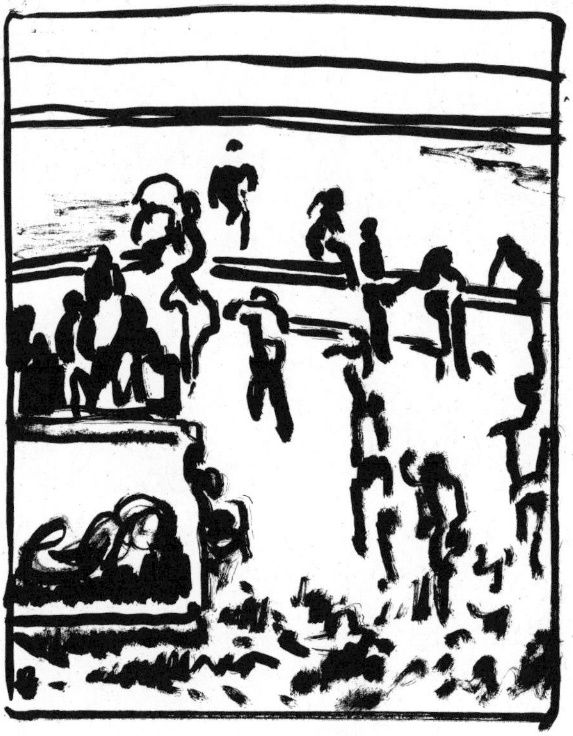

I FOUND THE TERM *DYAA* (PAGE 62) IN A BOOK ABOUT THE MALIAN PHOTOGRAPHER SEYDOU KEÏTA. DYAA IS THE DOUBLE IN OUR DREAMS, OUR REFLECTION IN A MIRROR OR OUR IMAGE IN A PHOTOGRAPH. I HAVE TWO PICTURES OF OUR FAMILY TAKEN AT A PHOTOGRAPHER'S STUDIO DURING OUR THREE-YEAR STAY IN BENIN. I HAVE NEVER DRAWN THESE IMAGES UNTIL NOW. PHANTOMS OUTSIDE THE FRAME. TARZAN.

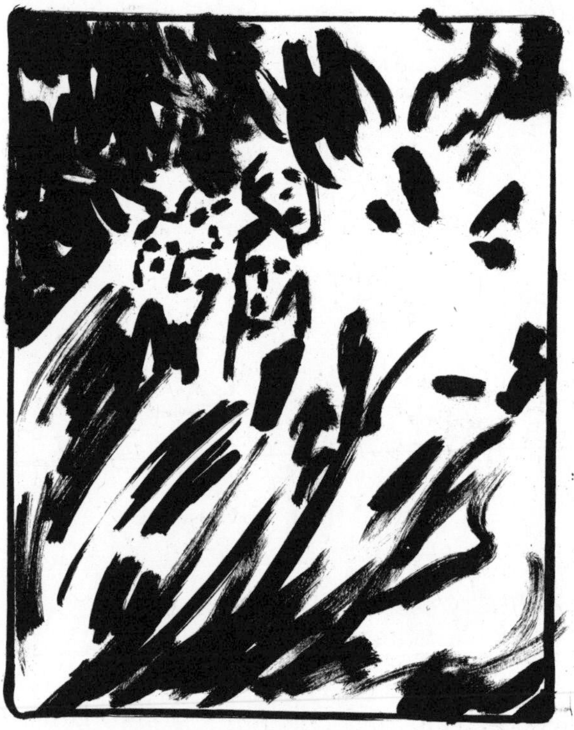

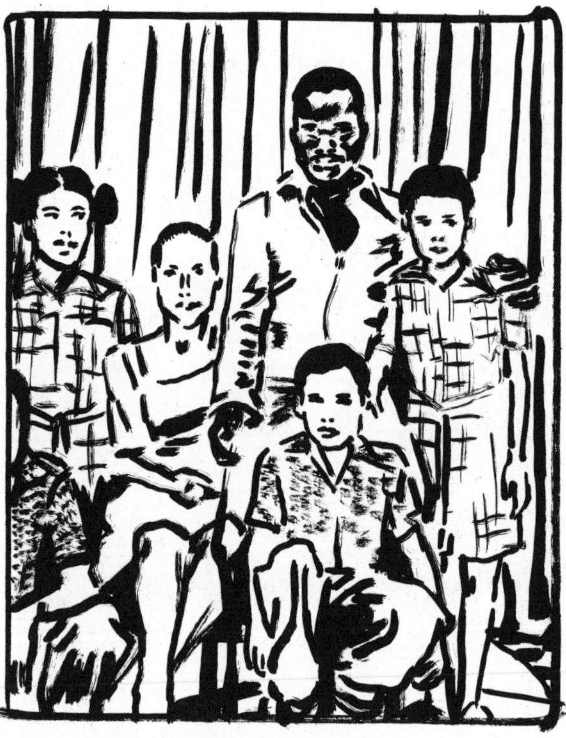

"A DIEU ALASSANE." GOODBYE ODIOUS ALASSANE, GOODBYE TO ALL THE ODIOUS. THE DEMONSTRATOR IN THE PHOTOGRAPH ON WHICH THIS DRAWING IS BASED MEANT SIMPLY "ADIEU ALASSANE" (PAGE 103). I WROTE THIS POSTSCRIPTUM AS A RETORT TO THE STATEMENTS AND ACTIONS OF PEOPLE WHO SHOULD BE ASHAMED OF THE WAY THEY EARN "A PLACE IN HISTORY."

TELLING TALES IS THE BUSINESS OF SURVIVORS. TALES OF PHANTOMS. MASKS. WORDS. FLESH. REMOVED FROM MYSELF, I REMAIN ALONE BEHIND THE BOOK. NO. I LIVE WITH THE DEAD. WITH THE MOORS, THE BLACKS, THE MAD. MY FRIENDS THE NEGROES, AT THE BOTTOM OF THE OCEAN, DEEP IN THE SANDS AND STREAMS OF ELDORADO. I DWELL WITH THE LIVING. EVERLASTING JOY.

REMOVED FROM MYSELF, I REMAIN ALONE ON MY LIPS. THE LIGHTNESS I ONCE HAD I HAVE NO MORE. CAN THE WORLD HOLD ALL OF THE WOES OF THE WORLD? CAN MY LOVE?

ALSO AVAILABLE
FROM NEW YORK REVIEW COMICS

ALMOST COMPLETELY BAXTER
Glen Baxter

AGONY
Mark Beyer

PEPLUM
Blutch

THE GREEN HAND
Nicole Claveloux

WHAT AM I DOING HERE?
Abner Dean

PRETENDING IS LYING
Dominique Goblet

VOICES IN THE DARK
Ulli Lust

FATHER AND SON
E.O. Plauen

SOFT CITY
Pushwagner

THE NEW WORLD
Chris Reynolds

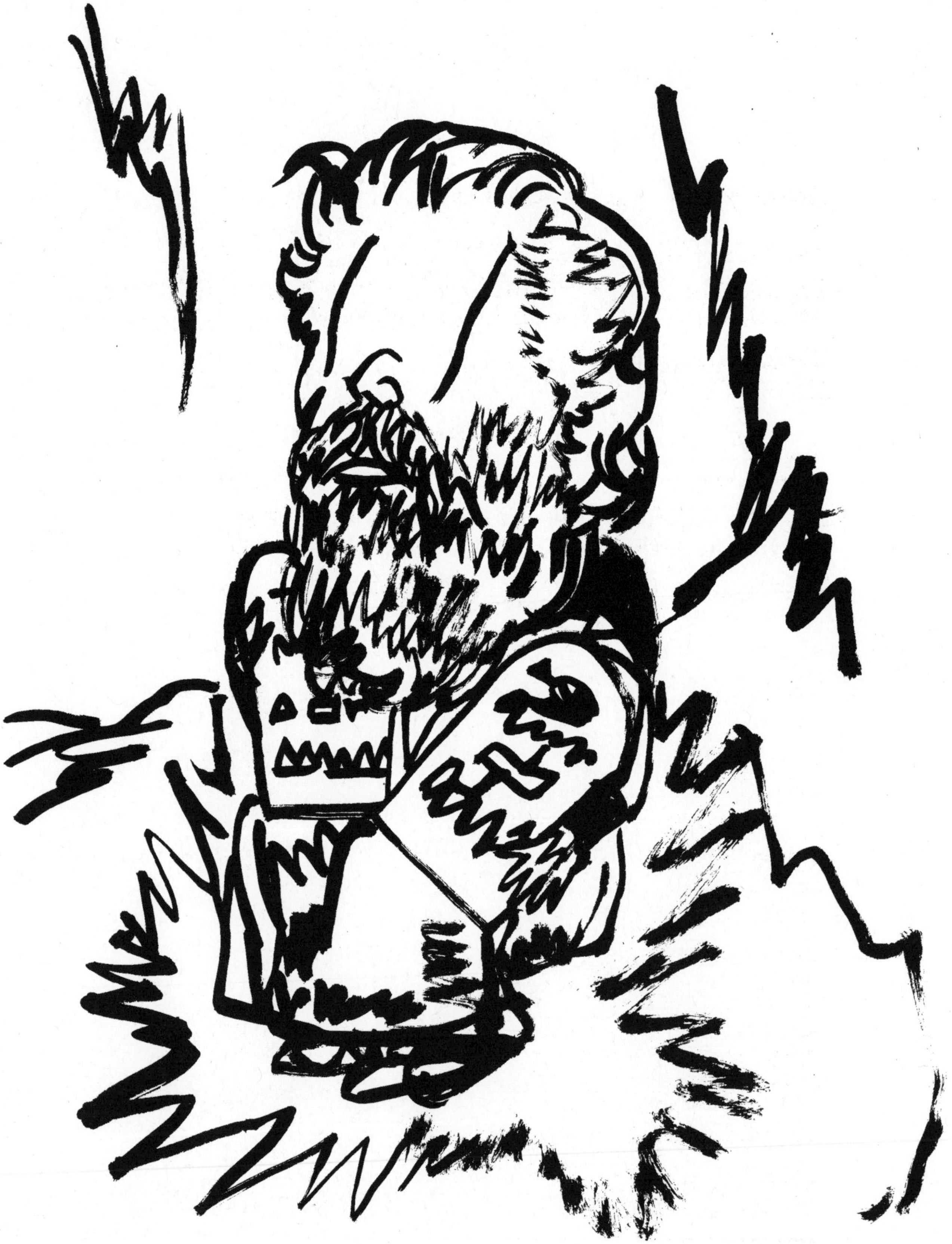